Be the Parent Your Child Deserves

Take Back Your Parental Role to
Motivate, Inspire, and Lead Your Child

Be the
Parent
Your Child
Deserves

Rae Turnbull

New Page Books
A division of The Career Press, Inc..
Franklin Lakes, NJ

BE THE PARENT YOUR CHILD DESERVES

Cover design by Design Solutions

Printed in the U.S.A. by Book-mart Press

To order this title, please call toll-free 1-800-CAREER-1 (NJ and Canada: 201-848-0310) to order using VISA or MasterCard, or for further information on books from Career Press.

The Career Press, Inc., 3 Tice Road, PO Box 687,
Franklin Lakes, NJ 07417

www.careerpress.com

Library of Congress Cataloging-in-Publication Data

Turnbull, Rae.
   Be the parent your child deserves : take back your parental role to motivate, inspire, and lead your child / by Rae Turnbull.

      p.   cm.

   ISBN 1-56414-508-5 (pbk.)

   1. Parenting. 2. Parents—Conduct of life. 3. Parent and child. 4. Parent and teenager.
I. Title.

   HQ755.8 .T85 2000

   649'.1—dc21   00-033256

Dedication

Dedicated to my parents, Vincent Anthony and Raphael Frances Prudente, from whose loving example I continue to learn.

Acknowledgments

I thank my daughter Gwynn Turnbull, whose perceptive writer's insights guided me patiently through this book's critical early drafts, and gave me the courage to continue.

I thank my son Ian Turnbull, and his wife Paddy, for their conscientious effort to be the parents their sons deserve. Their heartfelt commitment strengthens my resolve and gives me hope.

I'm grateful to my dear friends and colleagues Marsha and Larry Brady, Sandra Estrada, and to my brother Vince Prudente, for their unfailing faith in this project.

I thank juvenile probation officer and writer Tara Flewelling, who believed in my work and brought it to the attention of others. I thank freelance editor Susan Leon, who helped make this project presentable for publication. I thank Bonnie Waltrip, my readers, and my Forum participants for their honesty and encouragement.

I'm grateful for my extended families, the Vonas, Prudentes, and Turnbulls. They accepted parenthood with willingness and honor.

I thank my husband George, whose steadfast support and unconditional love sustain me.

Contents

Preface

I am a teacher, and I know your children. I am a parent, and I know you. For 40 years, while I raised my own children, I taught yours. Your children were in my classroom in schools in many different parts of this country, in affluent as well as low-income neighborhoods. I taught your children in public schools, in private schools, in exclusive preparatory schools, and in small rural schools. In schools for exceptional children, where the gifted child was the norm, and in schools for children with learning disabilities or language limitations: In all of these, I taught your children.

I watched the effort you made to be an effective parent, and I watched as that effort became an increasingly difficult struggle for you. So difficult that you began to lose your confidence in your ability to be the parent your child deserves.

I saw a great need for parents to believe in themselves again, and in response to that need, I created the *Forum for Parents: The Parent as a Teacher.* The sole purpose of the forum is to teach you how to regain your confidence and reclaim your rightful parental role as teacher to your child. I opened these forums to all parents from many different cultural backgrounds and various levels of formal education.

You are reading this book for the same reason other parents attended my forums: You sense that something is seriously wrong with today's approach to parenthood. Some of you seem to be doing everything right, but you still see your children heading for destructive choices. Some of your children are managing fairly well in the moral minefields today's child must march through, but you're not sure why, and you're worried that it may not last.

You're tense, anxious, unable to truly enjoy parenthood as the fulfilling experience you know it should be. You are looking for reasons. You are looking for answers. You are often overwhelmed, and you are looking for hope. To discover the reasons, and search for the solutions that will offer hope, we must first define the problem: We have forgotten our primary parental responsibility: *It is to teach.*

We must teach our children not only how to pick up after themselves, or how to do math, but also teach them principles and values and concepts, like how to respect themselves and others. As parents, our primary purpose is not to make our children happy. Finding their own happiness is their responsibility. If we teach them how to become self-reliant, well-balanced individuals, capable of loving themselves and others, they will be able to have the satisfaction of finding happiness for themselves. As parents, we usually find ourselves in one of three different categories:

1. Those of us who do too much for our children.
2. Those of us who do too little for our children.
3. Those of us who do too little or too much at the wrong times.

Most of us fall into the third group, and it is this confusion over how much to do and when to do it that keeps us from being truly effective parents.

In our well-intentioned desire to make life as easy as possible for our children, those of us who do too much for them are crippling those very children by robbing them of the skills they will need to provide for themselves in the real world. In our mistaken belief that it is our job, as parents, to make our children happy, we buy them everything they ask for, we do their homework for them, we give them no responsibility for chores. Then we wonder why they are unmotivated, unproductive, and most distressing of all to most parents, unhappy.

No matter how much we profess to our children that we have confidence in them, our actions tell them something very different. When we do everything for them, we are convincing them that they are not capable of doing for themselves. We unwittingly teach them that struggle is to be avoided. We forget that the struggle to reach goals, and the effort it takes to make dreams come true, is what gives real value to those goals and dreams.

When we indulge our children's every whim, we are taking away their right to struggle for rewards, and their right to own the rewards they receive as a result of their struggle. Indulging our children may make us feel good about ourselves, but it will only produce self-indulgent children, incapable of taking on the realities of adulthood, unable to ever find for themselves that happiness we so desperately want them to have.

Those of us who do too little for our children also cripple them by robbing them of their childhood. By doing too little for them, under the guise of preparing them for a harsh world, we force them into adult responsibilities long before there is any real necessity for them to take on those burdens. Children left with no playtime and no real opportunity to just be children become those adults who continually seem to be searching for the childhood they never had. Their perpetually adolescent behavior, long after they are physically mature, keeps them from ever becoming completely self-reliant adults.

Physically or emotionally, or both, when we make our children's lives too hard, they want to avoid any other kind of struggle. Trying to keep up with our unrealistic demands requires so much effort that they lose their incentive to make an effort to struggle for, or even have, worthwhile personal goals and dreams. Unable to believe in their own possibilities, they resign themselves to never finding their own happiness.

Those of us in the third category, who are confused about when to do things for our children and when to insist that they do things for themselves, need to find the balance between the two. Doing too much and doing too little are both extremes. In our discussion of each one in the preceding paragraphs, we can see the results of our actions when we go to either extreme. Understanding why these results occur can help us better evaluate what our actions need to be, when it is helpful to do something for a child, and when it is harmful.

You may have the best of intentions, but good intentions alone will not raise a child. You must let the results of your actions be your yardstick for measuring what you need to change to achieve that goal.

Whichever category you find yourself in, there is hope. I will teach you how to reclaim your rightful responsibility as a parent to your child. But the parent's role is one that must be earned. To earn it, you must actually do the work. You must make the effort. You cannot call yourself a parent unless you are willing to *be* a parent: to set standards and have expectations; to prepare your children and yourself for their eventual independence; and to enable them to find their own personal happiness.

Introduction

10 Stages in a Journey

efore you can reclaim your parental role with any real conviction, you need to join me on a journey. Think of me as your guide, because that is what a teacher truly is. You and I will not be traveling alone. There will be many parents accompanying us. Some of them you will recognize as friends and neighbors. Some will seem to be total strangers. Yet all will have in common one singular determination. They are taking this journey, as you are, to become the parent their child deserves.

There are different stages to every journey. This one has 10. Before I describe them, let me shed some light on some of the reasons why this journey has become necessary. What happened to so shake our confidence in our ability to be effective parents? The many people traveling with us and their stories will help you understand. Their names are not important; their stories are. Some we'll see more than once as we travel this road. Some we will meet and never see again, but it will be enough. Each of them will have something to teach us, if we pay attention. Let's begin.

Fellow travelers

Robert is 15 years old and lives with his mother, a full-time nurse employed in the largest of two area hospitals. Their city also includes a state university, as well as a smaller community college. The high school Robert attends has approximately 1500 students in its graduating class. Robert is already almost six feet tall and could pass for a 17-year-old at first glance, but his face betrays his adolescence.

His test scores show his intelligence to be above average. Yet his grade point is struggling to stay at a low C, with two failing grades pulling it down. He does nothing to help around the house. Surly disrespect colors any conversation he has with his mother, when he speaks to her at all. On two different days out of the past three weeks, he chose not to go to his afternoon classes. When he's home in the evenings, which is seldom, he spends all of his time in front of the television set or in his room surfing the Internet.

"I can't do anything with him!" His mother's hands twist in her lap as she sits opposite me. We're in a classroom in one of the schools that is hosting my parent forum. I've just completed the third of the 10 weekly sessions. Robert's mother is one of several parents who have asked me for some personal time after the two-hour session. I will later learn that Robert's father left the family several years ago and is no longer in contact with Robert and his mother. She is raising her son as a single parent.

As she speaks, confusion clouds her young face. I guess her age to be no more than 35, but the set of her jaw shows the aging signs of stress. Her expression makes it painfully clear that she is giving up, and she says exactly that. "That's not an option," I tell her, with no hesitation or indecision in my voice. It's not what she expected to hear.

On another evening in another town, two parents stop me as I'm leaving the second session. They're the father and stepmother of a 7th-grade girl. They heard about the forum from a friend who attended the first session the previous week, and they want to know if it's too late for them to sign up. They, too, have a story to tell, about a child they cannot understand, much less control.

Elizabeth is barely 12 years old, yet she's wearing clothes that strongly suggest a sexuality far beyond her years. Her test scores, like Robert's, show strong learning potential, especially in the areas of math and science. But her math grades are poor at best. She refuses to clean her room, or anything else in the house for that matter. She has twice taken money from her stepmother's purse. When her father confronted her about it, she stormed out of the house and stayed out all night. Her stepmother was frantic with fear, and they never did learn where Elizabeth spent that night.

It's Elizabeth's father, the operations manager in a small metal fabrication plant in the area, who speaks first. Frustration tightens his facial features, as he spits out his words in brittle bites. "Liz treats her stepmother like a slave," he says angrily, "and I can't even talk to the girl anymore without losing what little patience I have left."

Elizabeth's stepmother turns away. She doesn't want me to see her face. But I hear the sob in her voice as she speaks. "We've tried everything. Nothing works. We've just about given up." I tell both of them exactly what I told Robert's mother. "That's not an option." They don't want to hear it either.

These are just two examples of children whose parents are completely at a loss to understand the why and how of their present problems. Their despair is destroying whatever hope they once had that they could be effective parents. The quick and easy solutions don't work, and they know that now. But they don't know exactly why, and they don't know how to change the present pattern. These parents realize that their children need to become responsible, motivated, and respectful of the law, their families, and themselves. But they want someone or something else to make that happen. These parents have gone beyond despair. They've declared defeat.

These are not evil people, intent on exploiting or abandoning their children. They care desperately about their children. They love their children. They want to continue loving them. They just don't want to *parent* them. They've been led to believe that being a parent today is such a mysterious job that it can only be done by experts, people with special credentials or advanced educational degrees. Even with the help of a variety of support systems that are available in most communities, parents are losing hope that the average, well-intentioned adult can successfully cope with being a parent in today's world. They're wrong. They can do it. But first, let's examine why they think they can't.

It is true that parenthood today is more difficult and challenging than it was 50 years ago. With ever-increasing speed each year, guidelines are changing. New information, often untested by time or any real measurement of results, is constantly being offered. Emphasis is placed upon short-term, speedy solutions, when emphasis should in fact be focused on long-range, enduring goals. Tossing the baby out with the bath water, we've discarded reliable, time-proven methods along with methods time has shown to be ineffective and harmful. We need to return to the understanding of a parent's primary role.

Accepting the parent's primary role

It's impossible to consider taking this journey unless you are willing to accept the fundamental truth stated in this book's introduction: The primary role of a parent is that of *teacher*.

It is a role that continues throughout life. Parents are among the most influential teachers their children will ever have. But society has so blurred the importance of the parent in the life of a child that parents themselves have forgotten that primary role. Sadly, there are many different elements in our society intent on diminishing that parental role. To satisfy their own sometimes admirable, sometimes selfish goals, various social, political, and educational factions seek to influence and control the child. They want no interference from those who are meant to be the rightful guardians of the child's welfare: the parents.

As parents, on the advice of one group or the other, we find ourselves continually vacillating from overindulging our children to being unduly strict. It's often hard to maintain our balance when we are pulled in opposite directions, forced into those directions by constantly shifting standards and expectations from society in general.

Many who wish to replace us as parents of our children do so out of a real desire to affect positive change. Under the genuine agenda of concern and protection for those children whose parents are unwilling or unable to be proper parents, government agencies have taken over the responsibilities once solely accorded to parents. They've been so successful in usurping the role that even parents willing to be parents find themselves losing confidence in their own ability to handle the job.

Many of these agencies began with the legitimate purpose of addressing serious problems and correcting significant wrongs committed against children by woefully incompetent parents. But many of them have expanded so much that they must continually manipulate power away from parents in order to keep their own huge bureaucracies in place. They have ceased to be a means to an end and have become an end in themselves.

They are often staffed by well-meaning people who honestly want to further the welfare of the child, educated professionals who are confused and frustrated by their inability to fix the problem. They are sincerely surprised by the seemingly wholesale slide toward complete dereliction of duty on the part of many parents. Some of these agencies and associations do not realize that they are part of the problem they are trying to correct. What they don't understand is that parents are surrendering only because they are increasingly overwhelmed.

Adding to the temptation to pull away from parental responsibility is the mesmerizing influence of the media. This is covered more completely in Chapter 7. For now, it is enough to understand the following basic truths: The media mass-markets products and ideas. They do this primarily with the major aim of maximizing profits, regardless of how that marketing may affect children. The media targets the young directly, because, as one media sage said candidly, "They are the ones most easily influenced." Theirs is a blatant sidestep around parental influence.

By making their pitch directly to our children, right in our own homes, via television and now the Internet, media marketers manipulate parents into relinquishing their influence on their child's upbringing. Instead of encouraging self-reliance and independent thinking in our children, the media encourages dependency on products and images. It encourages children to see *wants* as *needs*. Our children are being urged to take on the trappings of adulthood without taking on its responsibilities. It is a tantalizing idea, one that is especially appealing to immature minds housed in physically mature bodies.

It is not my intent to blame the government, the media, or any other specific organization. We live in a relatively free society and more than in any other country at any time in history, we have been granted great power to make our own decisions. If there is any fault to be found, let's fault ourselves. We, the parents, have fallen for the false promises. We have allowed ourselves to believe that a job of such importance as parenting could be done without careful thought and considerable effort. We stopped being parents and teachers to our children. But we must return to that role. When we do, we must respect the enormous power that goes with it.

For good or ill, intentionally or not, a child's first lessons in life are learned from his or her parents. This instruction does not diminish in its significance, even when children begin to be influenced by others. Every other teacher the child has, throughout his or her life, will have to contend with the teaching the child has received from the parent. It will color the way all other instruction is received or rejected.

Values will be set by the parents, and those values will be strengthened, weakened, tested, adjusted, enhanced, or eliminated by future teachers. Yet all those future teachers, whether they are playmates, schoolteachers, relatives, friends, or any others the child encounters in his life, will not have the powerful potential for influence that a parent has upon a child.

Ten stages in the journey

Before you can fully appreciate the importance of the parent's role as the child's most influential teacher, you must first accept the fact that everything you encounter on this journey applies, in principle, to children of all ages. Every example I use and every story I tell are gleaned from real families, my own as well as others. They are real parents in real situations. What I have learned and will share with you is based solely on my observations as a parent and a teacher. These observations have convinced me that there are constants in the process of becoming an effective parent, and these constants apply to all children at all times.

Honesty is honesty, whether the child is 18 months old or 18 years old, boy or girl, black or white. Honesty is honesty, whether the parent is young or old, single or married, man or woman. Because one particular story may have a 5-year-old as its central figure does not mean the message is not equally relevant to your teenager. In the same way, the stories about teenage situations are just as pertinent and will apply just as successfully, with minor modifications, to your 7-year-old.

Don't look for the section on toddlers or search for the one on helpful hints for your junior high school student. You won't find sections like that in this book. There are no segregated areas in this journey. This is not a collection of nice, neat, superficial solutions tailor made and targeted only to a particular, isolated age group. Children are already too much isolated in our society. They are crammed into convenient little compartments, then constantly referred to as members of that isolated little compartment, rather than as individuals. When we speak about them to others, we use terms like my teenager, toddler, or preschooler. Of all the parents I have observed, the most effective ones often have one striking similarity: They frequently refer to their children by their individual given names. One family in particular comes to mind.

There are three children in this family, relatively close in age. Close enough that all three were teenagers at the same time. But I seldom heard them referred to as such by their parents, even when it would have been convenient to do so. The first time I was struck by this was when their father mentioned that the family was getting ready for a camping trip. Instead of saying "We're taking our teenagers to the lake this weekend," he said, "We're taking John, Karen, and Matt to the lake this weekend."

It was not a conscious thing he did, naming them in that fashion. It was simply that he saw them so clearly as individuals that it reflected even in the way he spoke about them. Uniquely individual, all three of these children were and are conscientious, responsible, and productive human beings. They are a credit to their parents' acceptance of the importance of their parental role. These parents recognize that real life is not neatly marked by age and gender. Its realities and constants cross gender lines and blur color boundaries.

If you expect a child to be a responsible individual, you must treat that child as an individual, not an anonymous member of some large group, isolated from any meaningful contact with anyone outside that group.

When we allow society to crowd our children into convenient cubicles, the individual child can be lost. When individuality is lost, it becomes increasingly difficult to be individually responsible. Without individual responsibility, individual happiness becomes harder and harder to find.

As a parent, you must accept your role as teacher to your child and not flinch from its responsibility. In the broadest sense, when you accept a child into your life, you must also accept the weight of your power to influence that child and bear it with grace and honor. Only then will parenthood become the joyful journey that it needs to be. You must understand how the responsibility for teaching that child will change you and how it will better you if you allow it to.

The responsibility of teaching your child will lead you into unexpected places and make you face and conquer your own fears, because accepting a child into your life connects you with a life force greater than yourself. It allows you to linger in this world beyond your time. This child guarantees that years from now, long after you are gone from this place, a part of you will still exist, perhaps in a note of music perfectly played, or a baseball soaring high into the brilliant blue sky of July, or a principle honorably defended.

When you accept the gift of this child in your life, these children who allow you to touch eternity, you must also accept the responsibility of raising them. You must become the teacher each child deserves. Will this be difficult to do? Only if you resist the idea that you must earn your right to be a parent. Only if you intended to take the name and not make the effort to be all that the name implies and requires. If you are reading this book, you are ready for the journey that will take you to this acceptance.

Because I believe in your willingness, we will travel through the journey's 10 stages together. In the process, it will become impossible for you to ever again minimize your own importance to your child. Within yourself, you will find the ability to be a much stronger, more effective parent than you ever thought you could be. In the process of teaching your child, by your example, you will not only teach yourself how to be the parent you need to be, you will also teach yourself how to be the person you want to be.

When I travel, I like to have some idea of where I'm going, and how I'm going to get there. I also like to have some idea of what I can expect to find along the way. With that in mind, I prepared this overview for you so there will be no surprises. At any point in time, you can refer to this and know where you are and where you still have to go. The stages have titles to make them easier to remember and find when you need to return to them.

* **Take the journey.** **Stage 1** is the foundation. It defines your primary parental role as the teacher of your child and explains why teaching by example is so powerful. It will help you understand how the role of teacher was taken from you, and how you can get it back.

* **Take the time.** **Stage 2** urges you to discover your child, to understand the child by learning exactly who he or she really is. You will learn how to appreciate and encourage the individuality of your child by observing the clues that are always there, if you make the effort to see them.

* **Be the guide.** **Stage 3** explores what a parent must do to be an inspiration to a child and a guide the child will want to follow for all the right reasons. You will clearly see that you are perfectly capable of inspiring your children to be productive, self-reliant, decent human beings.

* **Build trust.** **Stage 4** clarifies the challenge of choices and how the parent must set the pattern for making good choices. It will help you help your child determine which choices generate freedom, and which choices cause the loss of freedom.

* **Show the way.** **Stage 5** explains the inherent value of work as a way to earn personal satisfaction. It will tell you how you can bring your child to an understanding of work's importance, and how it can be your child's miracle maker.

❄ **Have faith. Stage 6** shows you how to provide true help for the homework dilemma, without actually doing the child's homework yourself. You will learn how to allow your child to own his or her homework, and thereby own the satisfaction that comes with the knowledge that they are capable of completing it themselves.

❄ **Take the lead. Stage 7** details how you can successfully control the powerful media influence on your child. You will learn how and why the media seeks to manipulate your child. You will also learn to understand the value of the media and to see it as a useful servant rather than a destructive master.

❄ **Find the good. Stage 8** explains how the true source of self-esteem comes from self-discipline. You will understand how self-discipline can help your child find his or her full potential for self-reliance. You will learn how self-reliance is the true key to your child's happiness.

❄ **Look in your mirror. Stage 9** insists that you can and must always move forward by reinforcing positives and reversing negatives. You will understand that it is always possible, though not necessarily easy, to improve your situation. It will impress upon you the importance of never giving up on your child or yourself.

❄ **Be a beginner. Stage 10** describes what lifelong learning truly is. It will show you how your own life experiences, good and bad, can help your child, and you, welcome productive change as an invigorating challenge. You will see how joyful the journey can be when you are always willing to be a beginner.

The pledge

Before you begin this journey, I want you to make a pledge. When you make a pledge, you give your word. Like all pledges, this is a promise, a solemn statement of intent. Like our country's pledge of allegiance, it is clear, direct, and brief. It is designed to help you remember your allegiance, your responsibility to your child:

> *I will be the teacher my children deserve. I will prepare them for their eventual independence by teaching them how to become self-reliant, self-confident adults, able to love themselves and others, willing to lead decent, useful lives, and capable of pursuing their own happiness.*

Stage 1

Take the Journey

ow that you understand why you're taking this journey, you also need to understand what you have to do to make yourself ready. So you can be confident of reaching your destination, you will be following a map of sorts. It will not necessarily indicate a direct route from one clearly marked point to another, but there will be markers every so often, guides to keep you heading in the right direction.

These guides will move you from one location to another, and the guide for each location will appear in the form of a question. The answers to each question will prepare you for the next. By using examples and stories in the text that follows each question, the answers will make themselves clear.

You will want to spend a little time at each location, absorbing, learning all you can, before you move on to the next one. Some will require a longer stay. There may be more history there that you will want to know. Some locations will offer side trips, and you'll need to take them to fully appreciate what that place has to offer. If you feel the need to return to any location in any stage, don't hesitate to do so. As with any journey, every time you travel that way again, you will see things you may have missed the first time.

Approach each place with a willingness to accept what it has to offer. There will be a different set of guides in each of these stages. In this initial stage of your journey, expect to find the answers to five questions.

Why must you keep your word?

If you are to be an effective teacher to your children, they must trust you. You build trust by keeping your word. Because the best-remembered lessons are always learned by example, logic tells us that parents' most effective teaching is done by the example they set for their children to follow. As a parent, how your own life is lived is extremely important. When you become a parent, inherent in your acceptance of that responsibility is the promise to be a good role model and teacher of your children. In effect, you give your word. Therefore, as a parent and a teacher, it is absolutely essential that you keep your word.

To make it easier to remember that you have given your word, say the parent's pledge out loud, as you would with any serious pledge. Make it repeatedly, to reassure and remind yourself. By saying it out loud, by verbalizing your intention, you are also making a promise to yourself. The pledge is nothing short of a commitment to action, a promise to earn your privilege to be called a parent. As with all pledges, it should be repeated from time to time.

You may find yourself using part of the pledge, adjusting its language to suit the particular situation, to remind yourself and your child of your commitment. For example, if your 14-year-old is complaining about having to clean up the mess she made in the laundry room when she dyed tee shirts for the homecoming rally, your pledge may sound like this: "I'm your mother. An important part of my job is to teach you how to be self-reliant. I'm not doing you any favors when I allow you to depend on me to do things you can do for yourself."

Using the word *can* is a subtle way to remind her that you believe her to be a capable individual. The best part about restating your pledge, even in this modified form, is that you can indicate that you expect a certain behavior and you can do it without raising your voice or getting into a shouting match. If she has heard this part of the pledge spoken by you before, maybe in slightly different words, she will still know, the minute it begins, that it's a signal of your firm resolve.

It also lets her know that you expect her to be responsible. She can then accept that cleaning up her mess is not giving in to some arbitrary whim of her mother's. It's simply being responsible. It's the logical thing to do. When she sees it in that light, she's much more likely to simply do what you rightly expect her to do with no additional fuss.

There is great power in the spoken word. Each time you make your pledge to be the teacher your child deserves, you strengthen your own resolve. You remind yourself to keep your word. You also increase your child's respect for you, which increases his or her sense of security. No child wants to be parented by someone who doesn't seem to have any firm conviction about his or her job description. There is no security in that, and children flounder without that security. They may not be able to put it into words, but children instinctively want parents who are willing to be responsible for the role. They may challenge you every step of the way, but it is only to test your resolve.

Every time you prove your resolve by keeping your promise to keep your word, your child is relieved and reassured. Your child knows you can be trusted. That trust builds the base of honesty every child needs in order to become what we all profess we want our children to become: confident, self-reliant adults.

At this point in our journey, it's necessary to take a short side trip. Since we are speaking of honesty, we must be honest with ourselves and recognize that some parents may not want their children to become self-reliant. They may not even realize it, but they really want their children to remain children indefinitely. Children who are never encouraged to grow up make it convenient for their parents to also postpone facing the prospect of their own mortality. Some of us are so afraid of growing old and dying that we don't want our children to become adults. As long as our children remain children we are not old, and as long as we are not old we will not die. Absurd? Yes, but sometimes subconsciously true.

On the other hand, let's suppose that your child is the one avoiding the process of growing up by ignoring responsibilities and generally behaving like a spoiled toddler even though she's almost 16 years old. This same child wants the benefits of growing up, such as driving a car and being able to determine her own hours. As her parent, you know you need to make it clear to her that she must accept some "grown-up" responsibilities, such as picking up after herself and completing chores and homework in a timely manner, before you can believe she's capable of the larger responsibility of driving a car. Yet, even though she manages to continually avoid those responsibilities, you pick up the learner's permit for her 16th birthday. Ask yourself why.

Perhaps because her irresponsible behavior allows you to continue to feel needed and important. As long as she clings to childhood when it's convenient for her to do so, it allows you to cling to the role of provider of all necessities, the omniscient individual you had to be when she was a baby. Keeping your children children also allows you to continue using them as an excuse to avoid taking charge of your life.

Maybe you're afraid of taking the necessary steps to realize your own potential, steps such as getting your high school diploma, or freeing yourself from drug dependency, or going back to college, or getting off welfare. When you have a dependent child who needs you, no matter how old that child is, it can be a very acceptable excuse to avoid your own personal responsibilities, even though the child should actually be your reason for accepting them. If you have more than one of these child/adults, it becomes an even more potent excuse for procrastination. So even though you're having difficulty with the children you already have, you decide to have still another child, to give yourself one more excuse to postpone your obligation to yourself.

This is one of the reasons many teenagers get pregnant or deliberately sire a child. With a real baby, an actual child, they can become instantly grown up without actually growing up to the reality of what this new element in their life will mean in terms of responsibility and commitment. Not only is this grossly unfair to their child, but it is morally wrong to burden the world with yet another dependent, demoralized, and potentially destructive adult. The damage done to families in particular and civilization in general by criminally irresponsible adults can be found on every dark page in history.

We skillfully subvert acknowledging most of these motives, because it's painful to face the facts of our own dishonesty. But it has to be done. Keeping our children children is a luxury society cannot afford. When we don't teach our children, gradually, step by step, how to gain responsible control of their lives, they remain emotionally childlike, even as their bodies mature and their minds gather more and more information. But the information is of no use or is manipulated and becomes dangerous in the hands of a maladjusted child/adult. We like to blame things like drugs or television for society's problems. But it's how we use and abuse those things that pose the problem, not the things in and of themselves.

If we truly want our children to be safe and happy, how is that possible if we keep them from becoming self-reliant? If we sincerely care about our children's welfare, then we will insist they develop self-reliance. The sort of self-reliance that will enable them to evaluate what they find in the world, the good and the bad, and be able to know the difference and act accordingly. Face the fact that we cannot walk ahead of our children, all through their life, sweeping away all the destructive elements of society so that they arrive at life's end unscathed and uncorrupted in mind and body. If they are to cope with the cruelties and champion justice and fairness in the world, they must be able to rely on their own good judgment to recognize both for what they are.

This is not something that can be done by passing more laws or adding more cumbersome restrictions. We cannot legislate or superimpose protection from all the negatives in life without compromising the personal strength and freedom needed to find the positives in life.

Good judgment, strong character, and self-reliance cannot enter the mind and heart from the outside. They must develop from within. They must come from being exposed to good examples, and having the opportunity to practice, to model those examples, so that those qualities become part of the whole person.

Let's return to that 16-year-old who refuses to pick up after herself. You promised to be her parent and teach her self-reliance. Keep your word. Use your ingenuity to teach the lesson she needs to learn. First, be certain that you do not leave your own trail of coats, notebooks, shoes, and so forth through every room in your house. You're going to tell me that you already do pick up after yourself, but she's not getting the message. Keep doing it anyway. If she continues to miss this lesson you are teaching by your example, then remember you have many more years of life experience than your daughter. By virtue of that fact alone, you are wiser than she is, if you will only remember to use that wisdom. Use your accumulated experience to make her realize the importance of keeping track of her own belongings.

Try this strategy: Begin by realizing that most of us need to be uncomfortable before we willingly change a behavior. Make her uncomfortable. After she's gone to bed, don't pick up her backpack from the middle of the living room floor and place it by the door so she doesn't forget it when she leaves for school. When she calls you from school and asks you to bring her backpack, tell her you're sorry but you can't. If she asks you why, give her an honest reason: " This isn't an emergency. You need to keep track of your own belongings. I can't leave what I'm doing every time you've neglected your responsibility. That wouldn't be fair to you or to me." When you say that you let her know you believe she wants to be responsible. Be consistent in your refusal to do what she's perfectly capable of doing for herself.

To be consistent, you have to take the same approach with everything she neglects to do. Don't remove her favorite shirt from the dryer before it wrinkles. She's the one who left it there. Let it still be there when she wants to wear it in the morning. Don't help her find the curling iron, her lipstick, or her hat. You get the idea. When her behavior inconveniences her often enough, she will change her behavior. Above all, don't resort to leaving your belongings all over the place to teach her a lesson. The only lesson you will be teaching is a negative one. You want to always be an example of positive behavior.

If you understand the absolute necessity for your children to develop self-reliance for their own personal happiness as well as for the good of society, then you should be able to more readily put aside your selfish need to keep your children perpetual children. It will take effort. But it will not only bring you ultimate victory, it will bring you moments of great joy. It will also bring you the peace of mind that comes when you realize that should chance take you from them, your children will be able to seek and find their own happiness.

Why is example such a powerful teacher?

Example is a powerful teacher because it is so direct and honest. When I speak about honesty, I do not mean the tactless, sometimes brutal bluntness some parents use to verbally lacerate their children in the name of so-called honesty. I'm speaking of the kind of honesty that requires effort, the honesty of actions versus words.

Whether the behavior we model or the character we display is good or bad for our children, they learn from it either way. Negative example is as powerful a teacher as positive example. If we want to motivate our children in a positive direction, one that is in their best interest, it's important that we do more than just tell them what we expect. It's far more effective if we show them by our own example. "Don't scream at your sister!" loses its effectiveness as a directive to your 12-year-old when he hears you shouting at your spouse.

In fact, the more we show our children what we expect by our own behavior, the less we have to tell them. The more they see that we are willing to do what we expect them to do, the more they trust us. There is leadership in that kind of teaching and a fairness in that kind of leadership that makes resistance difficult and earns genuine respect.

The commander who leads his troops into battle is followed because he is trusted. He is not ordering anyone to do what he is unwilling to do himself. Even though the situation is full of danger, his troops follow his lead. He doesn't deny the danger. He affirms it, and they respect him because he is willing to guide them through it. He is willing to take the same risks he is asking his troops to take. By doing it himself, he is showing them how. In order to do this, his troops realize he had to confront his own fears. It is his ability to do that for the sake of those he must lead that makes him the best kind of leader: a teacher by example.

What is lacking in many parents today is the willingness to confront the changes they may have to make in themselves in order to be effective parents. They are unwilling to lead, to accept the responsibility of being a parent. Parents in earlier generations seemed to have a better grasp on this basic component of being a mother or a father, even when they became parents while they were still relatively young. It's important to remember that teenage parents are not the new phenomenon they are made to seem. In the early part of this century, many people began their families at a very young age, often when they were 16 or 17 years old. Many of them were our own parents or grandparents. But most of those young men and women fully understood that parenthood meant they must now become responsible adults. They fully expected to raise the children they brought into the world by teaching them values and working to provide for them.

Those parents also expected something of their children. They expected them to be a useful part of the family unit, with chores and responsibilities that began at a very young age. Those parents understood the power of example as a teacher. They had learned their own basic values from the example of their parents and grandparents. On farms and ranches, parents and children worked alongside one another, not in some idyllic setting, but in real-life situations.

Even in towns and cities, children often helped in family grocery or hardware stores, barber shops or shoemaker shops, carpentry or dry goods or any number of other small businesses. They ran errands, they swept the floors, they tended the smaller children, they did whatever had to be done to be a useful part of the family. I'm not condoning abusive situations where children are forced to work in "sweatshop" conditions. I'm speaking about a reasonable amount of responsibility for the age and physical capability of the child.

Throughout this journey, I use examples from my own personal family history. You also have a personal family history, and your values, both good and bad, have been shaped by that history. Refer to it often, and it will help you determine what you want to keep and what you want to eliminate in terms of worthwhile values for your children to follow.

For example, in his late teens my father worked alongside his immigrant father laying miles of railroad track in western Pennsylvania. All the time, my father was absorbing his father's pride in precision and his honest work ethic. My mother's oldest sister, my Aunt Rose, while still a teenager, was my grandmother's capable "right hand" in the family delicatessen. At my grandmother's side, she observed and absorbed lessons like how to buy the best produce at a fair price without compromising her standards or her integrity—integrity that earned respect for both women in the community. My father's father and my mother's mother didn't preach these values. They lived them, and their example taught those values to their children.

Were those perfect times? No. Was life often difficult and labor hard? Yes. But there was purpose to it. Life was expected to be something that required effort, not something you slid through, with no particular purpose, knowing neither pain nor joy.

Parents regarded the raising of a child as something worthwhile, and like all things worthwhile, it required effort. Children shared the purpose of the whole family to better itself and provide for itself honorably. There was a balance that is often missing in our modern approach of isolating children from any real function in the family unit. We regard them as beings we should pamper and provide with all manner of things. We are frustrated when our children fail to accept responsibility, yet we have taught them, by our example, that it is not necessary. We promised to be parents, but we failed to keep our word.

Whenever I made a mistake with my own children or with the students in my classroom, it was always because I said one thing and did another. I did not keep my word. When that happened, my integrity was weakened, and the children or students I was trying to teach no longer trusted me. Nothing is as effective a teaching tool as honesty. Trust is its by-product. Parents who are trusted to keep their word are free to be the teachers they need to be.

There is an old saying: A man does not truly become a man until he accepts the responsibility of raising his child. It very rightly affirms the fact that it is not the siring of a child that proves manhood. That only proves that he is male. Equally true is the fact that it is not giving birth to a baby that makes a woman a mother. That only proves that she is female. Becoming a parent, in the true sense of the word, is not something that just happens. Becoming pregnant or siring a child can happen without intention, and sometimes with very little thought. But being a parent, the actual raising of a child, does require a great deal of thought, good intention, and effort.

Being a parent requires purpose, and that purpose is to raise a child who will be a decent, productive, well-adjusted, self-reliant human being.

If you have doubts that this should be the primary purpose of parenting, then return to the earlier section on self-reliance. To fulfill this purpose as parents, we need to make every effort to be good role models for the children we are preparing for the adult world. We get so caught up in being our child's pal, buddy, or sports director that we forget that first and foremost, the child needs a parent. It is the parent who must raise the child by teaching the child. It's a role you can never abandon.

Remember Robert and Elizabeth from the first introduction? Their parents wanted to relinquish the role of parenting their children. It was not a deliberate dereliction of duty on their part, nor was it an indication of any lack of love for their children. They only considered giving up because they sincerely thought they had done all they could do. Robert's mother said, "I can't do anything with him," as though he was something that needed to be fixed. She was not yet aware of the fact that before she will effectively do anything with Robert, she has to first "fix" herself.

Perhaps the necessity of teaching our children by our own example is the true miracle of procreation. All the great religions of the world admonish us to continually strive to improve ourselves, to come closer to their ideal of God as that image is embodied in the qualities of honesty, forgiveness, justice, and integrity of character. Our children can be the greatest inspiration for us to continually re-invent ourselves as we try to reach that goal. It is often painful to rework ourselves, to correct our faults, to labor toward that ideal. It requires effort. Often it can only be something as powerful as the love we have for our children that will force us to make that effort.

As we go through each stage of our lives, our children watch us carefully, and we are teaching them, by our example, how to do it.

In the following two stories, you can see how my own parents' efforts to deal with extremely difficult situations became a life lesson for their children. Their awareness that they were still serving as guides, teaching by their example, actually helped them with their heroic struggles.

In the last year of his life, my father showed me how to face the fear of death not only by the things he said, but by how he conducted himself. At age 89, he was still my teacher. I watched him wage a valiant battle to remain as independent as possible during his last few years. A barber by trade, my father was still barbering two days a week at a local shop until a worsening heart condition and kidney complications finally made it necessary for him to go on kidney dialysis during his last six months of life. He knew that at his age and in his physical condition, dialysis was not a cure, but rather a way of extending his life for a short while.

My father enjoyed the camaraderie of the merchants he met as he strolled through town before he went to work. He enjoyed genuine friendships with many of his loyal customers. He was reluctant to see those pleasant and productive days disappear from his life. I knew it was difficult for him to declare, the month he began the daily dialysis treatments, that he would finally retire. But he had always known there would come a time when continuing to barber would not only put a strain on his physical condition, but would cause concern to the rest of the family.

I knew by his acceptance of this one activity leaving his life that he was preparing himself and us for the inevitable. Yet even then, he still saw the positive side of the situation. "That will give me more time with the boys," he said, speaking about his beloved great-grandsons. Indeed, their frequent visits were the highlights of his last days.

Did my father struggle to live in the active, vigorous sense of the word, for as long as he could? Yes. Did he resist death and fight for his life? Yes. But he also showed me the acceptance side of that struggle. He showed me how to be gracious in that acceptance. Although I know he felt great sadness to see his struggle ending, he never let us see him succumb to despair. He always knew how much he was loved by all of us in the family. In my heart, I hold the hope that in those last difficult days, he was helped by that knowledge of our respect and devotion. When my own calendar is closing, may I follow the example of his grace and courage.

At 83 years old, my mother, too, is still my teacher. She is showing me how to cope with the loss of a beloved spouse, someone she happily shared her life with for 63 years. I know she is aware of our concern for her, and she does her best to ease that concern by keeping herself as

active and independent as her health allows. Her grief is great, but her gratitude for what she still has is as strong as my father's was. A hospital volunteer, she still performs those weekly duties. Her adjustment to life without
my father by her side is a mighty one. But she is helped in that adjustment
by the knowledge that her actions give her children a guide to follow.

She knows we are watching, learning by her example how to continue
to live a useful, happy life without succumbing to her sorrow. Our need to
still learn from her gives her strength to get through this difficult time. To
continue to grow and reinvent ourselves for the sake of our children is
one of the blessings of parenthood, if we only will see it as such. When
we improve ourselves for the sake of our children, the quality of our own
lives improves immeasurably. My mother will prevail. Always a strong
and determined lady, I sense that she is even stronger now, for the strength
that comes from being strong for the sake of someone else is a powerful
thing.

Why is honesty with ourselves so critical?

Nothing will change, no improvements will take place, as long as we
deceive ourselves about *why* we are doing what we are doing. Once we
become parents, we must recognize that we may need to change some of
our own behavior. We can't, if we're not honest with ourselves about the
real reasons for that behavior.

How will you know if a particular behavior of yours needs to be
changed? Ask yourself if that behavior is something you want to see duplicated in your child.

When you observe your actions from that viewpoint, it will be much
easier to realize what needs to be corrected. It's one thing for an adult to
shout and stamp his or her feet and storm out of the house, and call it a
harmless "letting off steam" form of behavior. It's quite another to be
publicly embarrassed by seeing those same actions duplicated in your 10-
year-old, especially if you are honest with yourself and recognize that
behavior as your own.

Sometimes just acknowledging our reason for doing what we do can
make it easier to correct our behavior. For example: Instead of seeing that

your child has meaningful chores to perform so that he will learn to be a useful part of the family unit, you don't hold him responsible for any chores. Acknowledge that you find it easier to just do it yourself, rather than see that he does it and does it properly.

Perhaps you tell yourself that you don't want him to be too tired to do well in school. Yet if you are honest with yourself, you know that a few simple chores will not unnecessarily tire him. The truth is you want to be the "worker bee," doing everything yourself, so that others will see you as unselfish and sacrificing. Yet by keeping your son from developing some pride of his own because he is sharing the workload, you selfishly take away his opportunity to be useful.

The sacrifice you are making is, in actuality, his self-esteem. When we fail to give our children guidelines for responsible behavior, we are not making life easier for them. We are making life easier for ourselves, if only for the short term, and we are making life much harder for our children for the long term. If we don't want the discomfort of having guidelines for our own behavior, we must always remember, whether in the home or the classroom, it's the child's mental and physical welfare, not ours, that is at stake.

If something about ourselves must change, then so be it. It does not require advanced degrees to understand and act upon the simple, singular fact that change requires that we stop doing one thing, and start doing another. Stop and start. I said it was simple; I did not say it was easy. Change requires effort. But everything worthwhile requires effort, and changing bad habits in yourself in order to be a better example for your child is well worth the effort. Remember, if you don't want to see your poor behavior and bad habits mirrored in your child, then change them. No matter how difficult that change may be for you to make, do it. It will be one of the best things you ever do for your child. It will be one of the best things you ever do for yourself.

When we're not receiving the results we want from our children, it's often because we're not being honest with ourselves about why we do what we do. In one of my sessions, an attractive woman in her early forties, the mother of high school-age children, said, "It's hard for me to follow through on a consequence when my son's broken a rule. I'm too kind-hearted. If I told him, 'No TV for a week,' after a few days of him saying he's sorry, I figure he's learned a lesson and I ease up.'"

She had been attending every session faithfully, so I knew she was sincere in her effort to improve herself as a parent. But her comment is typical of the well-intentioned, yet confused thinking that prevails in our quick-and-easy solution society. "Yes," I told her, "He has learned a lesson. He's learned that you do not keep your word."

The logic of my response reached her quickly. I could see it by the look of surprise that appeared on her face. It was clear to me that she had never seen her behavior in this particular light. Then I addressed the second fallacy in her thinking. "As to being kind-hearted," I said quietly, "How kind is it for your son to repeat the same mistake simply because you want to keep a certain image you have of yourself?" She liked the perception of herself as a kind individual. There was nothing wrong in that. But she was not thinking about true kindness as much as she was thinking about being perceived as kind.

During the course of the forum sessions, she began to see where and how she was putting that need to feel good about herself above her child's need to have a parent willing to set guidelines for responsible behavior. She was not being truly kind to her son. She was being kind to herself. She was settling for feeling good right now, instead of making the effort to raise her son in a positive way. Gradually, she concluded that some discomfort on her part now would result in her feeling much better about herself later on.

We can reverse our own poor behavior and when we do, it always results in deeper satisfaction with ourselves. We do it for the sake of the child, but we also reap the benefit. Once she corrected the habit, this particular mother was much happier with herself, although originally she thought that it might be a little too late for her to change. But after she struggled through the first few tries, reminding herself always that it was kinder to her son to be firm when firmness was called for, she found that she could change. "I never could have done it, though," she told me later on, "if I hadn't realized that it was the best thing I could do for my son." If you follow the basic logic of choices and consequences, I maintain that it is never too late to change your behavior for the sake of your child.

Why must you always think ahead?

If we want our children to think all the way through to the end of a course of action before they take it, we must do the same. Our behavior always affects them, sometimes directly, sometimes indirectly, sometimes soon, sometimes late. If we ignore that reality, we are not accepting the principle of choices and consequences. Consequences, good or bad, always follow every choice we make. There is a logic to them when we follow them all the way through. Too often, we stop short, and then we're sincerely surprised at the end result.

We live in a world where speedy results are valued. For many reasons, quick, short-term solutions can be good. When we're trying to finish a week's worth of dirty laundry, the quick turnaround time of an automatic washing machine and its companion automatic clothes dryer are exactly what we need. But when we're trying to form positive behavior patterns in an impressionable child, we need to think in the long term. That means we need to look beyond how our actions affect an immediate goal and anticipate how those same actions will affect the child's behavior later.

Here are a few examples. In both of these, remember your long-range goal is to raise your child to be a confident, self-reliant, responsible adult.

In the first example, your immediate goal is to straighten up the living room before some unexpected visitors arrive. Your 7-year-old has toy trains and wooden tracks scattered all over the floor. He's been setting up a little train layout complete with imaginary locations for the station and all sorts of other arrangements that mean something to him in this game he is playing. It's a stormy Saturday, and you told him earlier that he could bring his train stuff into the living room because you didn't anticipate anyone coming by on such a miserable day. He's been inside all morning and entertaining himself pretty well. You've been doing some paperwork at the dining room table nearby. Suddenly, the entire scene shifts from one of personally interesting, relaxed activity for both of you to a frantic effort to accommodate the unexpected interruption.

Scenario one: You get down on your hands and knees and start scrambling to gather toys and tracks, as you say repeatedly, "C'mon,

Sam, hurry and get these picked up! Two of my friends from the library club are coming, and this room is a mess! C'mon, hurry up!" Your son senses your urgency and gets an urgent tone to his own voice. "Mom, wait! Stop! You're messing up my track layout! Wait! Why do we hafta hurry? You're wrecking my stuff!"

You're both frustrated. It's taking twice as long to put the room in order, because you're both stubbornly staking your claim on having things your way. You ride roughshod over his desire to not disturb what he built. "That's enough!" you say. "You can build it again! I can't wait for you to pick this stuff up! I'll do it!" He wails as the results of his building efforts are rapidly dismembered and tossed into the box.

Your child has just learned some very undesirable lessons in behavior. First, he learned that if he argues about it long enough, you will do what you're asking him to do, so he is encouraged to ignore your requests in the future. Second, he is learning that his belongings, his arrangements, and his dreams have no value. They can be easily scooped up and put aside arbitrarily when someone "more important" comes on the scene. Third, he is learning to resent visitors, because their arrival creates what he sees as unreasonable demands.

The living room will most likely be very presentable when your guests arrive, so your short-term goal is realized. However, you've made your long-range goal of your child's self-reliance and confidence much harder to reach.

The next time you ask him to do something, he will have a stronger argument to delay the process, because he has learned that arguing about it keeps him from having to do it. He has also learned that you really don't place much value on his creations, because you can so easily sweep them aside on what seems to him to be pure whim. He's much more likely to stop making the effort to create anything, for fear it will be wasted effort, and he will feel foolish for having placed any value on it in the first place.

Scenario two: You tell your child that you need to have the living room floor cleared because some friends from your library club are coming. They will need to sit in the living room while they are helping you decide which books should be ordered from the new library lists. You tell him to pick up all the loose train cars and tracks and put them in the box. Then you tell him that you will carefully move the track he has already arranged a certain way into a corner of the room so it won't get stepped on, and he can play with it later. He complains about the disruption, but you persist, carefully moving the track as you continue to urge him to gather up the other pieces.

You keep your voice calm but firm. "Sam, you can see that your track is staying together, and you won't have to rebuild it. It's a nice layout and I'd like to show it to my friends when they come. But let's hurry, because they'll be here soon. C'mon now, you do your part, and get those bits and pieces into the box quickly." He is reassured that you're doing what you said you would do, but he just doesn't feel like picking up all the other stuff. He'd much rather just go over to the corner and continue playing with what you moved there for him.

Persist. "Sam, those extra pieces need to be picked up right now, or they'll be stepped on and broken. I did my part. You do yours. I'm waiting." Then you mentally put yourself on hold and stand there until he begins his task. If he dawdles, restrain your impulse to push him out of the way and do it yourself. He's testing your resolve. Lingering these few extra minutes will not seriously harm your quick clean-up plans. Encourage him without being effusive. "Good. Speed it up a little please. Thank you. I'll clear my stuff from the dining room table while you're finishing that."

If he still resists, try making it exciting, reminding him that the guests will be able to see what he's accomplished. "They won't believe that you built this all by yourself. Maybe you can build something else while they're here, and then they can see how you do it."

Your guests may arrive before it's all done, so your short-term goal of presenting them with an orderly dining room and living room may not be realized. But the long-range benefits of your actions are enormous. Your son learned that you keep your word. He also learned that you respect his work, because his "play" is, after all, his work. He learned that you expect him to be responsible enough about taking care of his things to pick them up and keep them out of harm's way.

He also learned to not resent visitors, but to welcome them as people who may be interested in him and in his work. By taking the mental time to think your actions all the way through, you became a much more effective parent. You probably also slowed yourself down enough to put unexpected guests in proper perspective. It's your home, and they must be willing to accept whatever condition it's in when their arrival occurs with such short notice. When you are able to be comfortable with that fact, then you, too, will be more likely to welcome such unexpected visits simply as surprises, not unwanted intrusions.

🐝🐝🐝

Those two responses to situations are only one small part of any number of scenarios that can clearly illustrate the importance of thinking in the long term. Your children watch you for signs of what their behavior should be. They may not adopt that behavior immediately, but somewhere along the line, as they grow into adulthood, you will see your behavior mirrored in theirs.

Think about these examples:

- 🐝 If it's all right for you to lie to your wife about the real cost of the sports equipment you bought, then your child will automatically assume it's all right for her to lie about what she buys with her lunch money.
- 🐝 If it's acceptable for you to bring home office supplies from your job, then your child sees nothing wrong in bringing home someone else's jacket that was left behind in the classroom.
- 🐝 If you forgive the fact that your 8th grader took money from your purse, then he will expect you to forgive the fact that he took money from the register of the convenience store where he works.

The list is endless. Just remember that whenever you're tempted to take a dishonorable course of action because it's easy or comfortable, stop and think about how that action is being perceived by your child, and where that perception may lead. Remind yourself that children learn best by example. We have no idea how far-reaching the effect of our actions is on our children's behavior when they become adults. Childhood memories of a parent's behavior will sometimes surface many years later in a way the parent could never have anticipated. The parent, in fact, may have completely forgotten the entire incident, but the child did not.

Driving her old truck across the Southwest, my daughter was on one of those long, lonely drives between rodeos. She was tired, hungry, and except for a $10 bill in her pocket, broke. She pulled into the parking lot of an old diner in the middle of nowhere, she told me later, and went inside. She sat down and ordered a hamburger. The waitress was sullen, and the hamburger was so greasy she couldn't finish it.

When my daughter paid her bill, the same waitress was at the register. She took the $10 bill and handed back the change. Noticing that she was being given change for $20 instead of $10, my daughter, angry with the poor service and poorer food, never said a word. She jammed the money into her pocket and walked out. She told me she said to herself, "Serves her right!" as she climbed into her truck and drove away.

As she continued down the highway, a picture flashed into her mind. "I remembered when Dad went to buy a bunch of newspapers because there was an article in them about one of us, Mom."

She was telling me the story from a pay phone inside that night's rodeo arena. "It was raining," she continued, "and we kids were in the back seat of the car. I remember watching Dad, standing in the rain, carefully putting the full amount of change into the newspaper vending machine. I remember being old enough to realize he could have taken all the papers he needed even after he had put in enough money for just one, because the machine stayed open. But he continued to put in the proper amount. He didn't even realize I was watching him. It was raining so hard, he couldn't know that we could see him."

That mental picture prompted her to turn her truck around and head back to that old diner. She handed the money to the waitress and said simply, "You gave me the wrong change." Then she walked out the door, remembering the look of gratitude and surprise on the face of the waitress. "Mom, I haven't felt this good about the world and myself for a long time." The operator broke in, and my daughter hurried to finish, "I just wanted to call. Please tell Dad thanks!" My husband does not remember the newspaper-buying incident. But his daughter did.

What are learning styles?

Everyone learns a little differently. Recognizing that fact is extremely helpful to every teacher. If we expect each of our children to learn things in exactly the same way, we are doing them a great disservice and discouraging their desire to learn. I'm not speaking of academic learning only; I'm speaking of all learning.

There are basically three broad categories of learning styles: auditory, visual, and kinesthetic.

Briefly put, the auditory learner needs to hear something in the form of words, explanations, or lectures to understand it the first time it is presented. The visual learner needs to see something in the form of a drawing, diagram, or pictures to better understand it. The kinesthetic learner must actually do it, perform the task, or be physically involved before a new concept becomes clear. Most of us learn by using all three ways, but we are stronger in one or two, especially when we are learning something that is difficult for us.

Many parents are unaware of these disparities in learning styles. Knowing they exist helps the parent understand why one child seems to learn more quickly than the other. For example: Your son Brian doesn't seem to learn as easily as your son Mark when something is explained to him for the first time. It's because the information is not presented in the way Brian learns best. If he is primarily a visual learner, and Mark is an auditory learner, then Brian will never respond to purely verbal instructions as well as Mark does. Brian needs to see it in order to learn it.

When most of us try to teach something new to someone else, we usually present the information in our own predominant learning style. If you are a parent who learns quickly when you hear something presented, then you will most likely try to teach your child with purely verbal instructions. Chances are very good that you will not think to present the information visually as well as verbally. Because you understand it when it's explained with words, you forget that your son Brian will understand it better if he sees a picture or a diagram. Consequently, because your son Mark learns in much the same way you do, by hearing information spoken, he will grasp the concept more quickly than Brian. Brian is then perceived to be the slower learner, when in fact, the information is just not being presented in his learning style.

To help you have a better understanding of your own family's differences and similarities in learning styles, have each of them answer the questions on pages 47 and 48. They are the same ones I use in my forum sessions. They will help you be aware of the differences in the way each member of your family learns by showing you the different ways each member responds to the same question.

This won't take long; there are only four questions. There are no secret or right answers. This is merely intended to make you more aware of the learning patterns within your own family. Each person should just write or say the letter of the answer that corresponds to the way he or she feels.

Question 1: *When a lightning storm comes, what do you do?*
  A. Turn out all the lights in the house so I can see the outside display.
  B. Turn off the television and radio so I can listen to the thunder and wind.
  C. Go outside so I can feel the wind and watch the movement of the clouds.

Question 2: *What is your favorite kind of vacation?*
  A. Traveling to places I've never seen before.
  B. Reading in a quiet cabin, far from a lot of people.
  C. Camping, or fishing, or playing basketball, or baseball, or some other activity.

Question 3: When you dress for school or work, what is most important to you?

   A. I want what I wear to be comfortable, so I can move easily.
   B. I want to wear something colorful, or very individual, something others notice.
   C. I want to wear a uniform, so I don't have to think about what to wear.

Question 4: In a restaurant, as long as the food is good, what else is important to you?

   A. To be with people I like to talk to.
   B. To be in a place that has pictures or posters or paintings on the walls and is nicely decorated.
   C. To be somewhere where I can see outside and feel that I have plenty of room.

Don't be surprised if some members of your family, including you, want to give more than one letter as an answer to one of the questions. None of us learns in just one clear-cut way all the time. However, you will see certain tendencies come to the surface. For example, your 10-year-old daughter may pick answer C in questions one and two, answer A in question three, and answer A in question four. Although the last answer hints at a child who likes words, conversation, and probably learns best by hearing instructions or reading directions, her answers to the first three questions indicate a child who is very kinesthetic. She probably prefers to move and be active, and therefore will learn best when she can be physically involved in the learning process.

By no means should you use any of the answers to cram your child, your spouse, or yourself into one neat little learning compartment. These are simply meant to make you aware of preferences that indicate learning tendencies. Learning tendencies that often overlap can still show some helpful pattern for you to follow when you are teaching your child. However, it's always wise to offer instruction that uses all three learning styles so that you're certain the message is getting through.

For example, when you're setting up a list of chores with your 14-year-old, don't just tell him what they are. Write them down and give him a copy to post in his room. Better yet, change the color of marker you use with each different chore. Even better, make a little symbol, funny cartoon, or simple diagram that goes with each chore. If you really want to reach your hands-on, kinesthetic learner, have *him* write them down, make the drawings, and change the colors. You get the idea. You're taking into consideration all three learning patterns, and when you do, there's a much better chance that your child will learn what you want him to know.

Precisely because it is auditory, visual, and kinesthetic all rolled into one, teaching by example is still the most powerful teaching method. Children learn to behave by observing how others behave. Notice I use the word *behave*. More is learned from our actual behavior than from any one thing we say. Words alone are weak teachers, even to strong auditory learners. When all they hear are words, without any evidence of action to support the words, the lesson takes much longer to learn.

Remember the story of my daughter recounting her memory of her father's honesty at the newspaper vending machine? What part of her father's example of worthwhile behavior left the most lasting impression on his daughter? What she saw? What she heard? Or was it that she was actively involved in the whole physical process of getting the newspapers? Because it was a lesson learned by example, all three learning styles were involved.

If you want to be certain your teaching is reaching each of your children, then rely on example as your strongest method. The example doesn't have to be heavy handed or obvious. Often, the lesson can be learned with humor and just plain fun as part of the example.

Consider this father who rides his Harley Davidson motorcycle to work every day. One of the things he wants to impress upon his son is that being prompt and responsible toward one's job does not have to be a joyless burden. His teenage son knows how much his father loves to ride that motorbike. Wearing the riding leathers and lace up boots, the father looks a little like some renegade biker, the stereotypical irresponsible individual.

However, his son sees something quite different. What he is learning from his father's actions is that his father goes to work every day, gets there on time, and does both riding a vehicle he thoroughly enjoys. The son sees that responsibility can successfully combine with enjoyment. The father could preach about this to his son until his son was weary of hearing things like "it's important to get to work on time" or "you can be a responsible person and still enjoy your life." The son learns the lesson much better from the fact that his father actually does both.

Example instructs so well because it is seen as well as heard, and it is interactive with those we need to teach. Because example teaches in all three learning styles, it has the greatest potential to bridge the differences in learning styles in your children. Example is also the most honest, most direct form of teaching.

Throughout this book, you will see this statement proven many times. You will begin to recognize situations in your own experience that also prove its truth.

There has been much scholarly work done on learning styles and intelligences. Such noted psychologists as Harvard's Howard Gardner have exhaustively researched the ways in which we learn. Bettie B. Youngs, in her book *Stress and Your Child*, includes a fine summary of Howard Gardner's theory of the Seven Intelligences, which delves even more deeply into learning patterns. It is not my intent to take parents on a scholarly journey into the complexities of learning styles. I save that for other professional educators. I merely want parents to understand that we all learn in different ways.

It is primarily because of that fact that children so desperately need some stability in the whole process. They want a constant, something about the ever-changing process of learning that does not change. That constant should and must be honesty. As we move through this book, I will return again and again to that constant. You will begin to believe how critical it is that you keep your word.

Stage 2

Take the Time

---

his second stage of your journey is where you learn about discovery, dreams, and direction and how important all three are to your child. This is where, perhaps for the very first time, you begin to truly appreciate the individuality of your child. You realize what is meant by effort, as you learn to pay attention to the often subtle signals your children send to you. This is where you open your mind to positive possibilities and help your children learn how to find their own.

Why do you need to discover your child?

Your child is your constant companion on this journey. It's wise, then, to make every effort to discover who this person is who travels with you. To do this, you must pay attention. If you are truly observant when you are with your child, you will notice many clues that will enlighten you. What are his likes and dislikes? What are her real interests? Who does he look up to in the family? Who does she think is funny? What embarrasses him? What does she think of herself? Why? These are just a few of the questions you should be able to answer.

If you can't, then you are trying to communicate with a stranger, speaking in a language neither of you understands. Your child's acceptance of anything you are trying to teach will be made much more difficult, if not impossible, if there is no real communication between the two of you. Far too many parents have a better knowledge of the real interests of their friends or neighbors than they have of their child's interests. I see sad evidence of this at our school every year.

When a student is having academic or social problems, parents are asked to come to the school for a parent-teacher conference. First, the parent is contacted by the school counselor and a time is arranged for the conference. The parent's work schedule is taken into consideration, and a time is set that will be convenient for all participants. The participants are part of what is properly called a student study team.

The team consists of every teacher who is currently teaching the child, the parents, or guardians of the child and one or more of the school's administrators. The student is also present at this conference. The key word is *study*. When we sincerely want to learn about something or someone, we have to study that something or someone in order for discovery to take place.

The atmosphere during the student study team meetings is informal yet serious. The emphasis is on interest and concern, not punishment. The object is to identify the positives and negatives of the situation so that progress can be made. Each teacher gives a brief assessment of the student's classroom situation, beginning with the positive aspects, then the negatives. The current grade in that particular subject is noted, along with the classroom behavior and the overall attitude of the student.

Each teacher usually brings some examples of the student's work. The counselor takes notes, as does the administrator, and the parent and the student are encouraged to ask questions or make comments during the proceedings. In other words, this meeting explores what is happening that is good and where improvement needs to be made. The student study team meeting is an effort by the school to directly involve parents in the educational process, yet many parents are uncomfortable with this.

Their attitudes vary widely. Some parents are clearly appreciative of this combined effort to help their child. But I've also seen parents display clear annoyance and irritation at having to be inconvenienced by the whole procedure. Others are very defensive. Some parents are subdued and fearful, intimidated by the educational surroundings, almost as though they shouldn't be there among so many educated experts. Others clearly do not seem to care about their child's situation. Some seem to wonder why we can't just fix the problem without involving them at all. First impressions, however, can be very misleading at these meetings. As the conference progresses, all too frequently I see evidence quite contrary to what the parent or the student wishes to project. In short, I often see people being dishonest with themselves.

For example, a student may be dressed in the latest teenage style and appear to be clean and properly fed. Beyond these outward indications of parental care and concern, it soon becomes obvious to me that the child is truly unknown to the parent sitting there beside him. At one typical conference, I brought drawings completed by the 15-year-old boy whose poor scholastic performance and poorer attitude were reasons for the meeting. My intent was to show evidence not only of some artistic talent, but more importantly, to show evidence of effort and the ability to begin and complete a difficult project.

The boy's mother looked in astonishment at the drawings I displayed. In an accusatory tone, she turned to the boy and said, "I didn't know you could draw!" as though it was somehow his fault that she had no knowledge of this part of his persona. She had that defensive air about her that always signals fear to me. Fear that it will be discovered that this parent and child are, in reality, strangers. They may live under the same roof and share the same last name, but they have very little real knowledge of who the other one really is.

This fear cannot be given a name by the parent who feels it, because it is not recognized for what it is. It masquerades behind the disguise of righteous indignation. Indignation that this child is causing a problem. Indignation that the school, the teachers, or anyone else, for that matter, cannot seem to fix the problem.

The boy's mother quickly offered the excuse most parents offer: They have so little time. Rising to their own defense, they cite reasons such as both parents are working outside the home, it is a single-parent situation, or other children are taking up the parent's time. I contend that time truly is the problem, but not in the way these parents believe.

Let's assume that both parents are working outside the home because of necessity rather than choice. If that's the case, it's wise to remember that both parents earning the family income is nothing new in most of our family histories.

Both sets of my Italian immigrant grandparents found it absolutely necessary for mother and father to be working parents. My mother's mother ran a grocery/deli store seven days a week, and her husband operated a small shoemaker shop. My father's mother took in Italian immigrant railroad laborers as boarders and cooked separate meals for each one as they came off their shifts. Each boarder supplied the meat, but all the produce was supplied from my grandmother's ample veg-etable garden in her backyard, which she cultivated and planted herself. Her husband, my father's father, was a foreman on a track crew for that same railroad. When he lost his job during the Depression, he tended their backyard grapevines and did odd jobs while my grandmother con-tinued to care for the boarders.

The oldest child, my Aunt Marie, had to quit school to help supple-ment the family income. She used her facility with language (she was flu-ent in English and Italian) to land a job as part-time teller and interpreter for the local bank's many Italian-speaking customers. Her parents encour-aged her to try for the job because they were well aware of her skill with language. In spite of their heavy workload, all four of my grandparents could tell anyone who asked what each of their children's strengths and interests were. It wasn't because they had a lot of time. It was because they used what little time they had to pay attention to the signs that were there for them to see.

If anything, due to modern conveniences and lower expectations, most of us have more time than any of our grandparents did. We squander much of it on such things as sitting passively in front of the television set watching boring programs that cause us to constantly switch channels. We spend much of it sitting in our cars, driving from one function to another, keeping ourselves busy without being productive. As parents, we issue passing directives to our children as we rush from one thing to another, instead of having real conversations with them about dreams and goals and what it takes to reach them.

Yet, there are so many ways we can discover our children without prying or violating their privacy, and without drastically curtailing our own interests and activities. We just have to use our time wisely. We have to pay attention to them as individuals. How can we ever expect them to pay attention to us when we have so little regard for them that we won't even take the time to discover who they are?

How can you understand each child's individuality?

The greater the effort you make to discover your child, the better you will understand that child as an individual. Remember that you began this journey to learn how to be the teacher your child needs. Teaching to the individual provides a much greater opportunity for that individual to learn the lessons you are trying to teach. In the classroom, we call it one-on-one teaching, and it is most effective because it allows the teacher to use the child's individual interests as motivational tools. The interests a child has are also strong indicators of learning styles. As a parent, you are in the best position to observe the things that make your children the individuals they are. It will take effort, as well as time, but any sort of significant study takes both.

One way to discover your children's interests is to notice what they do with their free time. By free time, I mean that part of their day when they choose, not you, what's to be done.

Is your 10-year-old sitting with a pile of library books beside her, intent on the one in her lap? Is it yet another story about horses? Is your 5-year-old outside, pedaling up and down the driveway in his toy car, pretending to be in a race and cheering as though he's in some make-believe competition? Or is he looking around, letting the wind whip his cheeks red, just enjoying the exhilaration of the exercise? A glance or two can tell you things. These are the clues that can help you discover what will motivate that particular child. That knowledge can be a tremendous help to you every time you teach your child a new concept.

For example, if that 10-year-old needs a better understanding of how to handle money, explain it in terms of the cost of hay, veterinary bills, and necessary tack for the horse she hopes to have one day. If that competitive little 5-year-old needs to do a better job of picking up his toys, set the chore up as a timed game, complete with starting whistle and a chalkboard to mark the minutes it takes from one day to the next. Time? Do these approaches take up any more of your time than the usual nagging and harassing you have to do otherwise?

Why not talk with your child the way you do when you're with a neighbor or a friend? When we're with our children, we often shun real conversation. We don't ask questions about things we know interest the child, as we would with a friend. Instead, we bark orders, or worse, ignore any attempts at real conversation that the child initiates. We rebuff those attempts with comments like "I'm too busy right now." Would we say this to a friend? How much time does it take to stop for a minute and listen, as we would if a neighbor dropped in for a visit?

Remember Robert from the introduction? His mother complained that he spent most of his time in front of the television set and seldom spoke to her with any sort of civility. On those few evenings when he was home, I wondered if his mother made any real attempt to engage him in any conversation. Or did her idea of conversation with him consist of complaints about his lack of help around the house? Was his surly manner of speaking to her his way of dealing with the fact that he felt that she had no real interest in him, beyond what he might do for her? When she heard him laughing at something he saw on the television screen, did she wander by, notice what he found so funny, just to give herself some information about this stranger in her house?

When someone tells me their child is speaking to them in a disrespectful manner, I'm very interested to know how that person speaks to the child. What is the child learning from example? When we first meet a new neighbor, we try to be friendly, making them feel welcome by our tone of voice and by the interest we show in them. Try treating that recalcitrant teenager as if he or she was someone you just met. It may take many attempts before you get a real response, but don't quit. Be as patient with your family as you are with your friends. No matter how busy you think you are, you have the time.

As a teenager, some of the best conversations I ever had with my mother occurred as she and I prepared dinner. When I'd come home from school, distraught over losing a cheerleading contest or frustrated from an argument with a favorite classmate, she didn't put me off with "Not now, I'm busy!" She made me a part of what she was doing, as she might have done had a friend dropped by with some news. She'd hand me the potatoes and a peeler while she asked me questions that showed an honest interest.

Hers was a wise approach. It meant she never had to pry into my life. She made me feel what I had to say was important to her, and I found it easy to volunteer information. Information that helped her discover who I was and what mattered to me. She was a very results-oriented little Italian lady, and you can be certain she always had plenty to do with her time, but she was wise enough to know that counseling her own children was one of the most important of her many jobs.

Often, as parents, we think we know who are children are as individuals. To find out if you are truly paying attention to the signals they are sending your way, answer the set of questions in the form on page 60. Write them down and make a separate sheet for each member of your family. Be completely honest. For example, it's important to write down who your *child's* favorite friend is, not who *you* would like that favorite friend to be. This is the same questionnaire that I ask parents to complete in the forum sessions.

Your Child's Interests

Name: _____

What is his or her favorite form of entertainment?
(Television? Music videos? Be specific.) _____
_____

Favorite form of physical exercise? _____
Favorite food? _____
Favorite friend or friends? _____
Favorite relative? _____
Does he or she enjoy athletics? _____
(Not at all? A little? Very much?) _____
Does he or she enjoy reading?
(If so, what? Books? Magazines? Be specific.) _____
_____

Does he or she enjoy writing?
(If so, what? Stories? Poems? Song lyrics? Be specific.) _____
_____
_____

What is his or her favorite form of travel? _____
What is the favorite "hands-on" activity?
(Building? Drawing? Cooking? Be specific.) _____
_____

What does he or she dream of becoming?
(When we visit our next location, I'll explain exactly why I consider
this last question to be so important.) _____
_____
_____

When participants do this exercise in a forum session, many parents are
sincerely shocked to see that they have to leave many questions completely

blank. One father, a confident, friendly man who was a truck driver by trade told me he was so upset because he went home after the session and checked with his son to see how correct his answers were. He had missed the mark with every single one. His first reaction, he told me, was to hide behind the excuse that he was on the road so much and that was why he really didn't know his son.

"Then I remembered," he said, "that you told us to be honest with ourselves. When I was home, I just didn't really pay attention. Not only to my son, but to what my wife had to say, either. I figured I was doing enough to feed Kyle and give him a decent place to live. But what good was that if I didn't even know this kid I was supposed to be raising?"

I assured Kyle's father that he was not alone in missing the mark. Years ago, when I first developed this set of questions, I decided to answer them myself. Writing both of my own children's names across the top of two different copies of the questions, I confidently filled in the blanks. My daughter was about 13 years old at the time, and my son was almost 15. I was certain that I had a pretty fair knowledge of who their favorite family members were.

I was completely wrong. Their favorites were definitely not my favorites, though I was somehow expecting them to be the same. Had I really been paying attention, I would have noticed things like which relative my daughter seemed to spend more time with at family gatherings. I wasn't at all aware of who she really liked or why. The clues were there for me to see, but I wasn't bothering to look.

I missed the mark in other areas, too. For example, I thought my son had little or no interest in any sort of physical sport. Because he had never shown an inclination toward any team sport activity, I never thought to consider the possibility that he might find individual sports appealing. I was very surprised to see that he listed such things as hang gliding in the section on athletics.

Then I remembered how eager he had been to try it earlier that year, when a group of his father's students gathered for a practice session conducted by a professional hang-gliding instructor. My son was asked to participate, and he proved to be very good at it, especially for a young beginner. Had I bothered to see the clues in that bit of information, it could have been very helpful in better understanding the role athletics might have played in my son's life.

I reminded Kyle's father that the point of asking the questions is not to embarrass parents but to enlighten them. It's what we do with the answers that matters. Once I admitted that I didn't know as much as I thought I did about my own children, I was able to pay better attention and increase my knowledge of who they really were. That's exactly what Kyle's father did, and he couldn't believe how much more success he had helping to improve his son's attitude toward school when they started having real conversations instead of shouting matches.

He began taking his son along when he readied his truck for another long haul. Together, they checked the mechanics of the truck, filled it with fuel, and did a general safety evaluation. Kyle began to look forward to this work ritual as a way to prove to his dad that he was ready for more adult responsibility. The father realized his son was no longer a boy, but a young man eager for what the son saw as more manly chores.

His father put Kyle in charge of things like securing all the outbuildings on their small ranch when he was away. It was Kyle's responsibility to be sure everything was locked, and grasses and weeds were kept cut and clear of equipment so there was less fire danger when the dry desert winds whipped through their property. It was a chore to be taken seriously and Kyle knew it. He began staying home more when his dad was away, which was a great comfort to his mother. Kyle enjoyed the feeling of being trusted to take care of things. Something was being expected of him.

From their conversations, the father also learned that his son really enjoyed writing. Realizing his dad was truly interested in what he was doing, Kyle showed his dad a story he wrote for an English assignment. He liked to write about real events, in the way a reporter would, so his dad asked him to ask his teacher if he could write something about a day in the life of a truck driver. The boy was delighted when his teacher suggested that he accompany his father on one of his shorter runs and take notes for the story. Both of them saw each other in a clearer light after that trip. Father and son were together, as individuals, paying attention to each other.

Working together can be one of the best ways to encourage enlightening conversations with your child. Not only is the child learning to value work for its own sake, but he's also learning to value the individual who works alongside him. One reason we often develop strong friendships with our colleagues on the job is because we are paying attention to each other, just in the course of doing our job.

It is no accident that close camaraderie frequently develops between police officers who are partners on the job. It is not only that they spend a great deal of time together, but that they spend it in an atmosphere of work that they both consider important. In this environment, trust can develop between two individuals who may be very different in their over-all interests. The common interest of the work they do together makes it necessary for them to pay attention to each other. Their very lives often depend not only on how well they perform their duties, but on how well they know their partner. It is that knowledge that helps them know how that person will react in a given situation. It is that understanding of the other person as an individual that helps both partners feel secure in their knowledge of each other. How do they acquire that knowledge? By paying attention.

Why must you encourage your child's dreams?

Children who do not have a dream will never have a goal, a purpose, or a reason to struggle to achieve. Furthermore, a child with no dream is a child who becomes an easy target for those who sell the destructive dream of easy gratification and instant reward. What does your child dream of becoming? This last item on the questionnaire on page 60 is the one that I consider to be the most significant, yet it is often the one that parents are the least aware of, if they have considered it at all.

Most people are aware, for example, that their best friend always wanted to be a doctor but never got the opportunity. Most people are aware that the third baseman on their company softball team almost made it to the professional minor leagues. However, they have no idea what dreams their own children have for their futures.

Parents seldom realize that children's dreams begin early. Right now, that 5-year-old with the toy car wants to be a fireman. That 10-year-old dreams of training a horse to be a jumper. Encourage those dreams! Never mind that the dream may change. Each change is simply a shift in the general direction, but at least it is a forward momentum and not the backward pull that occurs when no interest and no direction are present.

No matter how often the dream changes and shifts, encourage each one because children learn from each one. They learn things they can carry with them and use in the next dream. They learn what they really value and what doesn't really hold their interest. They learn about possibilities in the world and in themselves.

"But," parents argue, "my daughter changes her mind every year. I can't keep paying for all her whims." I agree. The answer is not to discourage the dream, but to let most of the money for the dream's pursuit come primarily from the child's effort. I know a 14-year-old would-be guitar player who sweeps up and washes all the windows and glass cases at the local music store two afternoons a week after school in return for his weekly guitar lesson. A 12-year-old I know is cleaning animal cages at the pet supply store in exchange for a new puppy.

As a parent, you can and should help, but the child's investment of time and money is how he or she, and you, will learn if the interest is real or just a phase. If the child is willing to invest in the dream, then it's pretty safe to assume that dream is an indicator of that child's possible future direction.

Even when children change their dream often, parents who are paying attention will notice a pattern of interest common to each one. The little fireman may decide next year that he wants to be a policeman, and the year after that, he's enamored with the idea of becoming a paratrooper.

What is the common thread running through all of these? Is he interested in the challenge of life-and-death situations, taking care of others, or wearing a uniform? Whatever the common thread, it will weave through each dream and eventually resurface in the child's choice of an occupation. Sometimes that choice will at first seem unconnected to any of his early dreams. For example, he may become a doctor. But isn't a doctor duty bound to take care of others? Doesn't a doctor wear a uniform of a sort? Doesn't a doctor deal with the challenge of life-and-death situations?

Then again, the child may decide he wants nothing to do with any of these things. That's perfectly normal. Many of us find our true calling by the process of elimination. If we have dreams and we follow them for a while, we soon discover if they are what we thought they would be. If our interest wanes, then we can eliminate that possibility and go on to the next. Eventually, when we've discarded what didn't really hold our interest, we can see a clearer path to what we really want to be. Even if it is a phase, what children learn from the experience can be easily translated and used in pursuing the next passion that pulls them toward goals and what it takes to reach them.

Learning is not linear. It never goes in a straight, uncomplicated line. It bounces back and forth. It spreads out, like a river on a flood plain, picking up information, adding to itself, increasing its power as it narrows, regains its focus, and moves forward.

Childhood is the time when we should be encouraged to try on different dreams. Allow your child the freedom to fantasize and play different roles. My children had many different dreams as they moved through childhood and into adolescence, and we encouraged each one. In his early grade-school years, my son dreamed of becoming a train engineer. During junior high, that dream evolved into a fascination with model trains. He read about them and spent long hours at the local hobby shop. In a small room above our garage, he spent many evenings building little villages and learning to do the simple wiring for the train track layouts he designed.

Sometimes he was joined by friends who shared his interest, or some who were just curious to see what he did. Often, I joined him there, helping him paint the mountains for the scenery or attach the lichen we gathered to use as shrubbery on those tiny mountainsides. Just as often, he worked alone, engrossed in the project. Sometimes, he just went up there to play with the train set and dream.

All of these early experiences led indirectly to other interests that eventually resulted in a career as an electronic engineer. Yes, my husband built the train table for my son, but it was money my son earned mowing lawns and saved from Christmas and birthday gifts that paid for most of his model trains and his track.

You must allow it to be your child's dream, your child's investment of time and money, your child's dream to own. If you want to discover your child, you should know what that dream is. It's absolutely essential that you take the time.

Stage 3

Be the Guide

he places we visit in this stage of your journey will teach you about inspiration. In these locations, you become better acquainted with those traveling with you, and in the process, learn to better understand yourself. You will also visit briefly with others you are meeting for the first time and may never see again. Each of their stories will interest you. Some will surprise you, and some will sadden you, but each will help you prepare for the rest of the journey.

How can you inspire your child?

In order to inspire your children to set goals and overcome their fears, you need to overcome your own fears. Your willingness to accept that challenge will be the inspiration for your children to do the same. If not controlled, fear for their physical and emotional safety will constrict their confidence and keep them from setting goals that involve any sort of difficulty.

To overcome those fears, you must be motivated by a belief in the greater good you will achieve by putting them in proper perspective. When you do, your energy can be directed to helping your children learn the difference between necessary and unnecessary risk.

Please understand that keeping your children from any activity that involves risk can sometimes place them in greater danger. Physical and emotional risks are an inherent part of life. Neither can be completely avoided, nor should they be. We can take sensible precautions, but complete avoidance is not possible or even desirable. If we try to miss every single small pothole in this road we travel, we will be too preoccupied to avoid the greater chasm that may lie ahead.

Physical and emotional risks are always linked together. Protection from one may lead to greater exposure to the other. So many of us, in a misguided effort to keep our children safe from all physical harm, discourage their interest in anything we fear may be physically dangerous. We ignore the often more potent problem of lack of direction and its resulting boredom.

The child who is in real danger is the child who has no interest in anything. Yet it is highly likely that same child almost certainly did show an interest in something at an earlier stage in life, but the interest was dismissed, belittled, or completely ignored by the parent. Because the parent believed it to be frivolous, impractical, or physically dangerous, the child was never inspired to pursue it. If they tried to, the parent either discouraged it or forbade it outright. This is not only demoralizing to the child but can often be even more dangerous than the physical risks involved in the original interest.

Often parents are completely unaware that their reaction to a child's dream is a negative one. Suppose your 11-year-old wants to take dancing lessons. Her teacher took her class to a performance of the community college dance class, and your daughter was intrigued with the tap dancers. One of the college students is offering lessons in tap as a way to both earn some extra money and put her newly learned teaching techniques into practice. The lessons are reasonable, and she will come to the grade school once a week as part of her student-teaching requirement. What possible reason could you have to discourage your child's desire to take advantage of this opportunity to learn something new?

There's no great risk of injury. You're not afraid of where she has to go to take the lessons. Yet you find yourself saying, "Why do you want to do that? It takes hours and hours of practice, and you're not very coordinated. Remember the trouble you had learning to make the right moves in volleyball?" What motivates you to react in such a negative way? You tell yourself you're being realistic, sparing your child future disappointment.

The true reality is that you are stifling your child's willingness to risk learning something new. Learning to tap dance may be her way of dealing with the disappointment of not making the volleyball team. If you still want her to have a reality check, you can approach it in a much more positive way. "I'm sure it takes a lot of practice time, but it would be wonderful to be able to tap dance." Be thankful your child is willing to risk setting another goal.

What else motivates parents to stifle a child's natural desire to take a risk to achieve something, to risk having a goal? Often, beyond a healthy desire to protect a child, parents are motivated by a selfish desire to avoid facing disappointment in themselves. Sadly, sometimes parents don't want their child to have any interests that might make the child's life more exciting and meaningful.

This is never a conscious wish on the part of the parents. Parents who are bored and demoralized want to believe that it's not their fault that their lives have been so disappointing. If their child is interested in a goal or a dream and is actively pursuing it, the parents fear they will be left behind. They will lose their importance to the child. They will have to face the fact that their own life is dull and unfulfilling because of a failure on their part to do anything to change it. Unwilling to make that effort and unable to be honest with themselves, they unwittingly sacrifice their child, unconsciously condemning the child to the same disappointing existence they have.

Equally demoralizing and destructive are the parents who seek to fulfill their own dreams through their child. Under the guise of support and encouragement, these parents prod and push their child to achieve in an area of little or no real interest to the child. The parents are unwilling to make the effort to pursue their own dreams; they use the child to do the hard work of making that dream a reality.

"When I was your age," the parent may say, "I'd have given anything to have the chance to be a musician!" Children understandably rebel at this manipulation and arguments result that often leave the child feeling helpless and guilty for wanting to follow a different dream. If the child, in an effort to please an overbearing parent, does try to adopt the parent's dream as his own, it is usually at great cost to the child's emotional health and often manifests itself in physical illness.

Remember 12-year-old Elizabeth, who joined us at the beginning of this journey? Already physically mature, Elizabeth deliberately dressed to give the impression of a much older girl, and the money she stole from her mother's purse was used to buy expensive cosmetics. On the surface, her only interests seemed to be her physical appearance and the effect it had on her peers. Was this only a confused reaction to her early maturity? What were her real interests? Did either of her parents know?

From my first brief conversation with them, I already knew Elizabeth was desperate to be noticed. Her choice of clothes and the attention-attracting makeup were obvious clues that she wanted to be noticed and give herself some identity in the eyes of others. Apparently she felt there was no other way she could do it. As the forum sessions progressed, I realized there was very little at home to inspire Elizabeth to investigate any other interests she may have had.

Neither of her parents seemed to have any desire to do anything other than watch television. At least, that's what Elizabeth saw. Television was on night and day, whenever someone was home. Elizabeth's father had no hobbies to occupy his spare time, and he made it clear that he certainly had no interest in his job. One of his complaints about Elizabeth was that "she doesn't give a damn that my job has a lot of responsibility for little pay. I'm under a lot of pressure, and I can't wait to get to the house after work so I can relax and forget that place. And what do I get from her? Always asking for more of my hard-earned money to buy expensive makeup or add to her closet full of clothes!"

He was clearly the dominating influence in the family, and his beaten, negative attitude had apparently long ago stifled any interests and dreams his wife may have had. She too had a job, as one of several receptionists in a local dentist's office. But it clearly held no interest for her beyond her paycheck. She told me on one occasion that she was "basically pretty shy" and didn't like the way some of the other receptionists "visited" with the patients. "I can't do that," she said, failing to see that the receptionists she spoke about might actually be enjoying their jobs.

There was nothing about either one of her parents' examples to inspire Elizabeth to develop herself in any way but the obvious easy path to superficial attention. She concentrated on her outward appearance. Her young life was so boring that she wanted to rush through it, plunging headlong into the adult world by taking advantage of her rapidly maturing body and using it as a shortcut to what she perceived as a more interesting life. I asked her stepmother pointedly, "When Elizabeth was younger, what did she like to do?"

"Climb trees," her stepmother said. "We had a couple in the backyard of our old house, and I couldn't keep her off them. She was pretty limber and liked the monkey bars and climbing stuff at the grade school play ground." During the course of our conversation, her stepmother offhandedly mentioned that the only time Elizabeth seemed to really like school was when they did gymnastics in physical education.

"She tried out for the gymnastics team last year, and she made it," her stepmother said. "But at one of the practices after school, one of the girls broke her arm coming off the bar. That did it for me." The woman pursed her lips in a tight line as she continued. I sensed that she and Elizabeth had tangled over this one. "I made her quit. All we need is for her to get hurt and run up medical bills when neither of us has very good medical benefits from our jobs." I hoped in my heart that their medical benefits would not feel the greater challenge of the bills that might come later from a drug overdose or an unwanted pregnancy.

Why do children need to take risks?

Children are natural risk-takers, especially teenagers. It's how they test themselves, how they find meaning and excitement in their lives. The effort of overcoming the risk is how they keep themselves motivated and challenged. Parents can diminish the risk by teaching the child about safety and promoting safe attitudes. In that way, the child can still use the interest as a way to learn goal setting and the importance of effort.

Parents who discourage that interest are missing a golden opportunity to direct that child's need to take risks. The need will surface one way or another. Was Elizabeth testing her ability to take risks when she took money from her stepmother's purse? Was staying out all night putting her in less physical danger than swinging on the high bar for the gymnastics team, where Elizabeth could receive some of that attention she so desperately wanted?

This location in our journey provides some history that can help you understand how dangerous it is to stifle risk-taking instead of directing it. When my daughter was only 10 years old, she began saving money toward the purchase of a horse. It was a dream that began when she was 8. One of my well-meaning friends mentioned more than once that she personally knew several people who had been badly injured by horses. Her comments played on my own rather timid nature when it comes to things physical.

My lack of confidence in my ability to do things that required some physical courage was a direct result of my mother's well-intentioned but misdirected concern for my safety. She was only 19 years old when I was born and extremely anxious to prove herself to be a mother who would never let any harm come to any of her children. As a child, every time I tried anything that included some risk of physical injury, my mother cautioned me about it so much that her fears became my fears.

As an adult, I understood why she had been so overprotective, but during my childhood, it only made me unnecessarily fearful. I was determined that I would not continue the precedent my mother had set by transferring my fears to my daughter. I wanted my daughter to feel free to test her physical capability and not limit her possibilities, as I had done. In my heart, every time my friend reminded me of the dangers of dealing with livestock, I worried that I might be encouraging my daughter to follow an interest that could one day cause her serious injury. Thankfully, the logical part of my mind knew it wasn't my choice to make.

I reminded myself that my purpose as a parent was to help my children learn to have purpose themselves. The best way for children to learn how to direct themselves toward productive goals is for those goals to be of their own choosing.

As a teacher, I learned not to ignore the natural strengths and interests of my students if I wanted to motivate them. When I learned to channel their natural strengths and interests, I realized that approach could work miracles. It also worked wonders in my own home. When my daughter first dreamed of a horse of her own, we were living in a small tract house with the nearest stable two or three miles away. Wanting to encourage her, yet needing to be practical, my husband and I made her an offer. It was in three parts, each one prefaced with an *if.*

If, by her 12th birthday she could save enough money to buy a horse, if, in the meantime she would study the care and feeding of horses, and if she took a riding lesson every week on the "kid's horse" kept at the stable for just such a purpose, then she could have her horse when she reached that 12th birthday. Our thinking was that riding lessons would help her learn both basic horse skills and riding skills, which she would need to know when she had her own horse. We also felt that a 12-year-old would be better able to appreciate the importance of $30 a month for stall rent at the stable.

Our plan was to help her see how short-range goals lead to long-range goals. We also wanted to test her determination and discover if the interest was real or a passing whim. Four years was a good test of anyone's determination, and even if it were a passing phase, she would be learning valuable lessons along the way.

When my friend began worrying me with her fears of injury, we were two years into the plan. Already, the same small miracles I had witnessed in classrooms were occurring in my own home. A little girl who had shown no interest at all in subjects like anatomy and biology was now taking a keen interest in animal science information presented in school. That same little girl was getting up very early every Saturday and bicycling to the stables to help brush and wash a friend's horse in return for extra lessons.

"She's still two years away from her dream," I finally told my concerned friend. "In that time, she may be hurt pursuing that dream. She may also be hurt by someone running a red light and crashing into our car when I'm taking her to the library."

To my friend's credit, she never spoke of injury fears again. However, she never followed my lead and looked for clues of interest in her own child's life. Even when his interests became obvious, she ignored them, or did her best to stifle them.

Her son was relatively slight in build, but he wanted desperately to play football. She adamantly opposed it for fear of injury. She was also afraid that her son would suffer feelings of rejection if he was unable to adequately compete with so many boys bigger and stronger than he was. She would later discover that her lack of faith in her son's ability to handle that possible rejection would prove to be far more damaging to him than anything that could happen on the football field.

At a gathering of parents in our neighborhood years ago, my husband made an observation that I wish my friend had heeded. Talking about our need to let our children test themselves, he said that small successes build confidence, and small defeats build character.

Even if her son spent most of the season on the bench, just being a part of the team would have boosted his confidence far more than never having the opportunity to test himself and compete in a game he loved. Being on the team would have given him a small success. Not playing often would have only been a small defeat. At least if he was on the bench there was always the possibility that he would play. She kept him from that possibility.

A year or two later, he wanted to wrestle in the bantam-weight division in school, but his mother thought it a brutal, pointless sport, and again feared that he would feel inferior if others defeated him. Without realizing it, she was the one who defeated him by not allowing him to participate. Every opportunity he sought to strengthen his body and his confidence was routinely denied him.

Her son was never injured from football or wrestling. In a desperate attempt to prove his manhood, he began drinking after school with some older boys who also had no meaningful goals to reach, no practices to attend, and no where else they needed to be. When he was 15 years old, after an afternoon of drinking, he was a passenger in a car driven by one of his buddies. It plunged into an irrigation canal and all four young men in the car drowned.

I do not wish to infer that teenagers drink only because of lack of involvement in athletics. I know too many equally sad stories of teens, very active in sports, who fell victim to drinking and in some cases, were themselves the drunk drivers who took the lives of others. But I want to stress the importance of allowing children to participate in activities that interest them, even when those activities involve some physical risk. If those risks are part of a larger positive learning experience, closely monitored by coaches, parents, or other responsible adults, then risk can be minimized by such steps as insisting on proper equipment and providing reliable drivers to take children to and from events.

As parents, we can't allow our own fears to build artificial fences around our children. The possibility of injury and illness are always part of the inevitable pattern of life. How can our children ever learn to cope with life's realities if we protect them from every opportunity to learn how to take sensible precautions and still stay in the game? Remember that children have a need to test themselves. Direct that need, don't deny it. By your own example, show your child how to pursue interests in a sensible, safe way.

In one of the first forums I gave, one mother was extremely worried about her 16-year-old son's interest in motorcycle racing. I encouraged her to talk to him about the safety issues, and together they agreed on the steps he should take to minimize the risks. His father, a welder by trade, had always impressed upon his son how all the safety steps had to be followed, so the concept of minimizing risk was not new to the boy. Her son gathered all the information he could on the safest local tracks and the best safety equipment to wear.

His mother was relieved by all the effort her son had made to insure his own safety. His father encouraged the boy to maintain the motorcycle's working parts himself, so he could be certain faulty equipment would not present a problem. He had learned from his father's example that safety was a sensible part of any pursuit.

His mother gradually began to see how this interest was giving some purpose to her son's life and keeping him from the boredom that is the downfall of so many 16-year-olds. It was also helping him develop some practical mechanical skills, as well as personal pride because of those skills. Yes, he was taking a risk, but he was directing that risk, not ignoring it.

As his mother realized the value of directed risk, she began attending some of the rallies her son participated in and found herself cheering loudly for him. She was proud of his courage, and even more, she was proud of the fact that when he lost, he was learning to handle defeat without being defeated. He was also learning how to be gracious in victory. The races helped him learn to set and strive for goals. I explained to her that taking risk in a responsible way was building her son's confidence in his ability to take care of himself. It's much easier to be gracious when we believe ourselves to be worthwhile, capable individuals.

Will he one day become a famous motorcycle racer or open his own repair shop? Will this interest exhaust his need for physical risk and shift his life's work in an altogether different direction, like computer programming? Doesn't a computer programmer need to be conscious of meticulous detail? Wouldn't a computer programmer benefit from the ability to dismantle, repair, and reprogram in much the same way that this 16-year-old learned these skills to maintain the overall quality of his motorcycle's performance? Perhaps his current interest will resurface later, in the form of a weekend hobby, but it doesn't matter.

How, when, or if he uses his motorcycle racing experience in some direct form later in his life is not important. It will still have served its purpose. It built his self-confidence and increased his ability to handle competition, accepting its challenges and seeing its defeats and victories as part of a larger process. The confidence he gained from following his interest far outweighs the risks that were involved. His need to take risks was satisfied in a positive, productive manner. It kept him occupied, busy pursuing goals and too busy to be bored.

Confidence gained and skills learned increased this boy's choices about what to do with his life. By overcoming her fear and allowing her son to take that initial risk, his mother demonstrated her belief in his ability to learn to take care of himself. That in itself is a great confidence-builder for a child. By overcoming her fear, his mother taught him by her example something about her own courage.

What is so important about self-reliance?

Self-reliance is the foundation for self-respect. When we encourage our children to rely on themselves, we are proving to them that we believe them to be capable individuals. What is one of the first things that brings pride into a small child's eyes? When that child is able to complete a task and say, "Look, I did it all by myself!"

In that moment, the child feels the freedom of being able to do something independent of anyone else. Self-respect has begun to be a reality for that child. All sorts of examples come to my mind, but I will use only one, because it so clearly demonstrates the link between self-reliance and self-respect. It also illustrates how early this need for self-respect begins.

Daniel, my youngest grandson, is not yet 3 years old. One recent Saturday, I was spending the afternoon with him and his older brother, Jacob, who is 5 years old. The three of us just returned from a long walk, and the boys raced for the house to get a drink. Jacob, playing the big brother role, reached for two cups on the sink drain board and handed one to Daniel. How nice, I thought, that he's going to get a drink for his little brother.

As I watched, Jacob reached into the refrigerator, pulled out a fairly heavy plastic container of water, poured some into his cup, then put the container back on a low shelf in the refrigerator without pouring any water into his brother's cup. Daniel just watched patiently, with none of the whining I expected to hear because of what I perceived to be his brother's neglect. "Jacob," I said rather sharply, "Why didn't you get some water for Daniel?" Jacob's answer was quick and to the point, "Because he likes to get it for himself."

As he spoke, I watched Daniel struggle with the water container, needing both small hands to heft it off the shelf. Then he lugged it over to the table and heaved it onto the tabletop. Beaming proudly, he turned to me and said, "Me do it!" Jacob smiled knowingly and filled his brother's cup for him.

Apparently, the two little boys had already learned, probably through trial and error, that the container was too heavy for Daniel to also be able to pour the water. Daniel was perfectly willing to accept his big brother's help when it was really needed. However, he didn't want to be insulted by having his brother do the part that he knew he could do for himself. Jacob, by honoring his little brother's need to be self-reliant, allowed Daniel to add another small layer to his gradually building self-respect.

How had Jacob learned to encourage his little brother's self-reliance? The lesson was learned from his parents' example. From the time Jacob was Daniel's age, he remembered that he was encouraged to do things for himself whenever possible. His parents were ready to help when help was needed, but they were also willing to wait while the child took the extra time to try to do things on his own. This big brother was doing for his little brother what had been done for him.

I'm sure it would have been much easier in many instances for his parents to simply do the task themselves, thus providing Daniel with the result instead of teaching the child how to get the result for himself. It would have been easier for them and for Daniel in the short term, but much more difficult for all of them in the long term.

Unfortunately, many parents prefer the role of provider to the role of teacher. They want to provide everything for their children. If you are one of those parents, remember that one of the things you learned in the beginning of this journey was the importance of honesty with yourself. If you are being honest, you will see that clinging to the role of provider may be a way to avoid making the necessary changes that you need to make in yourself in order to be an effective teacher.

As a teacher to your children, you need to develop patience and consistency, and constantly keep your ultimate goal in mind. As a provider, you have no such constraints on your own behavior. Providing everything you think your child needs or you want him to have can be very personally satisfying as a short-term goal. It makes you feel important, necessary, and in control. Best of all, it requires no real effort on your part in terms of self-improvement. Without changing yourself at all, you can purchase, make, or do everything for your child. In this way, you believe that you insure your child's happiness. I urge you to understand that not only is that a selfish goal, but it is an impossible one. Here are some of the reasons why.

As a classroom teacher, I meet many parents who want to be able to say, "I gave my children everything they ever wanted." However, if they do, they are keeping from their children the one thing those children want and need most: the opportunity to respect themselves and their own abilities.

It's useful for us to remember that it is not our responsibility as parents to provide our children's happiness. Each of us must make ourselves happy. The self-reliant individual will be able to find his or her own happiness. Remember that's what your goal must be, for no matter how hard you try, as a parent, you cannot provide your child's happiness. That role is rightfully reserved for each individual.

Happiness is not an external thing. It must come from within the self. It cannot be given to someone. It must be gained by each individual for his or her own self. What better way to do that than to pursue our own interests, struggle toward our own goals, and claim our victories as our own? We must struggle. It is the struggle to reach them that gives true value to our goals. Without struggle, we may get the desired results, but there is no real achievement when that happens.

Self-respect is not enhanced when luck takes on greater importance than struggle. No one gains self-respect from accidental victories. We all like to feel that we are in control of our lives. When we stop the struggle and rely on luck to get what we need in life, we lose that control. In order for us to feel truly successful in our lives, we need to know that our success comes from our own effort, not from handouts or gifts. Both are fine in the right time and place, but as a way of life they are self-defeating and demoralizing. We do not want our children to be the victims of our own selfish need to make them happy.

Another reason for avoiding the pitfalls of the provider role is the fact that it's not the things we have that give us true satisfaction. It's the journey toward obtaining those things, the effort it took that marks their real value. On that journey to acquire what we think we desire, we learn much about ourselves.

One of the lessons we learn is that sometimes the things we think we need or want are not really that important to us after all. The thing itself is only the symbol of the journey and the goal reached, tangible evidence of the effort it took to acquire it. When too much is provided for us, it makes us lose confidence in our ability to provide for ourselves. Remember that one of your goals is for your child to become self-reliant.

One of the most important reasons for your child to develop skills in self-reliance is the somber fact that your role as your child's provider can change at any time. You can lose your job, become seriously ill, or be badly injured. Then your ability to provide is drastically impaired. However, none of these things alter the fact that you can still be a teacher of your child. How you deal with the challenges of job loss, illness, or injury can teach your child valuable lessons in how to cope with unexpected and unwanted change.

Now, I'd like to introduce Beth, the mother of three. Her oldest child, a 16-year-old girl, had been a student in one of my classes for only a few weeks when her mother came to the classroom. The family was new to our area, and Beth was checking with all of her daughter's teachers to see how she was coping with her new school environment.

"Melissa is doing well in my class," I told her mother. "I'm particularly impressed with how responsible she is, and how hard she works. She seems to get along well with others in the class, teasing and laughing with them before the bell, but she goes right to work when class begins. She's adjusting remarkably well to entering a new school so late in the year."

Beth smiled, and I could see that she was pleased but not surprised. "Melissa is my oldest," the mother said, "and she is one of three children I had." Beth was a well-spoken woman with a striking smile, confident and self-assured. Nothing about her prepared me for what she was about to say.

"My parents were both alcoholics." Beth began. She looked at me directly as she continued her story. "My own childhood was so hard, I wanted my kids to have as easy and pleasant a childhood as possible. Frankly, when they were younger, they were spoiled. I did everything for them, worked two jobs so I could buy them whatever they wanted. I never touched alcohol or drugs, because I was determined to break the cycle of substance abuse that had made my childhood so miserable.

"I knew I would be a better role model for my own kids because of that, but I wanted to do more," Beth continued. "I wanted to make their childhood as stress and worry free as I could. I figured I could protect them from everything by providing for them in a way my parents never provided for me." She paused, looked down at her hands for a moment, then spoke again.

"When Melissa was 11 and Jason was 9, my youngest son Todd was killed. It was one of those terrible freak accidents that happens, and you want to blame someone, but there's no one to blame, because it truly was an accident. Todd was 6 years old." She didn't tell me what the accident was and I never asked. It was not necessary for me to know.

"I'm so sorry," I said, feeling that stab of fear every mother feels, unable to imagine how I could endure the pain of losing a child. Yet this mother who sat across from my desk had not only endured it, but had allowed herself to learn from it.

She went on to tell me how Todd's death had devastated the whole family, especially the children. Jason and Todd had been friends and play mates as well as brothers. An important part of Jason's world was brutally cut away when his little brother's life ended. Melissa's older age helped her cope a little better, at least outwardly, but soon her grades slipped drastically in school.

"I had to tell her teachers that she was just going to have to work through this, because school was the last thing she considered important at that point in time." Beth said it took a full year for her children to begin to really cope with the tragedy.

"They had been so dependent on me to make everything right, to keep them from any disappointments, to provide smooth sailing through their life, and here they were, completely vulnerable, with no coping skills at all. They had no confidence in their ability to get through this. Why should they? I had always removed any obstacles for them, never letting them struggle through anything. Discovering the damage I had done to them by doing too much for them was almost as hard as losing Todd."

Beth stopped talking and sighed. Then she sat up very straight and a determined edge came into her voice. "That's when I decided that Melissa and Jason were going to learn to depend on themselves. I stopped running after them, providing everything. I think at first they thought I was being too hard on them, not understanding their pain. But I stuck to my promise to myself, and I've never regretted it.

"I started giving them more responsibility for chores and I saw to it that they did them," Beth said. "I insisted that they do their homework, instead of letting them use Todd's death as an excuse. Having to do these things for themselves helped to direct them away from their pain. They started to get some positive results in their lives and they knew it was coming from their effort. I honestly think that and time are what helped them survive their brother's death. It helped me, too. Now, I know my children will be able to take care of themselves one day, when I'm no longer around."

It would have been so easy for this mother to continue to cushion life for her children in the wake of such tragedy, but she realized that one of the reasons Todd's death hit them so hard was because they had never had to struggle through anything before. They had never had any practice in dealing with minor disappointments, so how could they cope with such a devastating thing as the death of a brother.

When parents see their most important role as that of provider, it gives them and their children a false sense of security, because the role of the provider is a temporary one. Even if all goes well in a child's life, as that child becomes an adult, he or she must begin to provide for his or her own well-being. If self-reliance is suddenly thrust upon them, life becomes much harder. Not having been taught how to do so, they can't provide for themselves, and their disappointment robs them of any self-respect they might otherwise have had.

We stopped at this location in our journey, looking for ways to inspire our children toward independence and self-reliance. Surely Beth's example of courage and the willingness to change herself is and will continue to be an inspiration to her children.

When do you need the help of mentors?

As parents and teachers of your children, your job is to guide, motivate, and encourage them toward self-direction. That self-direction comes from channeling natural interests toward productive goals. When you're not knowledgeable about a particular interest your child has, it's wise to learn as much as you can about it, and to seek out people who are proficient in that subject and can be used as mentors to help in the learning process.

The dictionary describes a mentor as a wise and trusted counselor or teacher. "Mentor" was actually the name of the trusted counselor of Ulysses, the Greek hero of the Trojan War, in the stories told of ancient Greek civilization. You need not go that far to find someone who can help you help your child. Often, mentors can be found right in your own family or in your neighborhood. You have to be willing to make the effort to find them, not only for your child's sake, but for your own growth.

Usually, when parents discourage a child's interest it's for one of two reasons, or sometimes for both. They themselves know nothing about that particular field of study, or they have heard horror stories about it from others. However, the wise parent will make the effort to become informed.

Learning more about the area of interest can often ease our worries regarding physical danger, unhealthy influences, or whatever else concerns us, and the horror stories can be put in proper perspective or disregarded entirely. Information is always helpful. Before we condemn something, we should be certain we know the facts about it. Reliable information can also keep us from falling for claims of false benefits for our child from a particular interest.

However, in order to search for information, we have to admit that we don't already have that knowledge. Wanting our children to see us as omniscient, we are often reluctant to admit ignorance. We selfishly want to be the child's only mentor. Why restrict your child's learning horizon by your own limits? Instead, as a parent, you should investigate that interest and learn more about it. By doing that, you allow your child's interest to broaden your own knowledge.

It's true that we are always teachers of values to our children, but they can teach us new skills, either directly or through a mentor. When you allow your children to teach you about something they are very interested in, they receive a worthwhile boost in their self-confidence. Finally! They can teach you something! They can be the all-knowing ones for a change. In the process, your child sees that you are not afraid to learn something new; the value of that will be made clearer when we visit the last stage in our journey. For now, remember that it is important that your child sees that you are still willing to learn and grow.

One of my son's interests in grade school was rock collecting. When it began, I knew absolutely nothing about geodes and crystals. I learned about them from my son. From every trip we made into Utah's high country where we often camped, he brought back assorted rocks and stored them in boxes in his room, along with his books on trains. I brought home some rock-hunting guidebooks from the school library, and one of them had maps of nearby places for good rock hunting excursions. Earlier in their lives, my husband had encouraged our children to read maps well, so that they were part of the process whenever we searched new areas for campsites.

My 12-year-old son poured over the rock-hunting maps, using them to plan the next family camping trip. Before long, his allowance money was buying rock hammers and books on how to recognize and label what he found. He and his father went on excursions to find a used rock saw so my son could cut and polish some of the specimens. Both of them were learning a lot about minerals and gems and the differences among them.

My son was also gaining some very valuable side benefits from this interest. He was learning to overcome a certain natural shyness about being a part of group activities. Because of his desire to become a "rock hound" (that's what they call themselves), he was willing to join clubs and attend meetings. My husband went with him to a local gathering that included a trade show. He was pleased to see his normally reserved child risk the embarrassment of being ignored as a kid and initiate conversations with adult club members.

Here were mentors who knew far more about rock collecting than we had been able to learn in such a short time. They had been following their interest for years, and they were more than eager to share their knowledge with any youngster who showed an interest in their hobby. One of them arranged for my son to give a talk on the hobby at the local library's Hobby Day. His grandfather built a portable display case made of glass and hardwood for him, and my son used it for the talk. His first attempt at public speaking was made much easier because he was talking about a subject that fascinated him. Not only was he building a rock collection, he was building self-confidence.

One day, the newspaper featured an article about a very old woman who was quite the rock hound and somewhat of a local celebrity. We were surprised to discover that she lived less than 10 miles away. I contacted her and she was kind enough to agree to let my son come for a visit.

I will never forget his face when she ushered us into her modest little house. In every room, there were boxes and crates full of her considerable collection. I watched my 7th grader listening intently to her wonderful stories and telling a few of his own, much to her delight. Her day was brightened by this boy who shared her enthusiasm. My day was brightened by seeing how my son's pursuit of his interest had helped him form positive friendships outside his peer group and in the process develop the ability to treat people of all ages with honest respect.

Did my son make gems and minerals his life's work? No. Did what he learned about planning and studying and communicating help him with his life's work? Most definitely, yes.

From the careful cataloguing of his early rock collection, he developed the beginnings of the meticulous thoroughness he uses to good advantage in his work today. His ability to chair important business meetings and skillfully present complicated concepts in various professional and political forums was born in those library talks he gave as a boy.

In every place we visit on this journey, there are stories that help us understand what we came to this place to learn. This one's about Robert, the 15-year-old who began this journey with us. Remember how Robert's mother complained that he spent so much time in front of the television? Remember my suggestion that she should try paying attention to what made him laugh when he was watching it?

She did follow my advice and was surprised to learn that the comedy shows Robert liked best were the ones that featured stand up comedians. Somewhat embarrassed, she told me that one evening when he noticed her looking, he suddenly said to her, without any curtness in his voice, "That would be so cool to do that!"

Before she thought about what she was saying, she answered with "Oh, you have to be really funny to do that night after night." He hunched down on the couch, and in his usual surly tone, he shot back with "What do you know about it!" She was hurt and sincerely confused.

At the time, she didn't realize that Robert was giving her an opportunity to discover something about him that she never knew. He wasn't even aware that he was giving her that invitation. He was just caught off guard when he noticed that she was paying attention to what he was interested in and he opened the door to his dreams just a crack. Her comment made him slam the door shut.

"Don't give up!" I told her. "Keep watching television with him, whether he makes you feel welcome or not. There's a clue there. Maybe he's tried to do that, and found a little success, enough to harbor a secret dream. Stay with it. It will lead to a way to turn Robert around." I wasn't sure exactly how, at that point, but I was certain she had stumbled onto something that would help her reach her child.

Two sessions later, she was happy to tell me that her persistence had paid off. She learned from one of Robert's friends that on those two occasions when Robert had skipped school in the afternoon, he had gone to another friend's where a party was in progress. When she first heard that, she was sure Robert was into drugs, and she confided to me, "I almost didn't ask anything else. I was afraid to find out. Of course, the kids were smoking pot. No one was going to tell me that, but I could figure that one out for myself. That was bad news, but it didn't surprise me. Why else would they be having a party when school was on, if it wasn't to drink or do drugs!"

The only reason Robert's friend was telling her anything was because his parents had discovered that he was also at the party, and the boy was grounded. They were the ones who told Robert's mother she should talk to their son if she wanted to know what kept Robert away from school those two afternoons. Robert's friend cooperated, because his parents were in no mood for games.

"Robert was mostly telling funny stories, and keeping us laughing," the boy told her. "You know, like, he's a crack up! He has this way of saying stuff that's just, you know, funny! He gets invited because he's sort of like, you know, the party's entertainment!" Robert's mother couldn't believe it. Her surly son was making other people laugh.

Then she told me she remembered how funny Robert's father had been. "Always a joke a minute," she said, then her voice softened. "Now that I think of it, Robert used to be that way. He was a little kid who was always clowning around and making the other kids laugh. After the divorce, he turned so serious. Maybe because I wasn't in the mood for anything funny, especially when we stopped hearing from his dad altogether. That's when Robert stopped being funny at home. I thought...," her voice trailed off and she looked away.

"The humor was still in him," I said quietly, "he just took it somewhere else." She nodded, unable to speak.

If she had been a little more perceptive when Robert first started withdrawing, she might have been able to encourage him to keep his ability to make people laugh. I reminded her of what I told her the first time we met: Giving up is not an option.

She might not know anything about the entertainer's craft, but she will find mentors who do. Maybe the drama teacher at the school will be able to help. It's a place to start. If Robert has some encouragement from his mother, in the form of finding mentors, it could well be what he needs to find a direction again. We'll meet Robert's mother again on this journey, because she has every intention of arriving at its destination. At each location, she learns a little more, and she uses what she learns.

When you evaluate your child's choice of an interest, keep your mind open and flexible. Many people view certain professions or trades as bad influences on their children. But if the child's values have been properly set by conscientious parents, they will be able to withstand the negative elements of that particular profession or trade.

When my daughter first began working in the entertainment industry, an industry whose perils are well documented, I was a little apprehensive. However, we already had a mentor right in our family who was familiar with that industry. It was my brother, who had played first trombone for some of the greatest jazz legends in music and had traveled the world practicing his craft. I knew that he had always managed to maintain his high standards of personal integrity.

After a year in the industry, my daughter's conclusions were essentially the same as my brother's observations had been. One of her friends, unduly impressed with the idea that my daughter was in the movie business, asked eagerly, "What's it really like?" My daughter quickly dispelled the notion of glamour that most people associate with this form of earning a living.

"The entertainment industry is like any other business," she answered. "It has its share of people who want something for nothing. But I notice that the people who are good in this business work really hard at their craft." She made it a point to keep her own values intact and associate only with those who had respect for those values.

If you want to inspire your child to set goals and gain self-direction, watch for his or her natural interests and guide and encourage those interests. Use friends and family as mentors if your own knowledge is limited. Knowledge is power, so find out more about your child's area of interest. Search out people who will give you accurate information, and don't rely on hearsay and rumor. Trust that the values you are practicing every day will be learned, through observation, by your child.

Have faith that your children will be strong by letting them know you expect them to be. By all means, keep an eye on them, monitor who their friends are, but give them some breathing space, too. Let your child face risk, physical and emotional, and learn how to find his own safe passage through it.

Your children must travel life's road on their own. To do so, they will need to know how to get from one place to another. Encourage their natural sense of direction. You can't take them where they need to go, but just as we have done for this journey, you can help provide a map for theirs.

Stage 4

Build Trust

O ur journey so far has shown you why your primary parental role is to be your child's teacher. You were shown why your best teaching is done when you are honest with yourself and your children. You've seen that example is your best teaching aid, and you've observed its power, both positive and negative. You've been encouraged to inspire your children to find productive interests that will lead to their own happiness. You glimpsed bits of history that clarified the necessity for your children to become self confident, responsible individuals. Now you will learn to build the trust your children will need to make that happen.

Why must there be a code of conduct?

Without a code of conduct to follow, your child will be much more susceptible to the arbitrary push and pull of peer pressure. Peer pressure is not something only teenagers face. Desirable and undesirable outside influences begin very early in a child's life, and when that influence comes from peers, it is much more powerful. As parents, we can respond to that influence in several ways.

We can rigidly control it by severely limiting our children's access to the influence of anyone else beyond ourselves. We can allow children to have unlimited access to outside influence and hope that they do not blindly follow, making no distinction between positive and negative behavior. Or we can give them guidelines, and reasons for those guidelines, so they can have a code of conduct to follow, one that will help them make responsible choices even when they are pressured by peers to do the exact opposite. Clearly, this last choice is the wisest. A code of conduct will enable your children to face the *challenge* of choices with a much greater guarantee that they will make responsible ones.

We all face the challenge of choices every day. Responsible choices cannot be made without rules, and rules that promote responsibility cannot be made without reasons. When a rule is made for a good reason, it becomes a reasonable rule, an intelligent guideline for desirable behavior rather than a rigid form of control.

Children can make much healthier decisions within a guiding framework of sensible rules, because the rules provide a foundation upon which they can build their own personal code of conduct. When they have ownership over the code of conduct they are following, they will also accept ownership of their choices. Their choices then become part of their self-reliance, and they are much more likely to make them in their own ultimate best interest.

It's unfair for parents to expect children to make good choices without the benefit of any guidelines. When we do this, we are abdicating our parental role of teacher and expecting our children to teach or parent themselves. For their own sense of security, children need to have rules to follow for their conduct, and they rightly expect those rules to be clear and consistent. As a parent, where do you start?

The best place to begin is with your own example, of course. But even if you are setting good, clear examples with your own positive behavior, children still need to have a set of guidelines to follow. This need for rules is as ancient as mankind's history. Reasonable rules are the foundation for every great civilization, and every enduring religion. Every great religion has its equivalent to the Judeo-Christian Ten Commandments: a set order of rules for acceptable conduct that can be referred to and followed by all who profess to believe in that religion's teachings. These rules apply to the high priests as well as the laypeople in the religious community. Rather than restrict, they provide stability for their members, giving them the security that comes when we know which road to follow to take us where we need to go.

The family unit is, or should be, a community, and as such, its conduct must be guided by a reasonable set of rules. In other words, the whole family needs to be governed by the same code of conduct. This includes parents as well as children. Human nature being what it is, we all need to be reminded of our responsibilities from time to time, as well as being made aware of our rights. This is especially true for children. Who is to set these guidelines?

It is the parent's responsibility to establish the basic structure upon which a solid set of guidelines can be built. However, the parents need the cooperation of the whole family to refine the guidelines so they can be understood and followed by all. If parents abdicate this essential responsibility, then their children, searching for some guidance, will follow the rules of whatever group is handy.

We may think our children crave complete freedom, but the direct opposite is true. With no family guideline structure in place, young minds searching for some stability and a set of rules to answer to find other guidelines to follow.

If they have no family code of conduct, they will seek out other codes, sometimes criminal codes such as those found in gangs. A big part of the appeal of gangs to children is the structured, iron-clad code of behavior that each member must follow. Guidelines... rules...and when rules are broken, there are consequences. If you want your children to face the challenge of choices with some hope of making the right ones, then you need to be certain they have some practice in making choices and understanding consequences.

This logic applies to the classroom as well. Step into any classroom where actual learning is going on, and you will soon see that there are guidelines in place that are being followed. The classroom may be noisy, depending on the activity or the subject, but everyone will be occupied and on task; no one will be interfering to any great degree with any one else's right to learn.

Step into any classroom where very *little* learning is going on, and you will quickly discover that there are no guidelines. The teacher is trying to get the attention of an unruly collection of children. Some students are trying to concentrate on the task at hand, others are confused about what the task actually is, and still others are bored and inattentive. There is no stability in this situation, and without stability, reasonable choices are difficult to make. Children in this classroom who have made the choice to learn are unable to because they are not being supported in that choice. The result is that many of those students will later make a choice to not even bother to try to learn. As my teaching career evolved, I discovered the secrets for making effective rules, and these secrets apply in both the family and the classroom setting.

What are the four secrets of effective rules?

The first secret is the key to the other three. Each one will be much more effective if this one is clearly understood.

1. There must be a reason for every rule.

Unless rules are reasonable, they cease to be the consistent guidelines they need to be and become merely a means for arbitrary control. People are much more likely to follow a rule if they understand why it is necessary. Once I accepted this, I never made a rule in my classroom unless I had a clear reason for it. I always made certain the reason was understood by those who were meant to follow the rule.

Guidelines, rules, and requests that are made within a classroom or within a home should never be made on whim. That makes them arbitrary and subject to change. Children need guidelines that are there *for a reason.* That's why it's so important for the whole family to make the rules together. When they do, the rules that result will almost certainly be stronger, because the family will have to agree on the reasons for having each particular rule in the first place.

Rules that do not have a real reason for being are indecisive, weak, and ineffective. They can't be defended if they are challenged, and believe me, they will be challenged. A child, even a very young child, will sense the indecision. As a parent or a classroom teacher, that indecision will be your swiftest downfall. That's why it's extremely important, imperative even, that you think something through before you set a rule. When your indecision shows, you're much more likely to be given an argument.

Watch a small child's reaction when you make a request. If you don't follow it with a reason that he can understand, he will give you an argument. It's his way of reacting to your indecision. It may show only in his body language. Let's say you've asked him to play on the other side of the yard, but you've given him no reason why. His reluctance to move quickly is not necessarily stubbornness or disobedience. It's probably a simple case of him not understanding why he has to move his toys to the other side of the yard.

His reaction to your request may take the form of a mild objection. "Why?" he asks. That's nothing more than a blunt reminder that you haven't given him a reason for what you've asked him to do. He's not being hard to get along with, he just wants to know why. Be glad that he does. It shows that, at least at this age, he's not willing to blindly follow a direction unless he has a reason to do so. It shows that he has a mind of his own and that he questions arbitrary requests; you will be grateful for that as he grows older.

Try making that same request to that same child, only this time give him a reason. "Jacob, move your toys over onto the grass. I want to hose the dust off the patio, and I don't want your toys to get wet." Jacob is only 5 years old, but the reason makes sense to him. He says okay and picks up his two toy trucks and heads for the grass.

This is exactly what happened just this past weekend with my grandson. The same little grandson who, when I simply said earlier, "Move your toys over on the grass," resisted and asked why. When there's a purpose, a reason for your request, a logic behind the rule, you will encounter much less resistance. Why? Because you're not building a restrictive wall that your child feels compelled to resist. You're building a firm foundation to support him, to lift him, and to guide him as he grows.

When you offer a reason for every rule, no matter what age the child is, you are effectively implying that you consider that child to be an intelligent human being, capable of understanding the logic of the request. When a family expects its members to understand reasonable requests, each member is much more inclined to rise to that expectation and respect the rule.

2. For a rule to be respected, it must apply to everyone.

This applies to the classroom, the home, and society. Because rules are meant to be guidelines for conduct, their intent has to be trusted for them to be effective. No one trusts the integrity of a rule that applies only to some of the people some of the time. Rules subject to change are not rules or guidelines. They are misleading methods for outside control.

Does this mean that everyone in the classroom, including the teacher, must respect the same rules? Yes. Does this mean that everyone in the family, including the parents, must respect the same rules? Yes. The following story is a perfect example of how this secret works.

High school teachers have a continual struggle with students arriving late to class. It seems no matter how long or short the passing time between classes, many students dawdle along and drift into class after the tardy bell. Teachers try all sorts of complicated policies to get students to class on time. Detention after school, clean-up sessions, referrals to the principal...the list is endless, but the problem continues.

I maintain it's because students often see tardy policies as an arbitrary effort at control, applying only to them. They're not convinced of the necessity of a policy that is not fairly practiced. Why must they be on time, they reason, when the teacher is often late? What difference does it make if they're late, students wonder, when the teacher doesn't really begin the lesson until five or sometimes 10 minutes into the class?

In both rationalizations, the student cites a lack of need for the rule and a lack of equity in its application. The rule is not trusted because it's not applied in an evenhanded manner. In short, it's not fair. The tardy policy I've followed with great success for many years is simple and fair, and because of that, it is respected: If students arrive after the bell without a note from a teacher or parent indicating a legitimate reason for their tardiness, I write "Five points off – Late" on their grade sheet.

In my classes, effort results in points earned, and points are hard to earn. Five or 10 points can ultimately mean the difference between an A- or a B+, a C- or a D+. The students know the rule and understand its reason. As I explain to them at the school year's beginning, "Tardiness is not tolerated well in the workplace. Why? Because it affects not only your performance, but it affects the performance of others. How long do you think a firefighter would keep his job if he misses a fire call because he's late, and his fellow firefighters must fight the blaze with one less man?"

"In this classroom, when you're late, you distract others with your entrance. You interrupt concentration on the lesson already in progress. You give yourself a disadvantage because you may have missed something critical to your understanding of the lesson. As a student, you have the right to learn. You do not have the right to interfere with anyone's else's right to learn."

There's an additional explanation for the success of my tardy policy. The second part of the policy is this: If I am late to class without a legitimate reason, all students have five points added to their grade sheet. This is the reason I give to the students: "This is our job, yours and mine. We all have a responsibility to be here on time."

Many teachers are very uncomfortable with this second part of the rule. They may not admit it, but they don't want to give up their special status. They want to be exempt from the responsible choice (punctuality) that they should be teaching by example. Unfortunately, they are missing an excellent opportunity to solve the tardy problem in an equitable, effective way. Does this work? Ask the students who run to get to my classes before the bell, yet saunter unconcernedly to many of their other classes. I make no exceptions for them or for me.

Here is where a small historical side trip will further prove the effectiveness of an evenhanded code of conduct. One year, in spite of my tardy policy, one of my classes still had two habitual latecomers. They were trying, but the habits of a lifetime, even a young lifetime, were proving hard to break. One of them had 20 points already marked off; another had 15. On a day dark with a drenching downpour, I pulled into the school parking lot just as the tardy bell rang. Hurrying from my car, I could see my students clustered at the locked classroom door, saying "You're late, Mrs. Turnbull!" On that particular day, both of my latecomers happened to be on time.

In an attempt to win my favor, one of them, obviously used to always blaming something or someone else for his shortcomings, said, "It's okay, Mrs. Turnbull. It's raining so hard, you probably could hardly see, and you had to drive a lot slower." I knew he meant to help, by providing me with an excuse in much the same way he provided himself with excuses. The whole class was waiting, expectantly, as I unlocked the door, to see what my response would be. Calmly and clearly, I replied, "You're right, Marcos, but I should have allowed myself more time."

As soon as I reached my desk, I added five points to the ledger of every person present. One student, seeing what I was doing, said in amazement, "You're really gonna do that?" I answered, "I said I would, didn't I?" Neither of my two habitual offenders was ever late again to my class. They respected the rule, because they understood the reason for it. They also respected the rule because they trusted me to make it fair. The rule applied to everyone.

3. Keep rules simple and few.

The good Lord recognized this principle when He gave Moses those Ten Commandments I spoke of earlier. God proved His infinite wisdom by realizing that if the rules are too complex and too many, mere mortals, in their confusion, will ignore or disobey them.

Unfortunately, many modern legislators have yet to grasp this truth. Many school administrators and teachers have also failed to grasp it. Rather than simplifying and refining rules, they heap more and more onto the already cumbersome pile of largely ignored rules and regulations, then wonder why students and teachers alike are becoming more and more belligerent and resistant to anything that even sounds like a rule.

Too many rules and laws are attempts to subjugate individuals, rather than encourage them to be responsible. Rules should be guidelines within which an individual can function with a certain amount of freedom. Too many rules result in placing people in the position of feeling unnecessarily restricted. Too many laws make criminals out of ordinarily law-abiding people, simply because they cannot possibly follow all of them. Choices have to be made, or the individual can't get through the day without confusion. Which rule, or law, do they follow, or honor? Which one do they break, or dishonor?

In the case of children, especially teenagers who cannot yet make a clear distinction between the two, often the unimportant, petty rules are followed, while the truly significant ones are ignored.

4. There must be a consequence whenever a rule is ignored.

Master screenwriting teacher and writer Robert McKee maintains that good scripts always include difficult choices that the story's participants must make. Because, to quote McKee, "True character is revealed in the choices a human being makes under pressure." Consequences add the element of pressure that defines our character. To follow or disregard a rule is a choice, and choices always have consequences, good or bad, depending on the choice. The consequence must be appropriate, and fair in its application. Don't even use the word punishment. Consequence is a much better and more accurate word. It reminds us that the consequence is a direct result of our choice.

The consequence should be direct, never arbitrary, never screamed out in unthinking rage or pent-up frustration. If consequences have been determined and agreed upon beforehand, that will save much stress in administering them. Consequences that include loss of privileges are usually the most effective. Privileges are earned and deserved. When rules regulating a privilege are disregarded, the privilege must be lost until trust can be regained.

In my senior year of high school, I decided that I wanted to be seen by my peers as a more sophisticated soul. I saw myself as too one dimensional. An achiever scholastically, and a participant in many school extracurricular activities, I also wanted to be thought of as someone daring and worldly. In an effort to prove this to my peers, I began smoking cigarettes. After all, I told myself, movie star Lauren Bacall smoked, and I thought it would be fun to be as powerful and sophisticated as Lauren Bacall.

Because of my many extracurricular activities, I often stayed after school for meetings with the yearbook staff, the play production group, or any other current project groups. These were necessary meetings accepted and understood by my ever-vigilant parents, but I was required to call and tell my mother where I would be and when I would arrive home. It was easy for me to use after-school meetings as a cover for my smoking sessions. The long walk home was enough to clear away much of the telltale smoke, and for several months, my dishonesty went undetected by my mother.

At that time, the general public was just beginning to be aware of the seriousness of the health hazards of smoking. But it was still glamorized in magazines and movies, and most people still thought its dangers were highly exaggerated. My father was also a smoker, and I told myself that if my father was a good person, then smoking couldn't be so bad. I neglected to notice that my father didn't lie about smoking or try to hide his habit from the rest of the family. My mother began to believe that these after-school meetings were too frequent, and on some afternoons, too long. She called the teacher who was the yearbook advisor and complained about it. Confronted by my mother, my worldliness wilted, and I confessed.

She kept her temper under careful control, but she still made her deep disappointment quite clear. She knew smoking was unhealthy, but it wasn't the smoking that most disturbed my mother. It was that I had made the choice to lie. My consequence: No extracurricular activities for the rest of that month. I had made a choice that cost me a privilege that meant more to me than even the opinion of my peers. Furthermore, for that whole semester, when I had a meeting after school, I had to bring a handwritten note from the teacher.

The consequence of my actions caused me embarrassment among my peers, making me feel like a child, something especially hard to take for a girl who was attempting to prove she was *daring and sophisticated*. It was a good lesson about the loss of trust.

Every family will need to determine what the proper consequence should be within their particular family framework. What may seem harsh to some will be perfectly reasonable to others. For our family, this consequence was appropriate. The family rules were there to guide, to direct, to insure safety, and to promote trust. The wording of my parents' rules was very simple and direct, as were their reasons. What was the rule I had broken? *Tell the truth.* The reason: *So we can trust each other.* The consequence: privileges were lost, until trust could be restored. All four secrets were at work:

1. Every rule must have a reason.
2. For a rule to be respected, it must apply to everyone.
3. Keep rules simple and few.
4. There must be a consequence when a rule is ignored.

Why is consistency better than compromise?

A compromised rule, just like a compromised relationship, is not worth very much. The whole purpose of having guidelines and rules is to establish a firm foundation so that the family can function with freedom within those guidelines. If there is any compromising, it should occur when the rules are being formulated. Once the rules are established, compromise should not be necessary if the rules are fair and reasonable.

It's a good idea to review the rules every so often. That should take care of any extenuating circumstances that might make it necessary to modify and revise a rule if it no longer applies. Our aim is to create a framework of guidelines that will have good general application, rules that will be respected because they are logical and meant for the general good of the family. This includes single-parent families and families in which grandparents are raising their grandchildren.

Rules that are constantly up for revision and subject to change create confusing inconsistency for everyone. That inconsistency is especially unwelcome to the children in the family. Children thrive on consistency. Knowing what the rules are and what to expect is especially welcome to children in their adolescent years. That's when they need constants they can count on, parents they can depend on to be consistent. When everything about the child is changing, inside and out, they need to know that something will stay the same.

That's why divorce is especially difficult for children in their early teens. It destroys an important constant in their rapidly changing, very confusing young lives. Intellectually, teenagers can understand and even come to accept some of the reasons for their parents' divorce. But emotionally, at a time when they need it most, the balance in their lives is destroyed. All the physical changes going on in their bodies and all the new emotional needs and urges combine to create confusion. Then, just when they thought they had all the confusion they could handle, more is created by their parents' divorce.

Part of the normal teenage rebelliousness toward parents is just rebellion in general to all of those changes within themselves. That's why it is so important for parents involved in a divorce to come to some agreement on a consistent set of rules for their children to follow.

Two people involved in dissolving their marriage partnership are dealing with the difficult situation of their own disappointments. But the child did not create the situation. The parents must put their own conflicting feelings aside and do everything they can to lessen the confusion their divorce is causing in their child's life. If the divorcing husband and wife agree on nothing else, they should at least agree that they will follow consistent guidelines for their children. On this one issue, at least, they must be the responsible parents they need to be.

Sometimes, this agreement is not possible. If, indeed, the reason for the divorce is one parent's lack of any real sense of responsibility toward the family, then the one who is willing to be the parent the child needs must still hold to a reasonable set of guidelines for the child. Now is not the time to be indecisive and arbitrary when what the child needs is stability and consistency.

This was the case with Robert. When his father left, Robert was 13 years old. Part of Robert's sullen withdrawal was his confusion and hurt over this sudden shift in the balance of the family. At a time when he needed a father's presence most, his left him. He could have handled it better if his father had died. The fact that his father left him by choice is one of the reasons Robert retreated from anything about himself that reminded him of his father. Things like his ability to make people laugh.

Robert's mother came to understand this later, but when her marriage was breaking up, she couldn't. In addition to her own hurt, she was aching for Robert's pain. In an effort to help him through it, she eased up on rules and regulations.

Trying to soften the divorce's blow to Robert, she removed any sense of structure to his life. She let him do pretty much as he pleased. This only made the blow harder for him to bear, because it left Robert without the stability that could have come from some structured framework. Nothing was expected of him, which only served to make him feel even more abandoned and less worthwhile. At a time when Robert needed guidance, in the form of some reasonable code to follow, some consistent family rules, she added to his insecurity by taking them all away.

How do you make rules that are respected?

The best way to devise reasonable rules that will be respected is to have the rules made by those who must live by them. It's the basic principle of democracy. I urge those who attend my parent forums to establish the family rules together, as a unified body of individuals. Even if it is a single parent family, like Robert's, it can still function as a family unit. Just as this country's most important governing document begins with "We, the people of the United States of America, do hereby solemnly resolve...," so should the family rules begin with "We."

The *we* must apply to adults as well as children. Remember, we are teaching our children by our own example. When fair rules govern everyone in a family, from the senior members to the very young, the rules truly become a code of conduct. As your family works to establish these rules, keep the four secrets discussed on page 101 firmly in mind.

One or two sessions of hammering out no more than 10 basic family rules will save countless hours of worry and derail frequent difficult encounters between family members. It will diffuse much damaging dialogue that might severely harm the self-esteem of parents and children alike. It will also eliminate those arbitrary and confusing "last-minute laws" that parents often inflict on their children. Depending on the mood of the parent at the time, the law will usually be too lax or too restrictive. It will also usually be ignored, because it has no firm foundation for respect.

Does this scenario sound familiar? Allison's date honks the horn, and she's on her way out the door, shouting a quick goodbye. Suddenly, her father, who is angry about the way things went at work that day, bellows, "Where do you think you're going?" Allison has already cleared things with her mother, but her mother isn't home. "Tell whoever that is to get out of the car and come in here if he's taking you anywhere!"

By now, Allison is thoroughly confused. "Didn't Mom tell you? It's Mark, Dad, you already met Mark last week. He came straight from work, and he's not coming in because we'll barely make the movie on time as it is!"

Now her father is further irritated by his daughter's tone of voice. "It's a school night," he reminds her. "You're not going anywhere on a school night until your grades get better. Tell that to Mark or whatever his name is!"

"But, Dad!" In tears, Allison protests, "That's not fair!"

She's right. It's not fair. Staying home on a school night is not an unfair rule, especially if Allison's grades have been poor. But this is the first time Allison has heard it. There was never any clear-cut discussion about the rules. Allison's parents make them up as they go along, seldom consulting with each other. The result is that Allison has no idea what the guidelines are at any given moment.

On this particular night, it would hardly be surprising if one of two things happened: Allison waves Mark on and runs to her room crying. Two hours later, her father feels terrible about his reaction and tries to make amends, but she's too hurt to hear him. There's no consistency in her life, because there's no agreement on what her guidelines are. In her mind, sneaking out whenever she wants to go somewhere starts to have an appeal.

The other ending to this encounter could happen like this: Allison shouts, "You can't keep me here! Mom said I could go!" and storms out of the house, leaving her father with no information about where she's going or when she'll be back. Two hours later, when his wife returns, Allison's parents begin to argue, each one blaming the other for the situation.

Had the family rules been established before this, the whole evening would have turned out very differently. When rules are in place and respected because they have been agreed upon beforehand, confusion is minimal, feelings aren't trampled, parents are kept informed, and children are much more likely to be kept safe and accountable.

Even children as young as 4 or 5 years old can be actively involved in the rule-making and rule-keeping process. Being part of the process will help them understand the idea of family unity and that rules are meant to apply to everyone. I am continuously reminded by my own preschool grandchildren just how aware and insightful their minds can be when it comes to recognizing fairness and honesty.

When individuals have ownership of a rule or regulation, they are much more inclined to honor it. In fact, children will often be quick to notice when adults are ignoring a rule, and they will just as quickly call it to the adult's attention. Be happy when they do. One of the best ways to learn is to teach, and when a child is teaching you a rule, he is also learning it himself.

One day, frustrated with myself and forgetting that my then 4-year-old grandson was in the next room, I let out a loud "Damnit!" Instantly, he came to the doorway with a stern look on his face. "That's a bad word, Mama Rae," he said seriously. Still frustrated, my first impulse was to tell him to mind his own manners and never mind about mine.

Good sense prevailed, and I accepted his admonishment as gracefully as I could. "You're right," I acknowledged. "Thank you for reminding me." He turned from the doorway, clearly proud of the fact that he was also the keeper of the rules.

Let's linger in this location long enough to really understand the rule-making process. We'll do it by actually making some basic rules. Sometimes parents are confused about where to start, when they finally have everyone together, ready and willing to establish the family guidelines.

The best way to begin is with the most important rule of all: *Keep your word.* It's the concept we were introduced to in the beginning of this journey. Without that rule as the foundation, the others will have no real clout.

Remember, we want these rules to be clear enough that the need to adjust and compromise is kept to a minimum when the rule is put into practice. To make it clear, we must give the reason for each rule we make. You will see, as we go along, that the rule addresses a specific issue, but the reason is part of the larger process that is the actual code of conduct.

It's helpful to use a few general areas of concern as starting points. Just as the guidelines for a society should be concerned with such issues as safety, respect, responsibilities, and duties, the guidelines for a family should do the same. Let's begin with the issue of safety. Each family will have its own particular needs in this area, but a general rule will work well for most:

> (!) **Rule**: When we leave the house, we let others know where we're going, with whom, and when we expect to return.

> (?) **Reason**: *Be Considerate.* All those who live in a house are affected by what the others do. Simple consideration makes life easier for all concerned.

This rule is a good one because it touches on respect and personal responsibility, as well as safety. Notice that the rule uses the word *we.* This means that when Dad leaves the house, as well as the children, he lets others know where he's going. Never mind using the excuse "I'm an adult, I can take care of myself." You're teaching by example, remember?

Besides, it's simple consideration and respect for others in the family for you to simply say, "I'm going to watch the softball game over at the park. I'll be back in a couple of hours." Suppose there's a family emergency and you need to be found in a hurry? Suppose your car breaks down halfway between the park and home and you can't get to a phone, or your car phone isn't working and you live six miles from the park? If you're not back in those couple of hours you mentioned, you'll be very happy to see your 17-year-old son driving down the road looking for you. It will also give him a pretty good perspective on why there's good reason for this rule.

Here's another example that touches on more than one area of concern:

Rule: Chores must be completed in a timely manner.

Reason: *Be dependable*. Your actions affect the welfare of others.

For example: Your chore is to feed the horses twice a day, once in the morning and once in the evening. Don't remember midway through the morning and feed the horses at 12 noon and then, because you don't want to go back to the stables after supper, feed them again at 3:30, on your way home from school. Horses not on pasture, where they can free-feed when they need it, will thrive with regular feeding times and decent intervals in between. Therefore, the health and welfare of the horse is directly affected by how you perform your chore. The reason is clear: Others are depending on you.

If your chore is to clear the table, then get it done quickly, so your brother, who has the chore of washing the dishes, doesn't have to wait for you. Are you the one who gathers the firewood for the campsite? Then it's going to be a cold campsite if night falls and the fire hasn't been started because you didn't gather the wood when it was still light. Again, others are depending on you.

You're beginning to get the idea, I'm sure, but let's mention some other possible rules, just to let you see that it's really not a difficult process, especially when you have the whole family involved. This one's a must if you have young drivers in the family:

Rule: No one may borrow a vehicle without the owner's knowledge and permission.

Reason: *Respect other people's property*. The person who owns and maintains the vehicle is the only one who should determine how and when it's used. Vehicles are expensive, powerful machines, and the owner is liable for any damage the vehicle does to individuals or property.

Need an example? With his summer paycheck, your 17-year-old son bought an old pick-up truck. He pays for the insurance and maintenance on it. You need to pick up some stuff from the feed store, and you don't want to clutter up the inside of your sedan. He's not home. You didn't ask him before if you could borrow his truck, but after all, you're his mother. So you borrow the truck. You're not being fair. What if he comes home and has plans to use his truck, and it's not there? Never mind that you left him a note. Unless it's an emergency, that's not fair.

What are you teaching by your example? Remember earlier in this journey, when we talked about following something all the way through to its logical end? For you to borrow his truck without asking means that it's all right for him to borrow your new sedan without asking. After all, you're not home, and he doesn't want to use his truck, dusty from hauling hay, for his date. That's where pulling rank and claiming privilege just because we're the parents leads.

The concept that family rules must apply to everyone in the family was one of the hardest things for Elizabeth's father to accept. He believed in rules, and, surprisingly, he was actually fairly consistent in insisting that rules were followed. But there was no equality in their application. This made his daughter see them as excessively restrictive and exercises in power, rather than guidelines for behavior.

For example, Elizabeth's father expected her to account for her exact whereabouts at all times, even when she was in the house. His wife told me that her husband would often call out, "Where are you, Elizabeth?" without moving from his place in front of the television set. "It's as though he doesn't trust her if she's not right there in plain view," the stepmother said.

I wanted to know if he ever left the television set long enough to just wander through the house and notice his daughter, and see for himself where she was, and maybe make a bit of polite conversation with her. "No," Elizabeth's stepmother said. "If she doesn't answer, he tells me to find out where she is, and when I do, it's as though he really doesn't care. I think Elizabeth doesn't answer sometimes just to see if he's interested enough to come and look for himself."

This conversation occurred after a session that her husband wasn't able to attend. As she was telling me this, Elizabeth's stepmother seemed to be realizing something else. "He does the same thing with me," she said, as though she saw this for the first time. During the course of the conversation, I was to discover that the father rarely accounted for his whereabouts, in the house or out, and, in fact, resented any questions about it.

I try to understand behavior by asking questions and interpreting the answers in a very direct way. I don't always question the person exhibiting the behavior. Often, my questions are silent, as I observe a situation. I look for clues. Not mysterious, hidden ones that require a trained psychiatrist to interpret, but straightforward evidence of cause and effect. This is something every parent and teacher can train themselves to do. I call it paying attention.

For example, Elizabeth's father has already made it clear that he hates his job and feels no sense of self-worth from his work. In his own home, his hunger for respect takes on a belligerent tone. He hasn't been able to earn respect at work, and his confidence in his ability to earn it anywhere else is at such a low ebb that he believes the only way to get it is to demand it. His wife's not much better off in terms of believing in herself, so she goes along with her husband's demands. However, it's obvious to any careful observer that she wants a better situation for her stepdaughter.

I always assume that parents want to do the right thing by their children. Whether it's a parent who is voluntarily attending the forum, or one who has been called in for a parent-teacher conference, or one who has been referred to the forum by an intervention counselor or probation officer, I always begin with faith in their good intentions.

I've found, over the years, that high expectations are the best expectations to have. People sense it and more often than not, because they believe that I believe in them, they will make a sincere effort to reach those expectations. It may not always be successful, but the effort must be honored. I find that when their effort is honored, whether it's in the forum sessions or in the classroom, my respect for their effort will usually result in a willingness to continue the effort, to try again to meet those high expectations.

Sometimes my faith is not rewarded. I always begin again from square one with every new situation, because more often than not, my faith is validated somewhere along the line. I have not given up on Elizabeth's parents, because they are both, each in their own way, not giving up on Elizabeth. In fact, two sessions later, Elizabeth's stepmother tells me that she finally persuaded her husband to sit down with her and Elizabeth, and together they made a short list of rules, complete with reasons for each one.

It's a good start. The family is finally beginning to adopt a code of conduct they will be able to follow. They are beginning to have a common purpose. Most gratifying to me is that this woman, who once seemed so without purpose and direction, is also gaining some self-respect. In this struggle to be the parent she now knows she needs to be, she is closer to becoming that parent. As we discovered early in our journey, the strength we gain when we are being strong for the sake of our children is a powerful strength.

If the first rule is to keep your word, then an equally important one should be to give honest answers to every question. The reason for this rule? If each member of the household can be counted on to be truthful at all times, then trust is the result. If you want your children to be able to withstand pressures of all kinds from their peers, then you must give them the opportunity to build the strength of character they will need to resist poor choices. Unless they have learned from a set of fairly devised and administered rules that choices have consequences, they will never be able to govern their own actions in a responsible way.

Think of rules as guidelines on the map for this journey you are taking to responsible parenthood. Without those guidelines, it's easy to lose the way, easy to forget the purpose for the journey in the first place.

In the same way, without guidelines your children will be left to poor choices and assigning blame to others for the consequences that result from those choices. They will never build the trust in their own ability to determine right choices, and they will be forever assigned to the unhappy role of followers of others, rather than leaders of their own lives. Let your family rules be part of the code of conduct, the trusted guidelines your children can use to lead them to responsible choices.

To help you begin to build that trust, I have included examples of rules from three different families who attended the forums: the McDonald family, the Delgado family, and the Knight family. As you read the examples, notice that some of the individual rules we discussed earlier in this stage of our journey were adopted (sometimes modified) by each family, but each *set* of rules is still very unique to that particular family's situation.

Remember that in each of these examples, the set of rules was devised by and agreed upon by the entire family and was intended to apply to every member. The family also had to come to agreement on consequences if rules were ignored. What you will find is that once rules have been agreed upon and it is clear that they apply to everyone, there is less and less need for consequences.

Inherent in these rules is the fact that the family making them expects them to be honored. This is the principle of high expectations that I spoke of earlier. Because they understand that this is how they are expected to behave, and why, the family begins to adopt the rules as part of a general code of conduct. In fact, take away the specific rules from each list, and you will have only the reasons left. One glance at the reasons and you will see the core of that family's code of conduct.

The McDonald family

(Two-parent household; one parent employed full-time outside home, one parent employed part-time outside home; four children, ages 6, 12, 15, and 17)

(!) **Rule**: When you make a promise, keep it.

(?) **Reason**: *Be truthful and dependable.*

(!) **Rule**: Leave a note on the kitchen bulletin board when you go somewhere. Tell where you are going and approximately when you will be back.

(?) **Reason**: *Be considerate and spare the family from worry.*

(!) **Rule**: Keep friends' home and work phone numbers posted and keep the list up to date.

(?) **Reason**: *Be available in case of emergency or change of plans.*

(!) **Rule**: Babysitting Sarah is divided equally between Mark, Jessica, and Ryan.

(?) **Reason**: *Be fair and respectful of each person's time.*

(!) **Rule**: Keep **your** "stuff" in **your** room.

(?) **Reason**: *Keep clutter under control.*

(!) **Rule**: If chores aren't done on time, privileges are lost.

(?) **Reason**: *Privileges must be earned.*

(!) **Rule**: Don't do Sarah's chores for her. (This includes you, Mom!)

(?) **Reason**: *Give everyone a chance to earn self-respect.*

(!) **Rule**: When you borrow something, return it promptly and in good condition.

(?) **Reason**: *Respect other people's property.*

(!) **Rule**: No loud music or shouting in the house.

(?) **Reason**: *Respect other people's right to have peace and quiet.*

(!) **Rule**: Don't use vulgar or obscene language.

(?) **Reason**: *Don't offend others with your speech.*

The Delgado family

(Two-parent household; both parents employed full-time outside the home; two children, ages 12 and 14)

(!) Rule: Keep your word.

(?) Reason: *Build trust in each other.*

(!) Rule: Check voice mail regularly and keep pagers with you always.

(?) Reason: *Be prepared for changes of plans or emergencies.*

(!) Rule: Do not accept a ride home with anyone unless they are on the list we agreed upon.

(?) Reason: *Keep yourself safe.*

(!) Rule: Do not borrow anything without first getting permission.

(?) Reason: *Respect each other's property.*

(!) Rule: Check the bulletin board every morning before you leave for work or school to remind yourself of meetings, lessons, practices, conferences, etc.

(?) Reason: *Be responsible to your commitments.*

(!) Rule: Save one weekend a month for family "mini-vacation."

(?) Reason: *Make time for each other an important priority.*

(!) Rule: Take care of your responsibilities in a timely manner.

(?) Reason: *Be dependable.*

(!) **Rule**: Resolve differences in a reasonable manner, through discussion or negotiation.

(?) **Reason**: *Treat each other with respect.*

(!) **Rule**: Do not put anything in your body that will harm your health.

(?) **Reason**: *Keep your mind and body healthy.*

(!) **Rule**: Be willing to accept the consequences for your choices.

(?) **Reason**: *Encourage yourself to make wise choices.*

The Knight family

(One-parent household; parent self-employed within home; three children, ages 14, 15, and 18)

(!) **Rule**: Always tell the truth.

(?) **Reason**: *Be able to trust each other.*

(!) **Rule**: Don't leave the house without telling someone where you're going and when you're coming back, and call home if you're going to be late.

(?) **Reason**: *Don't cause needless worry.*

(!) **Rule**: Don't ride with anyone who's been drinking. Call home for a ride from wherever you are.

(?) **Reason**: *Keep yourself out of danger.*

(!) **Rule**: Do your chores before you go anywhere.

(?) **Reason**: *Get things done on time.*

(!) **Rule**: Each person prepares dinner for the family two nights a week. Monday night, we each get our own.

(?) **Reason**: *Everyone does their share.*

(!) **Rule**: Pick up after yourself and put things where they belong.

(?) **Reason**: *Keep the house clean and organized.*

(!) **Rule**: Five percent of everyone's earnings goes into our summer camping trip fund.

(?) **Reason**: *Contribute to family fun.*

(!) **Rule**: Phone call time limits: one half hour per call, and no phone calls made or accepted after 10 p.m.

(?) **Reason**: *Be considerate of everyone's time and money.*

(!) **Rule**: No television during meals.

(?) **Reason**: *Communicate with each other.*

(!) **Rule**: We take turns running errands for Grandma Kate.

(?) **Reason**: *Help family members who need extra care.*

❋❋❋

Remember to be willing to revise specific rules as your family needs change, although you will probably find that the *reasons* will already be part of your family's code of conduct. For example, when the 14 year-old in the Delgado family is old enough to drive a car, I'm sure there will be a need for a rule governing the use of the family vehicles. However, the reason for the rule will most likely be safety or responsibility or both, already part of that family's code.

As long as your whole family is always involved in the rule-making process, there is nothing unfair or arbitrary about the procedure. As the parent, you must exercise parental discretion in guiding your children toward an acceptable code of conduct, but involving them in the formation of that code will allow you to build their trust.

Stage 5

Show the Way

You've traveled halfway in your journey. At each location, you've been diligently gathering information, studying examples, observing history, and using what you've learned to come to some significant conclusions. All of this work has been directed toward your goal of effective parenthood, and it has taken great effort to get this far. You are beginning to understand that the effort, the work itself, has value. At this stage of your journey, you will learn why.

Why is it important to value work?

Working for what we want and need provides purpose in our lives, and purpose increases our control over the kind of lives we lead. On a prominent wall in my classroom, there is an important sign. It consists of two sentences that I calligraphed, in large letters, long ago. It reads:

Believe in the power of work.
It can be your miracle maker.

I define work as effort made toward a worthwhile goal. That effort can include many things besides a paying job. It can be the rigorous practices athletes must regularly perform. It can be hours of volunteer work performed for hospitals and in schools. It can be the demanding job of caring for small children or aging relatives. These things may not bring in an income, but they are excellent examples of valuable efforts made toward a worthwhile goal.

Why think of work only as something that involves discomfort, difficulty, and mental and physical hardship? It often does. However, it also involves reward. That reward can come in many forms. It can be personal, financial, spiritual, physical, intellectual, or any of the other subtle variations of these general categories. The hardship, the discomfort, the difficulties only add to the value of the reward.

Working toward something helps us learn to delay gratification, to earn the reward we receive, and to be more fully entitled to receive it. Because work does these things, it increases our personal pride, adds to our personal satisfaction, and helps us maintain balance and direction in our lives. It even helps us find moments of joy.

In the 1960s, some segments of our society rebelled against the idea of work as a valuable, even joyful, pursuit. Reacting to a society they perceived as being about all work and no play, they swung the pendulum to the other extreme of all play and no work. But the pendulum must center itself somewhere between the driven materialist and the undisciplined "flower child." In that centering is the balance. Tossing aside any sort of real responsibility to themselves or to society, the counterculture of that decade claimed that freedom of spirit and creativity were somehow hampered by any sort of disciplined effort.

They forgot that true creativity does its best work within boundaries. Poet T. S. Eliot once explained it this way: "When forced to work within a strict framework, the imagination is taxed to its utmost—and will produce its richest ideas. Given total freedom, the work is likely to sprawl."

Historical examples of the wisdom of Eliot's statement are easy to find. All great artists, inventors, and discoverers have done their most creative work when they had problems to solve within prescribed limits or boundaries. Michelangelo's magnificent sculpture of David was created within the limitation of the 18-foot block of pure white, unflawed Carrarra marble from which the biblical hero was to emerge lifelike yet larger than life. Dr. Jonas Salk's discovery of the vaccine that would virtually wipe the dreaded disease of polio from the world was a creative solution to a particular problem. The musical genius of Beethoven did not diminish with the tragic limitation of the deafness that struck him in his later years. He saw his affliction as a challenge to overcome rather than a limitation to his creativity.

The work of those individuals produced rewards that are easy to see. But the following story clearly illustrates the hidden rewards that work can also bring. A few years ago, my son was faced with the engineering challenge of creating a design for a portable antenna tower. The tower had to be transported in pieces to remote locations where a radio link was needed. These were locations that did not have a high enough permanent structure to mount an antenna large enough for long-range distance transmissions.

Working within these parameters, my son designed a portable tower that could, when assembled on the site, safely extend to a full height of 55 feet, yet still be sturdy enough to withstand high winds in mountainous terrain. On-site assembly time for the tower also had to be relatively short and require only a few people to assemble or disassemble it. The whole idea was to be able to move it quickly, from site to site, as it was needed.

After months of work, my son's design was completed, and he proceeded to actually build the steel structure, to test the merit of his design.

After all of the parts were fabricated, he and a co-worker loaded the sections onto a truck and hauled them out to our ranch to test assembly time. He intended to prove that the tower could be assembled in only three hours by only three people. His father was the third man. Within three hours, it was fully erected and its steel cables precisely set, just as the moon rose, and flooded the field with its light. My son's co-worker returned to town and my husband went inside.

I stepped outside, looking for my son, wondering if he had left for home, and thinking it was unlike him to leave without saying goodbye. Then I found him. He was standing a little off to one side of his tower, his arms folded across his chest, his eyes focused on the moonlit steel cables soaring above him. No lines of poetry could have pleased a poet any more than the sight of those cables catching the moonlight pleased my son. On his face was that moment of joy that only comes when idea and effort combine and a new piece of work is done.

Except for some forms of back-breaking physical labor, work should never be viewed as drudgery, something to be avoided at all costs. Even hard physical labor, unless conditions are cruelly unjust, is an endeavor that has its moments of joy.

In our rural county, several immigrant Hmong families have rented unused fields and planted endless rows of strawberries. Their diligent physical labor and keen knowledge of the requirements of the crop have produced a thriving business selling their delicious strawberries at roadside stands beside those rented fields. It was a creative solution to the problem of unemployed families and unused fields. Many who happily consume the strawberries and marvel at the success of the enterprise have confided to me that they wonder if what the families have gained is worth all the hard work. They are missing the point entirely.

One of my Hmong friends, a hard-working man in his early forties, stood beside his son, a young man in his late teens. We were all near the strawberry stand, surveying the field behind us. I had just purchased an armful of the berries and commented on their fine quality. The father rested his hand lightly on his young son's shoulders and said with obvious pride, "Most of the work in this field is his. He plants beautiful straight rows, don't you think? When the spacing is right, the irrigating goes well, and the right amount of sun can get to the plants. He studies how to best do the work."

Clearly, their respect for each other's work helped the members of this family value each other. Once again, idea and effort combined to create a worthwhile result: work that provided a family with an honest income and increased individual self-respect.

Instinctively, we sense that our minds and bodies are kept sharp and our momentum kept in a forward moving mode when we perform honest work. Competing in the workforce encourages us to use the full potential of the mind and body our souls inhabit. Because we are designed to work, we are energized by it. Even if we have yet to find that meaningful work we most want to do, we are still using our minds and bodies while we search.

It's been clearly proven that when we are exercising our minds and bodies, we are healthier, illness occurs with far less frequency, and we can better ward off debilitating disease if and when it strikes. Whether our labor is mainly physical, or mental, or a combination of both, it keeps us functioning in the way our minds and bodies were designed to function.

That's one of the reasons why many people who have retired from their jobs after long years of service still continue to do volunteer work in various forms in the community. They are entitled to their leisurely schedule, yet they still crave that certain satisfaction, mental and physical, that comes from making an effort and contributing to society in a positive way. They still feel the need to have meaningful purpose in their lives.

Many people have the mistaken idea that to be free of the necessity to work is somehow the ultimate form of happiness. But people without any significant work to do are not automatically happy. In fact, the idea of rewarding people for not working has proven to be a miserable failure for many it was designed to help. That's why so many people on welfare programs search for a way to get off of them. Not working for what we need and want makes us feel provided for, worthless, and incapable; there is very little personal satisfaction and pride in any of those feelings.

Those adults who have successfully struggled to free themselves from the welfare roles, or from any other form of financial dependency, have a right to feel proud of that effort. Their children who witness that effort will be stronger for it, and better able to value work and believe in possibilities. When we are kept from earning what we want and need, it means others have control over our lives. Our destinies are not our own. That fact alone can make us feel enslaved, hostage to those who keep us from work. For no matter how fine their intentions may be, they hurt us more than they help us. Help in time of dire need is one thing; creating dependency is quite another.

Remember, very early in this book, when we discussed the goal of self-reliance for your child? I reminded you that it's not in your child's best interest to keep him or her perpetually dependent upon you. Why? It ultimately cripples the child. It destroys incentive, diminishes personal worth, and creates another dependent human being instead of a vigorous individual who contributes proudly to his or her own welfare and the society in which he or she lives.

Without work, we're without purpose and set adrift, deliberately severed from that society, on its fringes, with no meaningful goals or dreams to help us stay afloat. Never having had to learn skills, never having been able to develop ourselves productively, we have nothing to pass on to our children in the form of useful values and personal pride. We give them no reason to believe in possibilities, especially their own.

Why must we respect each other's work?

Whether the work brings in an income or not, it has value. Volunteering in hospitals, serving on school boards without pay, and donating hours to local charitable organizations is still useful work for you and for society. If you want children to believe in work's value, you have to show the way by teaching them to respect all work. The best way to do this is by your own example.

Remember our definition for work: effort made toward a worthwhile goal. Too many parents place importance on one member of the family's work, while demeaning the value of the work of other family members. This location is where we discover a relatively simple way to help the whole family learn mutual respect for each member's effort.

We do it by making a chart, a schedule that briefly describes the kind of work done by everyone in the family. When I say everyone, I mean just that. List each family member and a brief description of their work and the general hours that work occupies. Be certain to fill in the line that says "busiest time"; I'll explain its importance a little later.

In addition to each person's formal occupation, be sure to include volunteer work, community services, and so forth. Post the completed schedule somewhere in your house where it will be seen often. This chart will clearly show that each person's work involves time and effort. Each person's work has a purpose, and each purpose is important, even though it may be different. It's all significant work directed toward a common goal: taking care of the family unit by taking care of individual responsibilities. This schedule will remind each member of your family that they are all contributors.

Keeping in mind that times may vary considerably from family to family, look at this family's schedule:

The Family Work Schedule

Name: Charles (father)

Age: 42

Type of work: *Welder. Volunteer fireman.*

Hours:

Welding job: 8 a.m. to 5 p.m. five days a week, some days till 6 or 7. Occasional Saturdays.

Fireman job: Monday night meetings, plus fire calls whenever needed, day or night.

Busiest time: 6:30 a.m. to 8:30 a.m. gathering tools, driving to job, and setting up shop, and Monday fire station meetings (rushing from job to fire station).

❊❊❊

Name: Rachel (mother)

Age: 40

Type of work: *Homemaker. Kindergarten aide.*

Hours:

Homemaker job: Roughly 6 a.m. to 8 a.m. then 12:30 p.m. till 9 p.m., five days a week. 8 a.m. to 8 p.m. Saturday and Sunday. Occasional half-days on Sunday.

Kindergarten aide job: 8:30 a.m. to noon five days week.

Busiest time: 6 a.m. to 8 a.m. getting everybody, including myself, off to jobs.

5 p.m. to 7 p.m. getting dinner and getting 4-year-old Danny ready for bed.

🐾🐾🐾

Name: Annie (daughter)

Age: 14

Type of work: *Attending school. Babysitter.*

Hours:

Attending school job: 8:30 a.m. to 3:30 p.m., or later, depending on track meets or band practice.

Babysitter job: Any time from 7 p.m. to 11:30 p.m. or midnight, two evenings a week, usually Friday and Saturday.

Busiest time: 6 p.m. to 8 p.m. weekdays: homework and chores.

10 a.m. to noon Saturdays (babysitting Danny while Mom's attending class).

🐾🐾🐾

Name: Jason (son)

Age: 12

Type of work: *Attending school. Yard work.*

Hours:

Attending school job: 8:30 a.m. to 3:30 p.m., or later, depending on soccer games and practices.

Yard work job: Usually from 2 p.m. to 4: 30 p.m. on Saturdays, depending on weather. Sometimes one or two days after school, if weather's bad on Saturday.

Busiest time: 6:30 p.m. to ? p.m. weekdays: homework and chores. 4:30 p.m. to 8 p.m. if it's a yard-work day because it has to be done before dark, then chores and homework.

❦❦❦

Set the schedule up together, getting input from each family member, and helping each one to remember all that they do in a usual day. As each one jogs the memory of the other, you will begin to see how much of what others do with their day is taken for granted. The very act of setting up this sort of schedule immediately makes each member of the family much more aware of the contribution of the other members.

When Charles and Rachel's family was making their chart, the one who was most impressed with it was Rachel, the mother. She knew how hectic her own day was, but she didn't realize that Jason and Annie also had times of their day when they were extremely busy.

Charles also learned from the experience. He gained a new respect for the unexpected seriousness of Jason's attitude about his yard work for the elderly couple three doors down the street. So busy with his own work, Charles didn't realize that Jason worked for them after school a day or two if he missed a Saturday because of the weather.

The whole family gained a better understanding of each other's importance as contributing members in the family workforce. By having "attending school" listed as work, in the same way as their father's income-producing job, Annie and Jason realized that their parents considered it to be work of equal importance.

Perhaps the most enlightening part of this whole schedule is the "busiest time" part. Most of us need to respect the fact that there are times when other members of the household are just too busy to be asked for extra help or special favors. This line on the schedule basically announces "This is when I need everyone's cooperation. This is when I have all I can do to get my own work done. If anyone needs my help with homework or to get the car started, or whatever, then you'll have to pitch in and help me first. In other words, this is not a good time to ask me. Find a better time."

Children tend to expect parents to be at their beck and call, forgetting that their parents have other responsibilities placed on their time in addition to caring for the direct needs of their children. On the other hand, parents tend to forget how much of their children's day is taken up with their primary job of attending school, and that children also have their "busiest times." Parents are being unreasonable when they make unnecessary extra requests during their child's busy time. It's about respecting each other's importance and each other's work.

This is a good place to make an additional observation about the importance of being on the job when you are expected to be there. Remember, as the parent, you teach your child by your example that being where you are expected to be is a major part of the responsibility of any job.

Parents must be aware of the fact that attending school is one of the ways their child learns to accept the responsibility of being on the job.

If you keep pulling your children out of school to run errands or for appointments that could be scheduled during non-school hours, you are sending a message to your child that attending school is not serious work. Children will not value school as the important foundation for all other serious work if parents demean it by not respecting its scheduled hours.

What tools does your child need?

This location is where you learn how to invest in the tools your child needs in order to do his or her work. As we explore this area, you will quickly learn that tools are not necessarily tangible things. Many people assume that if they just invest in things that can be bought and given to the child, the child will automatically be successful, especially in school. Whole school districts do this. They furnish their schools with state-of-the-art libraries with the latest computer equipment, install computers in every classroom, and expect miracles. Then school board members are sincerely surprised when grades do not automatically soar and test scores show no appreciable improvement.

No matter how costly or sophisticated the supplies, if a positive attitude toward work is not fostered, and if students are not inspired by the example of teachers and parents to make the effort to learn how to use the supplies, then there will be no sudden "miracles." Remember the sign posted in my classroom. It's the work, not the equipment, that makes the miracles.

Clearly, then, before you invest in any equipment or supplies of a tangible kind, you first need to invest the time it takes to help your child develop a healthy respect for work. The last location provided you with some helpful suggestions for fostering that healthy attitude. So at this point in our journey, you understand the importance of mutual respect for each other's work, and you're ready to move on to additional ways to encourage your child's willingness to do his or her work.

What are the basic supplies, or tools, your child needs? I prefer to call them tools, because the word *tools* implies something used for work. One of the most helpful tools to prepare your child for success can often be provided without spending a dime. Or, if any money is spent, it will amount to very, very little. That tool is an adequate work space, which also means an appropriate work space. Remember this before you rush out to buy your child a new desk, lamp, or computer. Let's elaborate on what I mean by an appropriate work space.

An appropriate work space means one that is not only well suited to the work to be done, but even more important, it must be well suited to the child's basic learning style, which will also be the child's best way of working. Take a minute to review those three styles.

Auditory learners:

1. Learn best from what they hear.
2. Often read assignments aloud.
3. May be distracted by music with lyrics, because they pay attention to the words.
4. Prefer a relatively quiet area.
5. Will be helped by someone willing to read aloud or verbally explaining assignments.
6. Find television distracting only if they can hear the words.

Visual learners:

1. Learn best from what they see.
2. Prefer visually stimulating things like pictures and posters.
3. Are not easily distracted by lyrics if music is playing.
4. Respond to variations in color.
5. Respond to things like flash cards, different letter sizes, different letter styles.

Kinesthetic learners:

1. Learn best with physical involvement.
2. Need room to move around. Portable workstations often work best.
3. Often prefer to be "in the middle of things" when doing their work. They find it comforting rather than distracting.
4. Respond better to study guides that can be easily moved or separated (flash cards, blocks, and so on).
5. Learn more easily if they can act out or demonstrate the lesson.

Keep this general information in mind as we further explore the kind of supplies and workstations that would be appropriate for each child's dominant learning style. Begin with the workstation, because everyone works best when they have one.

The station will vary not only with the type of work needing to be done, but also with who will be doing the work. The workstation need not be large or luxurious, just personal. If you go to an office, have a shop in your garage, have a kitchen or a laundry room, or use a corner of the bedroom for your sewing machine, those are workstations. The workstation gives status to the work, attaches significance to what you do, and gives it value. Nothing will tell your child that you value his work more than having his own work space. Even in extremely crowded situations, space is one of the cheapest and most effective basic supplies or tools that you can provide.

Fine-tune that work space. Example: Your visual learner may benefit from an inexpensive blackboard or bulletin board where he or she can write or tack up assignments. But your auditory learner would get more use from a little hand-held tape recorder. Your *mover*, your kinesthetic learner, might prefer a portable work space, such as a small table with casters or wheels on it, and a place to stack different size flash cards so the child can move the information around, as well as the table!

Because your child's most important work is getting an education, the workstation will most likely be targeted to schoolwork. But your children are also getting an education from the sports they are involved in, the music lessons they're taking, the skateboard contests they participate in, and any of the interests they pursue that involve some form of concentration and effort. If you're wise, you'll make those interests part of the workstation. To do that requires more imagination than it does money.

One friend of mine shared a small apartment with her teenage son. She had been a widow for three years, and her job provided a very limited income. Her son was avidly interested in playing the drums and worked after school at the local music store. As he earned the money, he was acquiring a drum set, piece by piece. His bedroom was really a corner of the living room in their essentially one-bedroom apartment. However, his mother was a creative lady. With very little money, she and her son turned his corner into a workstation that suited him well.

They blocked off one end of the long living room with a neat room divider that was basically some large wooden panels attached to poles that suctioned to the ceiling and floor. Behind the panels, the son had his bed, a nightstand, and just enough space for his drums. Because they lived in an apartment building, most of his practicing was done on the small practice pad used by professional drummers. Dedicated musicians practice every day, but some instruments, like the piano or the drums, present a problem when the musician is in a hotel room or a city apartment. That's when portable keyboards and practice pads come in handy. Even though the boy seldom was able to use his actual drums in his crowded situation, he still wanted them in sight.

That left no real room for a desk. So he and his mother attached a desktop-size piece of plywood to the wall. The plywood was hinged so it could swing up flat against the wall when it was not in use. When he needed a writing surface, the plywood was lowered to a desk height level. On shelves beside the plywood desktop, he stacked his school books, CDs, paper, pencils, music sheets, a small CD player, and head phones so he could hear his music while he worked. On the underside of the plywood desk surface, the part that was on view when the desktop was positioned flat up against the wall, the teenager kept flyers and photos of favorite drummers or concerts in the area.

Anyone stepping into that corner of the living room knew it was clearly the place a young musician did his work. The time his mother took to help him create his workstation was probably one of the best investments she ever made. More than anything she could have said, it told him that his interests and his work had value. She was setting her son up for success. She was teaching him by what she did that his work was important, and there is always a way that can be found to get it done.

There are all sorts of similar solutions to personal workstations. One cardinal rule should be that they are off limits to others. Any good cook will tell you that their kitchen is sacred, and its tools are not to be rearranged by anyone else. No matter what work we do, or how old or young we are, we value our workstations. They are part of our identity. Even if our identity changes with every new interest, as it often does with children who are just discovering themselves and exploring new things all the time, that identity with our work is how we see ourselves in a positive way.

Just as it is important to respect a youngster's work and workstation, it is equally important to teach the young, by our example, to respect the interests and work of the senior members of the family.

This place in our journey offers a useful bit of history that beautifully proves this point. When my father-in-law came to live with us after the death of his wife of more than 60 years, he brought his favorite carpentry tools with him. Though a house painter by trade, he loved to make things with wood, like candelabras, lamp bases, children's toys, and similar items.

My husband, a teacher of design and an artist by profession, was also very handy with wood and small construction jobs. He built much of our furniture in the early years of our marriage. Wherever we lived, he always commandeered a section of the garage as his workshop. In that workshop area, he had a workbench where he kept his small tools, as well as a space for a large circular saw, sanding wheel, and other equipment suitable for larger wood projects. When his father moved into our house, he of course had access to all of this.

My husband respected the fact that his father might feel he was intruding on his son's work space. He also knew his father was particular about his own tools. So my husband built a large yet portable wooden cabinet and painted his father's name on it. Inside, there was a place for every tool his father had brought with him.

That portable wooden cabinet was a point of pride to my father-in-law. It was his workstation and assured him of his own special spot within his son's larger area. It represented the mutual respect each man had for the other's work, and their mutual need for their own space.

The transition from living in his own home to living in his son's home was a difficult one for an independent, proud man. My husband helped the transition by setting his father up for success in his new environment. In effect, he said, "You are not disrupting us, Dad. You are becoming a part of our lives, with your own identity still very much intact within the framework of the whole family." A personal work space is a sign of respect, an acknowledgment of each person's importance to the household. Respect for each person's individuality goes hand in hand with respect for each person's work.

Before we leave this location, we need to look at one last, very necessary tool for successful work. That tool is physical health. If anyone is to have mental strength and agility, the skills to solve problems, and the stamina to strive for success on the job, whatever that job may be, he or she needs physical health. I'm not just addressing the need for your child to receive sufficient rest, adequate nourishment, and exercise. I'm addressing the parent's need for those very same things. Treat your body with respect so your child will learn by your example to do the same.

In the classroom, I've learned that when I've received a reasonable amount of sleep and eaten reasonably nutritious meals, I'm much more capable of handling whatever problems may occur on any given day. My mind is sharper, more creative, more quickly able to come up with innovative, effective solutions. Even at the end of a long, tiring day, if I've slept well the night before, I'm still enthusiastic about my work, and able to look forward to the next day's challenge.

In the case of children, who are growing and changing physically, emotionally, and mentally every day, it's logical that proper rest and decent nutrition must be the first foundation for their success. An alert mind and a fit body are indeed tools to help us in our work. I use the word *us* because, as always, adults must teach their children by their own example.

If your 16-year-old daughter sees you skipping meals, drinking too much coffee, and staying up too late, how will she ever learn to care properly for her own body? This is an area where it's wise to remember what you learned early in your journey, when you were first introduced to learning styles. Teaching by example uses all three learning styles, and because of that is our most powerful teaching tool. The following story demonstrates making a positive health change for the sake of a child, in this case, two children.

When my children were still in grade school, they were made aware, in their science and health classes, of the horrors of cigarette smoking. My husband had quit smoking several times over the years, but always resumed the habit after awhile. Much to his irritation, the children began to nag him about his habit. He resisted their entreaties, but they were not to be dissuaded.

They were sincerely concerned for his health, and although he knew they were right, it was hard for him to admit it, not only to himself, but to them. They continued to bombard him with information that he already knew but was ignoring. Then one day, he saw the whole cigarette-smoking situation in a new light. He knew they soon would be, if they were not already, faced with choices to make about putting harmful substances into their own bodies. Drugs and teenage drinking were already becoming the terrible, destructive problem they are today. Like it or not, he knew he was being handed a perfect opportunity to show them the way.

One day, he asked them to gather around the kitchen table. On the table, he placed an empty cigarette pack and announced that this was the last pack of cigarettes he would ever smoke. The children were elated, feeling very proud of themselves and savoring their victory. Then my husband said, "Wait. There's one more part to this announcement." They began to calm down, wondering what the catch was. He continued, "I'm quitting this addiction because you've convinced me that it's bad for me. It will be hard but I will never again smoke. However, this promise has one condition to it, and that condition involves both of you."

Suddenly serious, they sat back down as their father explained, "If either one of you ever smokes or experiments with drugs, it will tell me that you don't really believe in taking care of your health, so I won't bother to take care of mine, and I'll start smoking again. This is not a threat," he said soberly, "this is a promise, one that's intended to help all of us have the strength and determination to take care of our own health."

It was a powerful promise, made all the more powerful because his children knew he always kept his word. They knew that if they violated their part of the condition, he would have to smoke again or break his word. To his knowledge, neither one of them ever gave him any reason to smoke again. That incident went a very long way toward insuring our children's physical and mental health, both extremely important tools for anyone's life work.

How can you prepare your child for success?

Preparing your children for success is not about spending a lot of money. Nor is it about placing undue pressure on children to be a star in everything they try. It's about assigning value to work, because the success we speak about is the self-reliance we want our children to gain. Therefore, setting up your child for success is about helping the child understand that work is how they achieve that self-reliance, that ability to reach the goals they set for themselves, that ability to become who and what they want to be. Work is how they gain and keep control over their destinies.

Children who know how to apply themselves to tasks, to take on the responsibilities of a job, however small, are the children who get things done. Each thing done, each task accomplished adds to their sense of worth and their ability to think through problems and make responsible choices. There is an old saying: We may not be able to change the world, but we can change ourselves. The one thing we have the most control over is ourselves. That control gives us power, the internal power that lets us resist harmful habits and dangerous companions.

When we help our children learn the value of work as a way of gaining power over their own lives, we are providing them with an invisible yet extremely protective shield against the people and things that would harm them. That is the kind of success we all want for our children. When they know they can, by their own skills and with their own intellect, work their way out of problems, they will be less likely to succumb to the often tragic solutions so many teenagers seem to opt for today.

Assigning value to work includes helping your child find work they will enjoy. Following their interests will help them and you discover the kind of work that will give them personal satisfaction. People who are content with their work always do a better job, and the better the job they do, the more content they become. It is a wonderful circle of accomplishment that gives the person a sense of identity and pride, things that must come from within the person, not from external forces or pressures.

An excellent example of this is the story of a father whose children I taught. An immigrant from Mexico, he found work on a large ranch in the area. A willing worker with a keen mind, he was soon recognized by his wise employer as someone worthy of advancement. When his employer offered him a job inside the office on the ranch, he was surprised when the young father turned it down. The new position would mean an end to long hours of work in the hot sun, better pay, and more responsibility with even greater chance for advancement. However, the young man explained that he loved to be outdoors and felt he would be most useful to his employer in that capacity. They compromised, and the young father was put in charge of a work crew, which still allowed him to be outside for most of his workday and resulted in an increase in pay. The employer had the good sense to recognize and reward good workers.

After several months of observing this young ranch worker, his employer noticed two things about him. One, the young man always carried his tools in a well-made leather bag with his initials monogrammed on it. It appeared to be handmade with leather of good quality. So good, in fact, it was nicely surviving the hard wear it was subjected to day in and day out on the job. There was great pride in the way the young man slung the bag over his shoulder, as he moved from one station at the ranch to another.

The second thing the employer noticed was that the young worker was very good at keeping the men in his crew content and at peak efficiency, yet he never pulled rank or lost his temper. "This is someone I don't want to lose," the employer told himself. Realizing the man was a very strong family man, the ranch owner arranged a better living situation for the family, right there on the ranch. In less than five years, the young man from Mexico, now the father of four, became the foreman for the entire ranch and a well-respected member of the whole community. Yet he was still most often found outside, in the fields, checking on his workers, often pitching in when a crew was temporarily shorthanded.

That fact explained one of the reasons why the man was able to earn such loyalty and hard work from his crew, no matter how large it grew to be. He was able to inspire them by his own example. He knew every aspect of the job he was asking them to do, and he kept his own skills sharp by actually doing the labor himself from time to time. Much like a commander who goes with his troops to the front lines, his was a respect earned, not bestowed by rank. He took pride in his position of foreman, but it was clear that his true pride came from the fact that he was earning a living for his family, outdoors, doing work he understood and did well. Early in his life, he had learned the value of work.

As to his handmade tool bag, the employer learned that the young man's father, a tanner of hides, had made the bag for his son. It had been made from scraps saved from the tough hides the old man worked with and fashioned into saddles in Mexico. It was to be his son's portable workstation, one that took him to another country, carrying with him his father's acknowledgment of the value of his work.

It also reminded the young man of the value of his father's work. Both men believed in the value of work. Needless to say, that ranch foreman's children were among my most diligent workers in the classroom. One is a law school graduate, one owns her own business, and the two youngest are attending college on merit scholarships.

Assign value to work, and insure that each child has a personal place and the right tools to do that work. Show them the way to believe in its power, and work will be their miracle maker.

Stage 6

Have Faith

S tage by stage in this journey you are learning to have faith in your ability to be an effective parent. In this particular stage, you will learn to also have faith in the ability of your children. You have helped them gain respect for the value of work in general. Now you will teach them to respect the real value of homework and practice, and the personal rewards they gain from doing both themselves. Pay close attention at each location; some of the answers to these four guiding questions will surprise you.

What is the real homework problem?

When you take control over your children's homework, you take away their responsibility for doing it. You also take away their right to the rewards, personal and otherwise, for its accomplishment. It's their work. Let them do it. True, they will often still need your help, but you must help them without doing the work for them. How? Have faith that they can do it, then prove it. If you really want to be useful, help your children learn how to help themselves. Their self-reliance is their key to confidence, and confidence is what they need to do their own work and earn their own rewards.

To do a good job at anything, confidence is required. But no one, neither child nor adult, gains confidence just by being told they can do something. It is the doing, the actual performing of the task, the relying on their own effort, that makes them believe in their own ability. Confidence is gained by actually going through an experience, witnessing the results, adding accomplishments, and ultimately reaching a goal.

When a responsibility is assigned to a child, let the task be his or hers to do. That's how your child discovers if he or she is having a real problem with understanding the work to be done. Before your children can learn to ask for help when it is really needed, they first must learn to discover if, in fact, they need help. If they do, from whom? Their teacher? A mentor? Their parent? Maybe it's just a simple case of needing an older brother to listen to their vocabulary words for the science test. Or maybe it's more complicated, such as a lack of understanding of the concepts of most of those vocabulary words. Maybe you and your child come to the realization together that some after-school tutoring is needed. The point is that a large part of homework is letting a child recognize what is and what is not clear.

If you do it for her, Sharon won't know until the next test that she really has no idea what those last three science theories mean. Instead of the small setback of homework done incorrectly, which will allow the teacher to recognize that more help in that particular area is needed, Sharon is now faced with the larger setback of a failed test. Helping Sharon with her homework by doing it for her may have helped your self-confidence, but it certainly didn't do much for Sharon's.

Maybe because I'm a teacher by profession, the whole issue of my children's homework was a difficult one for me. I had to learn to resist the impulse to "govern" the homework. Used to setting time aside in my classroom for students to begin homework assignments, I tried to do the same thing at home. In the classroom, it was a good idea. It allowed students the opportunity to see if they understood the assignment, and if not, I was available to answer questions before they took the work home.

As soon as I insisted on a set time period at home, it only served to release my children from the responsibility to determine their own best time, or to plan ahead far enough so that if they needed my help, I would be available. It released them from having to remember that they had homework to do and how long it would take them to do it. They knew I would remind them, and nag them if need be, because I was the one who took control of the homework.

I was so concerned with whether or not they were getting it done that I lost sight of the fact that it was theirs to do. If they were late finishing, I was hard-pressed not to jump in and practically do it for them. My wake-up call came one morning, when I heard, "Mom, quick! Type this up for me, please. It's a mess, and I have to leave in a half hour!" When I grabbed the paper and started for the typewriter, I realized that, once again, I had just taken complete ownership of that child's homework. This was the third or fourth time that this sort of last-minute scramble had taken place, and I had come to the rescue.

This time, I stopped myself, and said, "If you don't have time to do it, then you'll just have to turn it in like it is." The wail that went up was significant. "But mom! You don't have to leave until later! You have more time than I do!" That was right, and I was sorely tempted to come to the rescue one more time, but this was a lesson that had to be learned by both of us. As I went back to the kitchen, to finish the breakfast dishes, I said, "It's your homework, though, not mine. I have faith that you can plan ahead a little better next time."

To type that paper at such short notice might seem to be the charitable thing to do, but only in the short term. In the long term, it will be a disservice. It's one thing to occasionally come to a child's rescue when extenuating circumstances occur, but when rescue becomes a developing pattern, the child will begin to believe that your help is essential and the work cannot be finished without that help. It will be a step backward in that child's journey to self-reliance.

To help you understand how important it is for your children to have ownership of their work, keep in mind the following four statements. They apply to every type of challenging task they attempt to learn, but especially to school homework. Remind yourself that the best remembered-lessons are learned by example.

It follows then, that when you do your children's work, you are teaching them:

1. To deceive.
2. That they are not capable.
3. That work is something to be avoided or ignored.
4. That other people can and should do their work for them.

All four of these lessons will not only destroy confidence and seriously stunt the growth of the self-reliance needed to function successfully in the adult world, but they completely negate the real purpose of homework. That purpose is to assign work to be done outside the classroom, in order to see how well the child understands the material and to give them practice in using the material. A geometry principle is explained, then 10 problems are given so the student can practice using the principle. The goal of the teacher is not to receive a perfectly done assignment. The goal is to have the student practice the principle! If the practice produces a perfectly done assignment, then it can be assumed that the student understands the principle and can use it.

If the assignment is completed, but there are errors, then the teacher knows more study is required, more help is needed before that particular student can understand and use the principle. It's easy to see how the goal of the schoolwork is completely sabotaged when the work is done by someone other than the student. Often, when you first sit down to help, your intent is not to actually do the child's homework yourself. Your child is sitting there with you, but you neglect to notice that he is doodling or gazing off into space while you are laboring over the problem. However, whether or not you intended to, you are doing your child's work.

Some terrible lessons are learned when this happens. Not only is deception condoned, but children begin to believe in their inability to learn something difficult; they begin to believe that anything difficult should be avoided. How boring and limited their lives will be. How crippled their confidence will be. And how easy a target they will be for anyone who promises quick and easy satisfaction. In your effort to make your children's lives easier, you will have created more difficulties than you can imagine.

Every time they are faced with new challenges, they will remember that you did not have faith in their ability to meet them. Your children will encounter all sorts of challenges in the everyday business of living, getting and keeping a job, and providing themselves with the general necessities required to stay alive and maintain mental and physical health.

The greatest gift you can give your children is to help them understand that they are capable human beings. Then they will accept the normal challenges of life as what they are: a necessary part of living.

There's also something more. In order to maintain a healthy balance between the routine and the unusual, the human spirit unconsciously searches for challenge. If we aren't learning new ways of doing things, or investigating new areas of interest, stretching our minds and bodies, then mental and physical stagnation takes place. Depression and moodiness set in, as fear of failure drives us deeper into the routine we have established for ourselves, even when we are bored with it.

Avoiding normal risks associated with learning new skills or new material, your children still feel the need for risk, so they slip into the more dangerous area of "easy excitement." They try things designed to distract them from the real problem, things like alcohol, drugs, criminal activities, or adolescent sex. They try them because they appear to be an easy way to gain the sort of pleasure and satisfaction they are lacking in their lives. Too late they learn that the temporary satisfaction of drugs, drinking, or irresponsible sex is no replacement for the hefty dose of real excitement that comes with the mastery of new skills, new goals reached, relationships forged and improved upon, and all manner of other worthwhile achievements they can gain when they accept the challenges of life. Do you want to wish that sort of powerless existence on your child? Then help them to learn to help themselves.

How can you help your children help themselves?

When someone is faced with something new to them—a strange concept, a new theory, new words, whatever it is they must learn how to do—tell them the truth. The truth is that learning something new is never really easy. It requires a whole new set of responses, mental and physical. Like using muscles you haven't truly tried yet, it requires stretching and flexing and a certain amount of discomfort. It requires pushing yourself beyond your known limits. It is that very push and pull, that effort against those muscles, that stretching of sinew that makes the body grow in strength and physical endurance.

The barriers of our known limits provide something for us to struggle against. That struggle strengthens us in mind and body. Once we accept this, we realize that when we feel that resistance, growth is taking place. Barriers are being loosened, horizons are spreading wider: We are learning.

Why mislead someone, especially a child, by implying that what they are about to do will require no effort? Why dishonor the effort they will have to make? Besides, if you think it will smooth the way, or entice them to try, you are mistaken. If they are at all in doubt, telling someone that what they are attempting to do is *easy* only increases their apprehension and cripples their confidence. After all, if it's supposed to be easy, and they do poorly the first try, it only causes disappointment and creates an even stronger doubt in their own minds about their ability.

When your children attempt something new, let them know that it will take effort.

When you do that, you are allowing them to mentally prepare for struggle because they expect it. You are also keeping them from having the unrealistic idea of immediate success, an idea that will only hinder any real progress toward the goal.

When my students begin a project, I don't make statements like, "This will be fun!" or "It's so easy!" If I'm going to use the word easy, I'll say something like, "This won't necessarily be easy, but it won't be boring either!" Letting them know what they're about to learn will take effort shows them I respect their time. I'm not going to insult them by implying that what I'm asking of them could be done by anyone without any effort. I prefer words with some meat to them, some substance, words like *exciting*, *challenging*, or *innovative*.

Learning can't be done for someone, much as we might wish that were true. If you're trying to sing a song and you're having trouble reaching certain notes, your performance is not helped one bit by someone who sings the song for you. Yes, the song has been sung, but not by you. You are now convinced, more than ever, that you can't do it.

The same is true when you do your child's homework or chore. True, the work is done, but so is the damage to the child's confidence. On the other hand, if that same person who volunteered to sing your song for you gives you some basic instruction in breathing so you'll have more lung capacity to reach those difficult notes, that person is helping you to help yourself accomplish the goal. Seems logical, doesn't it? Then why do so many parents simply do the chore themselves rather than show their child how to do it?

The answer is also logical. Once we know how to do something, it is always easier and quicker to do it ourselves. To teach someone else takes effort. To show someone else how to do it takes time. To allow someone else to discover his or her own best way of doing the chore takes even more time.

All along this journey, we keep coming across examples of the harm done by settling for quick-and-easy solutions. Good only for the short term, the quick-and-easy path is neither quick nor easy for the long term. Shortcuts ultimately make us take longer to reach the goal. They don't allow us enough time to learn. Ironically, when enough time is taken and enough effort is made when we are first learning something new, the rest of the entire lifelong learning process is made easier. Shortcuts make us miss too many small steps in the learning process.

Confidence comes from attempting to take small steps and reach small goals by ourselves or with minimal help, and succeeding, by ourselves, then continuing on to the next small goal, eventually reaching the larger goal we were aiming for from the beginning. It is an incremental process that builds upon itself.

Confidence soars as we master, however slowly, one task after another. Small defeats are seen for what they are: temporary setbacks. They are put in proper perspective, much like the baseball player who stands ready at the plate, hits a foul ball, then turns to face the pitcher again. Hitting the ball foul is just a temporary setback, if kept in perspective. It can be seen as another chance to step up to the plate and face one more pitch, with a fresh opportunity for success. Keeping that in mind, when I'm teaching a child something new, I break it down into manageable steps. Then, if the child stumbles and falls a time or two, the damage to self-confidence will be negligible.

Why would you sidetrack your child's opportunity to build his confidence by never letting him do things for himself? Where will his confidence come from? Where will his character come from?

Yes, it may take time, but with increased confidence comes increased speed each time that child tackles something new and difficult. The child has faith that he can eventually do it, because the process of learning is not new to him. The concept of time taken and effort made is what he expects and in fact becomes comfortable with, as he meets with more and more small successes. He has done it before. He knows he can do it again. The child may not know exactly *how* yet, but he does know he will be able to *discover how*, because he has practice in learning new things.

My oldest grandson, now 5 years old, lives on the ranch next door. He has always loved to come to my house to play. Yet he knows that I have chores to do, and work to go to, and he knows those things take time. My time. More important to him, my time that could be used playing with him. One day, he arrived just as my husband and I were finishing dinner.

When his mother dropped him off at our house, she called out, "I'll be back soon," which made him very aware of time. In his mind, I'm sure, that translated to "not much play time." He hurried through his milk and cookies, then asked, "Mama Rae, can we play now?"

"After I clear the table and do the dishes," I replied. Though only 4 at the time, he already reflected the training his mother had given him in helping with chores like clearing the table. He quickly slipped from his chair and volunteered eagerly, "I will help you!"

My initial reaction, thinking about possible broken plates and glasses, was to decline his helpful offer and quickly do it myself. However, I am constantly condemned to take my own advice and learn from my own mistakes. Years ago, when my own children were this young, I made the mistake of doing far too much for them, when it came to basic tasks like clearing the table. I hadn't yet learned the value of these simple chores as a way for the child to build self-confidence and self-reliance. I was forever taking the easy way and quickly doing the chore myself.

Seeing myself as a self-sacrificing mother, constantly doing for her children, pleased me, but I was gaining an image at the expense of my children. It took my husband's interference to make me realize that what I perceived as kindness was actually selfish. Prolonging my children's dependence on me may have made me feel important, but it was making them feel incompetent. I wasn't about to make the same mistake with my grandchildren, so I accepted Jacob's offer of help.

I minimized risk by hastily removing the heavier plates, as he carefully carried the smaller ones and the silverware to the counter by the sink. He was so happy to be helping, because, as he declared with open honesty, "If I help, we get done faster, and then we can play." His help was actually making the process go a little slower, because his little legs couldn't move as fast as mine. Still, this wasn't about setting some new world record for clearing the table. This was about building a child's confidence.

Yes, it took effort and time to direct him. "Jacob, the butter goes on the side counter, and the shakers go beside the refrigerator." Yes, it took effort and time for me to rearrange the dishes and to explain why we don't just drop the dishes into the sudsy water. It would have been much easier and quicker to grab the first dish from him that first evening, with a sharp reprimand, "Don't touch that, you'll break it!" and clear the table myself. No dishes would have been broken, but he would have begun to believe that he is not capable of doing things for himself or for anyone else. I would rather break a dish than break a child's willingness to learn.

You must always keep the goal in sight. Now, less than a year later, this child knows how to be a real help. He can hand the right kind of screwdriver to his father when it's asked for, because his father took the time to show him the difference between a Phillips head and a straight-edged screwdriver. He can find the diapers for his baby brother because his mother took the time to show him where she keeps them. It's a real help when he gets them himself and hands them to her, while she readies the baby for his change.

At age 5, Jacob is already well on his way to being able to do all sorts of things for himself, and what he can't yet do, because of safety or size, he is certain he will learn later. "I have to be bigger before I can learn that," he says with confidence. In his mind, it's not a question of *can* he learn, but when. What a great gift is confidence. To have faith in our ability to solve problems, to learn whatever we need to learn, to do whatever we need to do. Taking the time to teach him how is the first step in helping a child learn to help himself.

Why must standards be maintained?

Think of standards as the destination toward which a particular task is directed. Set and maintain high standards for the work itself, but allow for different routes for reaching that destination. Often, when we have a set of standards, expectations, and requirements that must be met in order for a task to be properly completed, we become rigid in the way it must be done. We don't allow for individual solutions, and we stifle the child's desire to accomplish what needs to be accomplished. Remember what you discovered about your child's learning patterns earlier in our journey. Respect that learning pattern, and let it help your child determine how to perform the task at hand and still strive for the standard.

If you ask your teenager to set the table, curb your compulsion to rigidly direct how he or she will do it. One youngster might grab a stack of silverware in one hand and dishes in the other and pile them all on the table, then set the table from there. Another one might carry dishes first, putting one at each place, then return to the kitchen to get the silverware, place it properly, then the glasses, continuing in that ordered way until each place is set.

Neither way is right or wrong. The goal is to have a proper place setting for each person at the table. Respect the way your child wants to do the job. Tell them only how you want each place to be, then let them find, through doing it, their own best way of producing the required result.

Ultimately, they will discover, on their own, the most efficient way of doing the task. Discovering it themselves will produce more pride in the accomplishment. After all, on the job, aren't you much more comfortable, and ultimately much more efficient, when your employer allows you to find your own best way of doing your work? That's how creative solutions are born. By being allowed to solve problems in our own particular way. Guidance is helpful. Encouragement is valuable. Requirements are necessary. But the most creative and effective solutions always come when individuals are allowed to find those solutions in their own particularly ingenious way.

This does not mean that you are not allowed to make yourself available to answer questions, give advice, or generally support you child's efforts. Nor does it mean that you can't check the work to see that it meets reasonable requirements and assure that it is, in fact, actually done. This does not mean that you or anyone else has to accept poor work. Whether it's homework or household chores, high standards should be set and maintained. But expectations should always be explained clearly, and they should never be arbitrary. Reasons should be given why a certain result is needed.

For example, the essay needs to have enough margin so the teacher can make comments about each section. The dishes need to be stacked a certain way in the dishwasher so they can be cleaned efficiently. The dark clothes can't be combined with the white clothes if bleach is being used. Once expectations are explained, and reasons given for those expectations to be met, the child should be allowed to find his or her own best way of meeting them. Once fair and reasonable standards are set, don't demean the child's effort by compromising those standards.

In my classroom, standards are never lowered to accommodate different abilities. I have students of many varying academic abilities, and an exceedingly wide range of natural talent. Special education students, limited English-speaking students, Attention Deficit Disorder students, freshmen, sophomores, juniors, and seniors all work alongside one another. My standards are high, but they are carefully formulated to allow success, if effort is made, for all students.

Essentially, my students are competing with themselves, and they must show me progress and improvement. Those are two things students at all levels are capable of, with my guidance and their willingness to do the work. There is never any compromise made to insure an easier time for students with limitations, because they will need to learn how to get results in the real world in spite of limitations.

I want them to learn to overcome limitations, not be held back by them, or to use them as crippling excuses. If they are to build self-reliance and personal confidence, then I must maintain standards and at the same time demonstrate that those standards can be met, by helping each child find his or her own way of reaching the goal. I can pay attention to learning patterns and increase strengths and minimize weaknesses.

This has led to some inspiring achievements among students others considered to be less capable, achievements that have leveled the playing field for those particular children far better than any lowering of standards ever could. It has also encouraged students blessed with advantages to act as mentors and teachers to their classmates for whom the struggle is greater. I consider those to be equally inspiring achievements, for they are achievements of character. There are many examples of this every year, but this one will serve.

Ricardo is a limited English-proficient student who also has some learning disabilities. He is completing the final phase of the year's art requirements. In spite of his struggle with depth perception and visual space relationships, Ricardo has completed every assignment and earned enough points to receive an A+ for the year. His obvious improvement has been an inspiration to the rest of the class. They find it harder to make excuses to themselves for not making as great an effort as Ricardo does to meet the standards.

His secret: He works hard, asks many questions, and watches carefully whenever I give him instruction. But he also is helped considerably by observing the drawing techniques of several artistically talented students who sit near him in class. One in particular, David, has taken on the role of a mentor to Ricardo, helping him when I'm busy with other students. David is genuinely intrigued by Ricardo's improvement and is enjoying a teacher's satisfaction as he sees his pupil blossom and learn.

Ricardo is keenly interested in sports. The latest assignment is to draw a figure in action, and students are allowed to select what the figure will be doing, wearing, and so forth. As they pore over the magazine source material I keep in my room, they naturally look for people doing things that interest them. I make certain that there are plenty of sports magazines available, not only for Ricardo's sake, but for others who are fascinated with sports. But David went one step further.

A few days ago, he brought an armful of old *Sports Illustrated* magazines into the classroom. He plopped them on Ricardo's desk and page by page, the two of them searched for suitable figures to draw. David pointed out the photographs that were sharp and clear in their contrast, showing strong darks and lights so that Ricardo could more easily see the muscles and movement of the figure.

Using his own artistic perceptions, David guided Ricardo to choices that will help him meet the standards successfully. But even more than that, David's belief in Ricardo's ability to do the assignment makes Ricardo approach it with much more confidence. Equally important, Ricardo's enthusiastic response to his mentor's extra effort is also a confidence builder for David.

The standards are the same for both David and Ricardo, and each child is finding his own best way of meeting them. Remember that arbitrary, ever-changing standards are not true standards. They are confusing fluctuations that lead to poor performance and contribute to general apathy. This is as true for people in the workplace, who must suffer with constantly changing management expectations, as it is for students in the classroom whose teachers continually change the due dates on assignments, then wonder why more and more of their students don't bother to turn anything in on time.

There is not now, and never has been, anything arbitrary about personal responsibility. Then, it must follow logically, that you, as a parent, must not waver in your responsibility in that role. Set standards for behavior, as well as work, then don't be arbitrary about them. Be certain the standards are reasonable and just, then have faith that your children will be able to meet them. They will sense that faith. If you hold true to the standards, that is the most powerful demonstration of your faith in them and their capabilities. Don't give in to make yourself feel better. Remember, this is about your child's ultimate well being, not your temporary satisfaction.

Why teach your child to ask for help?

It may at first seem ironic that, in attempting to encourage self-reliance in our children, this location in our journey is all about teaching them how to ask for and get help. You must understand that seeking help to learn how to do something for ourselves is vastly different from getting someone to do it for us. If we don't know how to get the help we need to learn how to do something new, then we won't do it, or worse, we'll allow someone else to do it for us. Each time that happens, our self-confidence drops down one more level, making it harder and harder to climb back up to some satisfactory level of self-reliance.

Teach your children to ask for help when they need it. When you do this, you are making it possible for them to accept challenges. You are teaching them:

1. To do all they can do *without* help.
2. To recognize when they *need* help.
3. To arrange to *get* help.

Implied in this is that you trust them to do what they can without help, pushing themselves to go as far as they can with what they already know. You are also teaching them to go beyond what they know and ask for help to get through that new territory. The ultimate responsibility for getting the work done, whatever kind of work it is, must always rest with them. But to know help is there encourages a child to push their potential and not settle for the limitation of present knowledge.

Remember what you learned earlier about where to look for mentors. Begin with your own family and your own neighborhood. Some history in this location provides an example of how this works. When my brother first showed an interest in music, there was no one in our immediate family who was a musician. My enterprising mother discovered there was an excellent music teacher who gave private lessons in his own home and also taught at a local university. This teacher's home happened to be within walking distance from our working-class neighborhood.

The help my brother needed to get his first brass instrument was provided by that music teacher. Though the instrument my brother wanted to play was the slide trombone, he was still a small boy and it was difficult for his arms to extend the slide on the trombone to reach the farthest notes, but he loved its rich sound. The music teacher suggested beginning with the mellophone, an instrument similar in looks to a French horn. It produced a rich sound reminiscent of the mellow brass tones of the French horn and the trombone. He even helped my family locate a decent, used mellophone, and my brother's lifelong career as a world-class professional musician began.

On the late, great Duke Ellington's award-winning album, "Music Is My Mistress," the rich sound of my brother's slide trombone can be heard; one of his excellent musical arrangements is also featured in that wonderful collection of Ellington classics. There was challenge every step of the way as my brother pursued his music career, but each challenge met and mastered made his dream of making music his life's work become a reality.

This was only one of many times my parents saw signs of an interest, made it possible for us to pursue that interest, and provided ways for us to get the help we needed to learn what they couldn't teach us. But the practice, the schooling, the actual work, was always left to us. My brother's music lessons were held once a week, and his practice sessions were daily, and they were always his responsibility. My Saturday morning art classes had to be attended by me, and the drawings I produced at home had to be mine, the result of my effort and my growth.

Books and paper my parents could help with, lessons and instruction my teachers and mentors could help with, but the effort to learn the skills had to be made by me. The obvious result, of course, was that both my brother and I gained greater skills in our particular areas of interest. But less obvious, and actually more important, is the confidence we gained from the actual work. It helped both of us look upon challenge as an integral, desirable part of life.

If I made a list of all the gifts my parents gave us, at the very top would be their profound belief in our possibilities. If I made a list of all the ways I could hope to help my students, at the top of that list would be that same profound belief. I call my belief in their possibilities the gift of faith. Faith in their ability to accept challenge. Faith in their ability to learn to do the work themselves. Faith in their ability to find their own best way of working, to solve their own problems, one challenge and one step at a time. Faith in their ability to seek mentors when they need them to help them reach worthwhile goals.

You can give your children these gifts only if you are willing to invest your effort and your time. The effort it takes to pay attention, and the time it takes to teach. From your example, your children will understand that all learning requires both time and effort. They will also learn not to expect results without that investment of time and effort. With each new thing learned, their confidence will grow, as they become the self-reliant, well-balanced adults you have faith they will be.

Stage 7

Take the Lead

———————————————————————————

This part of your journey is where you begin to fully understand the power of the media, and why that power must be
safely managed. This is where you learn why time is a large
part of the problem, and how your leadership can teach your children to
strive for balance in the use of their time. Your travels through this area
also teach you more about your own power and that knowledge will
strengthen your struggle toward effective parenthood. There is much history to be found in this part of your journey, as well as forecasts for the
future. In these locations, you will find the constants in both.

Why must you balance the media message?

The electronic media possesses enormous potential for persuasive power. With its strikingly graphic visual images and state-of-the-art sound, television, for example, has literally revolutionized our ability to access information, both beneficial and harmful. We not only have access to this information, but we have it presented within the very homes in which we live, and therefore we are more easily persuaded by it. The greater the power inherent in something, the greater there is a need for striking a balance between its negative and positive potential. Balance is maintained by setting reasonable limits, not by arbitrary or extreme control. As tempting as it may be to do it, don't toss out your television set. There is an important truth that must be accepted before you can proceed in this location.

It has been said that once something is known, it can never be unknown. That perfectly describes the dilemma we encounter with all inventions. Once discovered, they are a part of our lives, a condition we must consider, a known factor in our existence. For example, whatever one believes about the benefits or the dangers of nuclear power, how to create it is now a known factor on our planet. We cannot wish it away or go back to not knowing it.

What we must do is learn how to use its awesome power in a positive way. We must learn to apply reasonable limits to its use and safeguard the disposal of its hazardous wastes. This is a truth that applies to all of the modern world's mixed bag of blessings and curses created by the human mind.

It is convenient to blame television, radio, automobiles, computers, and a host of other inventions and discoveries for our society's distressing lack of responsible, ethical behavior. But it's not *things* that tarnish our lives today. Rather, it is the way we allow these things to control and govern our actions.

We have all too eagerly embraced the power and the benefits these inventions provide, without giving much serious thought to the problem of their hazardous wastes. It's all about limits, and our willingness to establish reasonable limits to the way we use these things that our ingenuity and intelligence have introduced into our lives. We must learn to use that same intelligence and ingenuity to find solutions to whatever problems our discoveries and inventions may create.

The search for balance never leads to outright abolition or crippling censorship, nor does it lead to mindless acceptance. Though the human tendency toward oversimplification is always to swing precariously from one extreme to the other, the real human need is to find the balance between the two.

Consider the medical discovery of antibiotics, and the relatively recent realization that they can do harm as well as good. It's not the antibiotics that are the problem. It is our unwillingness to establish reasonable limits to their use.

Used appropriately and with care, these miraculous medicines save lives. Before the discovery of antibiotics, pneumonia took the lives of many more people than it does today. Treated early enough, with the proper antibiotics, pneumonia is curable, and patients can expect full recovery. But antibiotics, turned to too often when they are really not needed, have their effectiveness considerably lessened when a true emergency occurs. Their overuse destroys their miraculous potential, all the while creating a false sense of security in their users.

We can make a very similar observation about the electronic media. In its ability to present critical information in a timely fashion to huge numbers of people, the modern electronic media surpasses anything we've ever known. If there is an earthquake in an area where loved ones live, none of us longs for the days of the Pony Express to bring us news of the damage done or lives lost. We gratefully turn to our television sets to inform us quickly and directly. We depend on radios and telephones to tell us where to go for safety when floodwaters threaten. We are equally grateful for 911 emergency help when we are in distress, instead of having to rely on someone rushing on horseback to the nearest home for desperately needed help.

Reporting disasters, broadcasting storm warnings, alerting us to dangers of all types, the media can be a marvelous means of saving lives. This is certainly one aspect of it that we would not wish away. But this same marvel can distort information, dispense propaganda of dubious value, and lead those same huge numbers of people in unhealthy directions.

It's difficult for most of us to remember that the media is not a principled public servant, always directing itself toward the general good of humankind. It is, in fact, a very powerful tool of commerce, with buyers and sellers competing for control of our minds. Overly dramatic statement? Not at all. It's absolutely necessary to understand that every single minute of programming presented on your television screen is using extremely valuable time. Time that is paid for, at great cost, by those who want you to buy what they are selling, and that includes ideas as well as products.

In one of the forums that I conducted in an area of very low income, one father was concerned because he couldn't really afford to buy his son what he was convinced his son needed. The son was insisting on a particularly expensive brand of shoe to wear to school that year. The father had refused, for purely economic reasons, but was clearly upset that he had to turn down his son's request.

Why would a 14-year-old boy whose feet are still growing at a relatively rapid rate badger his low-income parents into buying him a pair of sneakers at the cost of $150? Was he just a self-centered child, unaware of the financial hardship this would cause his parents? No. His request was a direct response to skillful programming, not only of a product, but of an idea. He sincerely believed that the shoes would so significantly enhance his life that their cost would be worth it.

It was totally illogical for his parents, who were having difficulty making rent payments, to spend that kind of money on such a short-term satisfaction, but that fact completely escaped him. Not because he was insensitive, but because his young mind had been conditioned to accept this purchase as a need rather than a want.

Why would perfectly intelligent adults, who are reasonably responsible parents, agree to take such a request seriously, much less actually make the purchase? Because skillful marketing, bombarding them nightly via their television set, made them believe that this purchase would help their son find self-esteem, and they would be denying him a necessity if they did not fulfill his request. Why else would parents spend that kind of money for casual shoes that will be outgrown within six months? Why else would a child that age believe he was justified in making that kind of unreasonable request? Television is a medium that pushes and pulls at our sense of balance, frequently causing us to lose that balance and do things not always in our own best interest.

By its very nature, the media is not a provider of information that can be easily ignored. Think about it. When you walk into a room and a television set is on, what is being presented on the screen dominates the room. That is what it is intended to do. Highly qualified professional writers, designers, producers, and entertainers have put a great deal of effort into this product, their program, and they definitely want it to be something that will be noticed, something that will influence, something that will distract from all other activity in the room. If it doesn't, then they haven't done their jobs.

Remember, they're being paid for their time so that you, the viewer, will absorb the information they are presenting to you. That brings me directly to what I believe to be the major problem connected with the electronic media: time.

Why is time the primary problem?

What is wrong with this medium is not so much its overall content, but the fact that we allow it to take up too much of our *time*. We use so much of our time watching what other people are doing, that it keeps us from doing anything productive or rewarding with our own lives. It's entertaining to watch other people, especially if they are entertaining, engaging, witty personalities. The business of being entertaining is exactly how those who want us to buy what they sell hope to keep us watching every minute of their costly time. Even so-called public television has an agenda to sell. It, too, must entertain. It, too, must keep its audience watching every single minute, for its time is just as costly.

Entertainment is a business and a valid one. It is peopled by as many ethical, responsible individuals and as many charlatans and cheats as one will find in any other business. It is not the entertainment industry's fault that we are so captivated by it that we lose our perspective of time. After all, it is their business to entertain. It is our fault, not theirs, that we fail to see that a life given over to being continually entertained is a terrible waste of valuable time. As with other issues I've discussed, this one is also about balance. What is there about the media that throws us so off balance?

By media, I speak primarily of the electronic media, the potent visual forces of television, movies, videos, and so forth. Though magazines, newspapers, books, and radio are also powerful purveyors of fact and fiction, the added impact of vibrant visual images makes something like television doubly dramatic and its influence much more difficult to diffuse. It's been well documented with phrases such as "one picture is worth a thousand words" that words and ideas can be more powerfully presented when pictures are part of the package. When those pictures are also *moving*, accompanied by the emotional stimulus of music, they are virtually impossible to ignore, especially when those pictures are presented right in our own home.

When I was growing up, we loved the movies every bit as much as children do today. We went eagerly into the darkened theatre and sat dazed through double features while we dreamed that we were part of the drama on the larger-than-life screen. We fell into the hero's arms, we imagined ourselves as the lovers who met and kissed passionately, we longed for the fashionable clothes and fabulous cars, we listened to language we never heard at home, and we saw savage murders and daring deeds both right and wrong.

What's the difference between our fascination with the media and our children's preoccupation with it? You can argue that what our children see is so much more graphic today than what we viewed 30, or even 10, years ago. The language is much rougher and more sexually explicit. Violence and brutality of every sort is much more apt to be included purely for the sake of sensationalism rather than story. All this is true, but for our time period, the movies we saw were just as shocking and sensational. What's the real difference then?

I still contend the most damaging difference is the amount of time spent with our sight and our senses saturated by what is on that screen. That and the fact that the screen is now in our own home. During our youth, we had to leave our homes to watch the wonders on that screen. It made it an experience that was separate from our normal lives. Even if we spent all of Saturday afternoon in the theater and went to the movies every time the picture changed, which was usually every four days, we were in this powerful presence for only five or six hours a week, not five or six hours a day!

There was plenty of time for relatively normal life between weekly matinees full of crime scenes or passionate embraces or expensive clothes and cars. We teenagers left the theatre and returned to homes where usually well-entrenched family values and reasonably decent language could be found. Our world was peopled with mostly average individuals living useful, productive lives. Even if we had seen a blatantly sadistic movie at the theatre, its impact and influence would have been considerably lessened by the balance of the everyday business of work and play that went on between those weekly movie matinees.

There's that word again: balance. We didn't bring the organized crime boss, child molester, or sleazy pimp into our living rooms. We left them in the theatre, away from our family, safely removed from our lives, where we could continue to be children for as long as it took our impressionable minds to adjust to our adolescent bodies.

Today's children are constantly having their senses over stimulated for the sake of selling sneakers or blue jeans. Sensational, graphic pictures are pushed at them hour after hour. They see far too much, too soon, at too young an age. There is no time for balanced assessment, for processing, for any wisdom to be acquired about the value of what they see. When this happens repeatedly, these warped images get stuck in young minds not yet made strong enough to make good choices. Balance is destroyed, and much damage is done to the necessary growth needed to build character.

Today, children's physical senses are being dangerously over-stimulated, creating insatiable needs for quicker and easier sensual gratification. Yet their reasoning power, the part of them that must provide the balance, is receiving significantly less stimulation.

This overstimulation can be almost as destructive for adults. Too much exposure to the lives of the rich and famous on the television set in your living room can make that living room seem shabby, creating discontent. Discontent and dissatisfaction that can lead adults toward damaging habits that destroy families and futures. How much of Elizabeth's father's discontent with his life is fed by what he sees on his television screen? If he only saw it occasionally, it would most likely not make the same strong impression.

In the same way, if the boy who insisted on the expensive sneakers had only seen one glimpse of them, he would have been able to keep their cost in perspective, if he had considered them a possibility at all. But in both cases, these images are repeated over and over, in subtle and not so subtle ways, until the viewer begins to believe that he is somehow deficient if he does not have that way of life, that job, or that pair of shoes.

How can you control quality and content?

You must first believe in the necessity for that control. If you, as a parent, recognize that example is a powerful teacher, then you must also accept that television's examples are especially powerful teachers. Its presence in your home has the potential to be every bit as pervasive as the presence of anyone else who resides in that home. Far too many children spend more time being influenced by television than they do being influenced by their parents. Keep that fact in mind as we continue through this stage of our journey, and you will better understand why you must exercise some control over television's ability to influence and educate your child.

I'm always surprised when people refer to educational television as being somehow separate from all other programming in its ability to educate. This is simply not true. All television is educational. Whether the education is harmful or beneficial is a question of its content.

When your children watch a program filled with graphic portrayals of violence they are learning from it just as surely as when they watch an alphabet lesson on *Sesame Street*. When profanity is peppered throughout an action-adventure movie, your grade schooler is learning new words just as surely as he learned the ABCs in that segment of *Sesame Street* I spoke of earlier.

There is much admirable content in programming that is presented on channels not given over solely to education. There is also some very questionable content presented in some so-called public television programming. That's precisely why you need to be more aware of exactly what your child is watching when that powerful teacher is in the room.

Sit with your children. Watch what they watch. Discuss it with them. Make the effort to influence their perception of what they are watching. "That attitude may be funny on TV, but it's certainly not the way we speak to each other in *this* household," is a perfectly valid comment to make to an impressionable 10-year-old who is watching a 10-year-old actor speaking disrespectfully to a parent. You worry about negative peer pressure from some of your son's schoolmates. Remember that his "peers" on television are also exerting pressure on him.

At this point, some parents stridently cry out for government censorship. They want experts to tell the industry what they should and should not do. They want stringent regulations on nudity, violence, language, and a host of other areas of content that they find to be, at the very least, offensive, and at the very worst, downright destructive to their children's minds. Once they acknowledge the power of this demon teacher to influence and educate, they want something to curb that power.

I'm heartily in favor of curbing its power. However, I'm in favor of balancing that power with reasonable limits, not by outright government censorship or any other form of heavy-handed interference. I want to keep my right to freely choose what I will and will not watch or listen to. Government censorship is not the answer, any more than burning books was the answer centuries ago.

In the first place, it's almost impossible to get consensus on what should and should not be banned. Ideally, reasonable limits should be followed by those who govern the industry, those who produce, design, direct, and market what is presented. To be most effective, limits must come from our own individual effort. Once again in this journey, we are made aware of the importance of effort.

When we cry out for government censorship, we are trying to avoid effort. We want it to be made easy for us. We don't want to have to think, to make decisions, to set an example. Until we accept the responsibility of being a parent, our children will be doomed to be "parented" by everything and everyone else willing to make the effort to influence them. We cannot afford to assign the role of a parent to an industry whose sole purpose is to attract audiences to buy products or ideas. Remember that it's an industry that is very good at tapping into our base instincts and urges in order to sell those products and ideas.

For example, it is an unfortunate part of the human condition to be drawn to scenes of violence or brutality. We are compelled to slow down and stare at the site of a terrible auto accident, even though we are being hurried on by police already on the scene. We are equally drawn to displays of appalling violence and brutality on television, even though we had no intention of watching those scenes when they first appeared on our screen. Even when we are sickened by what we see, we can't seem to turn it off or walk away.

This contradiction in the human condition is something psychologists have tried to explain in many different ways. But none of the reasons for this human tendency alter the fact that media marketing strategists know it exists, and they use that knowledge of our contradictory nature to catch and hold our interest. If excessive portrayals of violence or vulgarity draw audiences who may buy those products or ideas, then limits to that excessiveness will be conveniently set aside in favor of profits. Therefore, content will almost always be controlled by what people will watch and for how long. No one is going to pay great sums of money to put programs or commercials on the air that no one is watching.

Ultimately, the best way to control content is to watch only what you consider to be worthwhile. If you or your children are busy with productive lives and are watching television for a relatively limited amount of time, then you will be much more selective about what you watch.

Face the fact that the best way to control the content of television programming is to control not only what you and your children watch, but how much time you spend watching it. We have come full circle again to the question of time.

Like it or not, if you want to be sure your children are being taught how to be decent, productive human beings, then you better be the one who is doing most of the teaching. If the best-remembered lessons are learned by example, then who or what your children spend the most time with is who or what will be their teacher. Ask yourself, are your children spending their time in a healthy balance of work and play? Are you?

Take a sheet of paper, preferably with your children watching, and in large letters, write "24 hours" at the top of the page. Then dissect an ordinary day into segments of time. Follow me. The result will startle and sober you.

There are 24 hours in a day.

Some of those hours must be devoted to absolute necessities that keep us alive and healthy, mentally and physically:

Sleep: *7 hours average* (the accepted norm for most adults).

Meals: *3 hours average* (a conservative estimate if you also include preparation).

Personal Hygiene: *1 hour average.*

We have used 11 out of 24 hours of our day.

There are also other necessary elements for a *balanced* life. They are earning a living and physical exercise. Sometimes these two overlap. Earning a living is what provides us with shelter and food. Included in this category is the *training* for earning a living. This training includes such activities as school, lessons, practices, and so on. Let's list the typical time taken up with all that is involved in earning a living.

Earning a living: *7 hours average* (some will need an hour more, some an hour less).

We have used 18 out of 24 hours of our day.

Physical exercise is necessary to keep the mind and body in healthy condition. It can come in the form of sports contests, gym workouts, games, dancing, or the like. If the way you earn your living is very physically strenuous, you can deduct some of the time in this category, but not much. Your mind and body still need physical exercise that is *separate* from your job.

Physical exercise: 1 hour average.

We have used 19 out of 24 hours of our day.

All of us have certain basic chores that are necessary for everyday life. These include ordinary things such as laundry, grocery shopping, running errands, and so on.

Daily chores: *1 hour average.*

We have used 20 out of 24 hours of our day.

Every occupation (or training for an occupation) requires some work at home, whether it's school assignments, getting gear ready for the next day, cleaning the equipment you use on your job, practicing a musical instrument, and so on. We'll call it homework.

Homework: *1 hour average* (a very conservative estimate).

We have used 21 out of 24 hours of our day.

We have *three hours left* for these three things:
* Interaction with friends and family.
* Relaxation.
* Passive entertainment.

Please remember that interaction with friends and family means activities such as conversation, games, and travel. Watching a movie or television with someone is not truly interacting. That is essentially a passive activity that can be done just as well alone. You and the other persons in the room are merely spectators watching others doing things.

If you're still not convinced you or your children might be devoting too many hours to television, consider this: If you watch only *4* hours of television a day, that totals *28* hours each week. That, in turn, adds up to *112* hours each month. All of which comes to a staggering *1,344* hours each year. Divide that by the original 24 hours, and you will have lost *56 days* or *2 full months of every year* of your life to television!

Two months lost that could have been used to start a project! Pursue a dream! Change your life! If you're watching more than four hours of television a day, you might not want to discover the total number of months of your year that television is taking away from you and from your children.

How can you tame television's power?

Take an active role. Instead of allowing yourself to be depressed by the time you've traded to television, take the lead and show your children, by your example, how to reclaim at least part of those two or more months of every year of your life. Yes, we're back to your life again. That's where change has to begin, with you. If you're plopped onto the sofa, absorbed in some gossip show, and you shoo your child out to play because he needs the exercise, it's not going to be nearly as effective as if you turn off the twaddle, pick yourself up and say, "Let's walk down to the playground."

Does that require some discipline on your part? Yes. Does that require some effort? Yes. As a way for your child to wean himself or herself away from the need for constant entertainment, does it work? Yes! If the television set is turned off, and you and your children are doing something else, it's not taking your time or theirs.

Is it easy to do this? Not necessarily, especially if you are the one addicted to television even more so than your child. However, we are talking about your child's welfare. Take a closer look at some of the more unsavory travelers hiding in the shadows as you move through this location. Do you want them to continue to accompany your family on this journey?

If someone pulled into your driveway, and if one glance at them, or one snatch of their overheard conversation indicated danger for your child, what would you do? Open the door and invite them in? Of course not. Yet you do just that when you invite people of even more questionable character into your living room every time you turn on your television set, with no regard for who or what is on the screen. People you would drum out of your neighborhood before they even had a chance to knock on your door, you invite right into the very home you regard as a safe haven for your family.

Many of you are actively involved, and rightly so, in safeguarding your children from human predators by lobbying for laws, joining neighborhood watch groups, monitoring your children's playgrounds, and other very effective and admirable deterrent measures. Yet you do not hesitate to use the television set as a convenient, inexpensive babysitter, with little or no investigation of the programming you are subjecting your children to. While you are out safeguarding the streets, sometimes terrible influences are infiltrating your own home.

One parent I know vowed, "I'll control television's influence! I'll get rid of the TV set!"

"Why would you do that?" I asked him. "Why would you remove the excellent opportunity your child has to learn about how storms are born, or why volcanoes erupt, or see someone like Tara Lipinski skate her way to an Olympic medal?"

I do not advocate the overly simplistic approach of "throwing the baby out with the bath water." I urge parents to take the lead in a more positive, productive way.

For example, look in your television listings to actually see what programs are offered in any given time period, then make some intelligent choices. If you just start bouncing all through the channels to see what's on, you may find yourself drawn into watching something that is a waste of your time, and worse, a possible harmful influence for your child.

Use some of the time you squander in those two months a year of indiscriminate television watching and actually investigate the exciting, entertaining, and positive influences that can be brought into your child's life and yours by that electronic genie. Don't be afraid to let him out of his bottle. Just be aware that you must be his master, not the other way around. It's your home. It's your child. It's your choice. Choice is what it truly comes to. Choice always requires thought, and purpose, and both require effort.

We have returned again to what a parent's purpose is. Remember your pledge to raise your children to be decent, productive, self reliant individuals, able to love themselves and others, capable of pursuing their own happiness. It's a description of well-balanced individuals. If you want to achieve balance in anything, you must make wise choices. Without well-considered choices about what we put on the scales, one side or the other will tip precariously and the balance is lost.

When a tightrope walker crosses the chasm, he is not rigid, never moving to the right or the left. In fact, though he may appear to be relatively rigid, his entire body is always shifting slightly, bending this way or that, to maintain his balance. Yet his feet move only in one direction: forward, toward the goal his eyes are firmly fixed upon, the other side.

In raising your children, you need to remember the importance of your purpose. Keeping that goal, that purpose in mind will tell you when to lessen the power and pull of influences your children may not yet be ready to withstand. It will also tell you when they need to have that exposure to those influences, and for how short or long a time.

Children are not born knowing who or what is worthy of time and space in their lives. As a parent, it's your responsibility to know.

When they walk the high wire over the awesome uncertainties of adolescence, would you tell them to look down? Of course not. Because you know that looking down for too long will only pull them off their balance. Then don't let their eyes be drawn too long into what can be seen on the television screen, or they will lose sight of the other side and fall before they've learned to fly. Take the lead. You're the parent. Show them, by your example, how to balance safely as they walk the wire.

Stage 8

Find the Good

This stage of your journey is where you learn how to honor your child's struggle for self-esteem. For the first time, you begin to understand how self-discipline and self-esteem are closely linked. You learn why you must have expectations and how to encourage your children to have them. You will meet parents who are learning to believe in their own worth in order to help their children believe in theirs. In these locations, you will also meet many of my students, and you will learn with them how to focus on the good in each individual.

Why is struggle necessary for true self-esteem?

Self-esteem comes from confidence in one's own ability to struggle for and reach personal goals. I use the word *struggle* because I want parents to celebrate it, to allow their children to go through it and to encourage them as they do, because only from struggle comes true self-worth. It is the difficulty of the task that makes its accomplishment an achievement; without personal achievement, there is no real sense of personal worth.

Telling your children that they are capable, worthwhile individuals is a good thing to do, but it will not automatically give them self-esteem. A sense of personal worth must come from the individual's own effort. Self-esteem cannot be handed to a child, as one would hand a child a coat and say, "Put this on, and you'll be warm." Much as we would like to, we cannot create the inside core of confidence a child needs as easily as we can create comfort for their outside. We can and must honor their struggle.

For that reason, it always amazes me when I hear a parent belittle their own child's struggle. It makes me angry and sad at the same time. Angry because of the sheer stupidity of this approach to raising a child. Sad because of the severe damage done to a child's self-esteem.

What could be more defeating to a child's struggle toward self-confidence than to be belittled by one's own parent?

If we as parents laugh at that struggle, children will avoid it in order to avoid the pain of being ridiculed by those they most want to please in this world—their parents. Parents need to support that struggle, to honor it by recognizing that in any struggle toward a goal mistakes must be made, but marvelous things will also be done. As a parent, those marvelous things should be your focus.

Meet Sam's father, who's traveling with us in this part of our journey. Sam and his friend Mark were students of mine. Sam's father once said to me, "I feel so sorry for Mark's parents. They're barely making ends meet, and it must really bother them that they can't provide for Mark and their other kids the way we can for ours."

Then he added, "Yet, Mark seems to be pretty well adjusted." That clearly puzzled Sam's father, but it came as no surprise to me.

Mark's parents were very supportive of their children, worrying more about feeding them well than providing extra niceties far too costly for their modest income. They attended every school function and encouraged their children in their studies and sports participation. They had, I'm certain, explained the facts of their financial situation to their children, and they expected their children to understand.

They also expected their children to set goals and reach for them. The whole idea of struggle was not new to Mark's family, and the children saw by their parents' example how struggle was celebrated as a way to achieve success, however modest.

Sam's father, on the other hand, placed far more importance on the outside than the inside of his son's well-being. I noticed the expensive clothes Sam always wore. The very latest in teenage style was his normal attire. The boy also never lacked for things like state-of-the-art CD equipment and expensive sports gear, while many of the other children in his class were making do with more modest or second-hand things.

I also noticed that Sam's father rarely attended any school function. When he did, his attitude toward his child's struggle was very negative. One particular incident comes to mind. After leaving my classroom one afternoon, I had stopped to watch an inning or two of the baseball game before I headed home. Sam loved baseball, and after one whole season on the bench, he was finally part of the regular lineup.

At this one game Sam's father finally attended, he watched as his son struck out for the second time. Clearly embarrassed, he shouted to his son, "For God's sake, Sam, hit the damn ball! No wonder they put you at the bottom of the lineup!" I was standing on the sidelines, not far from Sam's father. I heard every word. So did Sam.

The only thing that kept me silent was that I knew a scene would not help Sam's struggle. His face was already burning with embarrassment as he pretended not to hear his father's bellow, and he disappeared into the dugout to avoid further pain. I knew, at that moment, the boy was probably making a decision to avoid future participation in baseball, too. When I was certain that Sam could not see or hear us, I walked up to his father and stood quietly beside him for a while. His frustration was so strong, I could feel it in the air.

After a few minutes, he noticed me and recognized that I was one of Sam's teachers. "Hello, Mrs. Turnbull," he mumbled. I wasn't sure if he was embarrassed by Sam's performance or by his own.

Never one to be anything less than direct, when a child's well being is at stake, I said, "It's a struggle for Sam, but at least he's willing to go through it. Don't deny him, in front of the world. You should be proud of his courage to try." I walked away, giving him no opportunity for an explanation. I wanted him to think about my comment, and I wanted to keep myself from saying anything else.

I am well aware of the fact that when people don't know what to do, they do what's been done to them. It's one of the reasons why child abuse is perpetuated from generation to generation. For all I knew, Sam's father may have been treated that way by his father, and he was simply doing what he had been taught to do by his own father's example. I hoped my comment would make him aware of the fact that there was no need for him to be ashamed of his son and thereby ashamed of himself. He was looking for something to give him pride in his son, but he was looking with eyes that couldn't see.

In later parent meetings, as Sam's grades and attitude began to slide, I urged his father to spend less money on the boy and spend more time with him. "If you don't make that change," I warned, " you'll be wishing you had some of that money back to pay for the counseling or the bail money your son will need, because he's retreating farther and farther away from anything that requires struggle."

I was honest with Sam's father at all times, and I think he appreciated that directness. He was at least willing to understand that maybe he needed to change something about himself in order to help his son. I respected his need to maintain a good opinion of himself while he was making that effort. I wanted to honor his struggle for his own self-esteem. I hoped that from my example he could learn how to honor his son's struggle. I was direct with Sam's father, but never disrespectful.

Nothing is accomplished by showing disrespect for any individual. I learned that a long time ago from a beloved colleague. Joanne Harvey was a teacher's aide for the Migrant Education program at our school. For years, I watched her work with children in the classroom and in one-on-one tutoring sessions after school.

She often had to consult with parents, and I noticed that she always focused on how the parent-child relationship could be improved from a particular point forward, rather than focus on assigning shame or blame for the past. Mrs. Harvey maintained that no effort will be made to improve if a parent feels there is no hope that he or she can be an effective parent.

I followed her example and learned that when parents are treated with the respect their difficult job deserves, most of them respond by sincerely trying to do what's best for their child, and positive results are much more likely to occur. As parents, we have all made mistakes and we would change some things if we could. It's part of our learning process. Wrong turns are made on every journey, but we can head ourselves in the right direction again if we believe we are capable of reaching the destination. When we believe we can be the parents we need to be, then we're willing to make the effort that journey will take.

Sam's father proved to be worth my faith. Slowly but steadily, he was finding his own courage to change his demeaning, confidence damaging way of dealing with his son. He took his cue from Mark's parents and began attending more games. Because he was paying closer attention to his son, he was better able to notice that progress was actually taking place, not only in Sam's game, but in Sam as well. The father's change in attitude made possible a significant change in his son's attitude. They both made an effort to discipline themselves.

Sam's father learned to contain his frustration with Sam's slow progress in some areas, and the boy's progress gained speed in direct proportion to the father's ability to refrain from negative comments. Learning from his father's example of putting in more time, Sam also began to discipline himself to put in the extra practice time needed to succeed in the sports he loved. He was also encouraged to see the connection between extra time at practice and extra time at his studies. The extra work made it possible for him to maintain the grades that allowed him to participate in those sports. From their increased self-discipline came increased self-esteem for both Sam and his father.

Let there be no doubt about this: True self esteem comes from achievement, and achievement cannot come without struggle and self-discipline. The first will not occur without the other two.

Let's linger at this next location and learn more about this idea of self-discipline, self-esteem's powerful partner.

What is the value of self-discipline?

The value of self-discipline is that it allows the individual to be his or her own master. Existence in this world is precarious at best, with so many variables beyond our understanding or control. When we can create a state of being that gives us greater control over our individual selves, we also gain greater control over the direction our lives take. We become more self-reliant. Remind yourself that your child's self-reliance is your goal; recognize that self-reliance is one of the rewards of self-discipline.

A look in the dictionary at some of the synonyms for the word *discipline* is very enlightening. It lists words such as *development, exercise, practice,* and *cultivation*. All of these words imply a certain orderliness that leads to personal growth.

To take an idea and *develop* it is to discipline one's thinking in order to achieve a goal. To *exercise*, mentally or physically, is to discipline one's mind or body in order to improve that mind or body. To *practice* is to discipline one's way of doing something so that performance is enhanced. Discipline of the self is *cultivation* of the self, in order to control the self for its own benefit.

When discipline is involved, the goal is always toward some kind of improvement. Self-discipline, then, is the ability to control and direct oneself toward personal achievement. Discipline and control of the self is the very best kind of control because it comes from within the person. Because it comes from within, it is stronger than any kind of outside control can ever be, and it is welcomed rather than resisted.

If control comes from outside the self, sooner or later there will be rebellion in one form or another. The rebellion shows itself in anger, withdrawal, depression, harmful addiction, moderate or even severe illness, and extremely antisocial behavior. Parents who make their child's life completely struggle-free are actually insidiously imposing even greater control on the child from the outside because they are taking away the child's opportunity to achieve anything for himself/herself, including self-control. They rob their child of the need to develop any personal discipline.

Nothing that child gains is ever really a result of his or her own effort, so he or she gains no self-respect either.

A child whose struggle toward self-discipline is not honored will avoid struggle of any kind and will turn toward the easy path. That child is the one who falls under the control of those who prey on people who have no self-discipline, no self-esteem, and no meaningful direction in their lives.

In a misguided attempt to find the self-worth they so desperately need, these children grab at anything that will make them feel good about themselves, even if they know the feeling will only be temporary. They steal things in an effort to get things they believe they can get no other way. They get pregnant so that they can have something to love that is worth more than they think they are. They take drugs or drink alcohol to make themselves forget how little value they have. They destroy things in an effort to make others feel as vulnerable and worthless as they do. They take lives because their lives are so bereft of value that they view the lives of others as being the same. They are without the healthy balance of struggle and achievement, and without balance, it's very easy to fall.

It would seem that the parent who openly belittles a child is the exact opposite of the parent who loudly praises the child. But both are extremes and equally damaging to the child's sense of balance. Where the one virtually tells the child that he is so worthless there is no point to the struggle, the other virtually tells the child that he is so perfect that there is no need for the struggle.

The end result is the same. These children will not make the effort to get what they need to be proud of themselves. They will not be bothered with the struggle. Sadly, they will never be truly satisfied with their lives, because their lives will lack the necessary balance of effort and reward that creates confidence and genuine moments of joy.

Think about the things you've done in your life that give you the most pride. Were any of them truly easy to do? Of course not. If they were, you would have long ago forgotten them. They have no value. You never hear anyone describe a personal victory or a major achievement by saying, "I realized that if I was going to make something of my life, I had to stop doing anything productive and start drinking and doing drugs and damn any sort of personal discipline!" Those choices never lead to achievement; to make them is to embark on a fool's journey.

When any sort of personal awakening, real rebirth, or any worthwhile prize is won, people who have achieved it always speak about the struggle it took to reach that awakening, to experience that rebirth, or to gain that prize.

The students in my art classes are good examples of pride in the struggle. When they complete their projects, they are taught how to mount and display their finished drawings. In two glass cases in the main hallway of our small school, I display their work, changing the drawings every few weeks as new ones are completed. My classes emphasize the discipline of the craft, and the learning of basic drawing skills. The displays are proof of effort made and progress in skills acquired, regardless of talent.

Even the most creative of talents needs good foundational skills as a base from which to soar. Talent is God given and even so will never reach its full potential without effort. By following this approach, all of my students are provided with equal opportunity for success.

In this way, even those who have little or no natural drawing ability can still learn useful skills and earn a decent grade. By the same standard, those with strong natural ability who make no real effort and show only small improvement can find themselves earning a low grade. This is an evenhanded, fair approach to something as difficult to evaluate as art. Because of this, even though my expectations and standards are high, for behavior as well as work produced, my classes are always full. Students have seen the results in those glass cases, month after month, project after project, of achievement gained through honest effort.

Many times I have passed by those glass cases unobserved and have overheard students commenting on the work inside. There is always a significant group of admirers checking out the new drawings. Invariably, at least one of the students whose work is currently in the cases will also be in the group. Sometimes shyly, sometimes proudly, they will point out their work to the others. Always, one or more of the onlookers will make a comment like "you're good, Jake" or "I didn't know you could draw."

The response to these comments from the student whose work is being admired is always something like, "I put a lot of work into that one" or "that really took me a long time" or "it was really hard to get those colors just right." Each of these comments cries out loudly, proclaiming the difficulty of the task, honoring the effort made and acknowledging the struggle.

That is how self-worth is built, one thin layer at a time, each securely attached to the layer beneath. With each new layer comes the confidence that, with effort and self-discipline, nothing is beyond their reach. The subjects that I teach may be called art, calligraphy, art history, or speech and visual communication, but those are only convenient labels. What I really teach is self-discipline and self-motivation.

The results are not only seen in those glass cases or heard during speech performances on stage. Nor are the results seen only in the high grades earned by students of greatly varied natural ability. The real results of which I am most proud are the hundreds of students who have gone from those classes into the world, secure in the knowledge that they are capable of sustained effort, confident that they can achieve a goal. If this can be done by a teacher who is with these children for far less time than their parents are, then surely you, as your child's most influential teacher, can work even greater miracles.

How do high expectations promote self-esteem?

Do your children the favor of expecting something of them. That's what I did for the children whose work appeared in those glass cases. Today's children are constantly being criticized for their short attention spans and their inability to set and reach goals. If this criticism is true, why are parents and educators surprised? Parents gratify their children's every wish for fear they won't be able to do it for themselves. Educators keep dishonoring those same children by demanding less of their time and expecting less of them during that time.

It's as though we're afraid to offer them a full course of quality for fear they won't like or understand it. So we serve them "fast food" educations without providing any real nutritional value; then we wonder why school bores them. Can these children ever learn to challenge themselves? Of course they can, if we are willing to make the effort to educate them to their own greater possibilities, to actually expect something of them, and to allow them the time to fulfill those expectations.

Expectations must always be reasonable, taking into consideration the child's age and physical capabilities. Those expectations can then be

178 / Be the Parent Your Child Deserves

increased as the child's capability and confidence grows. The following story shows what can be accomplished by increasing expectations. Its setting is in the educational field, but its lessons are every bit as appropriate for the home.

Two years ago, hoping to increase the quality of our students' scholastic performance, our high school converted to longer class times. It's called a block schedule. Instead of meeting every day for short sessions, classes would meet on alternate days for a longer block of time. What used to be class lengths of 48 minutes became class lengths of 98 minutes.

The reasons behind the change were sound. It would encourage students to stay on task for a long enough period of time to really absorb information. It would be closer to on-the-job experiences, where attention and effort must be sustained for longer than bursts of 45 minutes. It would also allow teachers enough time to assess whether or not the students were actually understanding the information that was presented.

However, there was very real concern among the faculty about the ability of the students to sustain their attention for that long without a break. Those concerns didn't surprise me. In the last decade, parents and teachers have both shown a dismaying lack of confidence in the capabilities of the children they teach.

How have they shown it? By constantly making things easier for those children instead of recognizing that it is challenge that will keep their attention and gain their respect for themselves and for those who teach them, whether those teachers are parents or professional educators.

Fortunately, the general consensus of our faculty was that we would believe in our students' ability to meet the challenge of longer classes. In an effort to minimize the possibility of wandering student attention, the faculty generally agreed to provide enough variety in their lesson plans throughout the 98-minute span to maintain student interest.

Surprisingly, there was general concern among the faculty about their own ability to maintain focus for that long. I realized that most of our faculty ranges in age from late twenties to late forties, a generation that has grown up with television. Their idea of a long span of time is a 60-minute program. Even in their college training, most classes did not exceed that limit, except for some lab classes; and in those, breaks of 15 minutes were provided halfway through the session. Concerns aside, the plan was put into effect.

This year is our third year with 98-minute class times. The plan proved to be very successful. Students did learn to increase their ability to focus for longer periods of time. In fact, not only did their overall scholastic performance increase in quality, but students generally seemed to be much calmer, demonstrating less disruptive behavior. It was as though they actually welcomed the opportunity to be able to stay in one place and focus on something for longer than a few minutes at a time.

Good teaching practices kept their attention stimulated but focused. They no longer had to physically move from class to class just as they were beginning to grasp a concept or understand a new principle. They knew when they arrived in the classroom that they would have time to settle in, begin their work, and become absorbed in it. They had time to accomplish something! Even kinesthetic learners who need to move about physically seemed more willing to stay in one place. Most teachers recognized the kinesthetic learners and allowed for them by providing legitimate reasons for interaction and movement as part of their overall lesson plan.

Even those teachers who had feared their own attention would lag found that they were just as happy with the longer stretches of time as the students were. They, too, were able to accomplish more, felt more satisfied with results, and were personally pleased with the increase in their own ability to maintain focus.

Parents who had worried that their children would not be up to the task of adjusting to longer classes began to see that perhaps their own expectations of their children had been too low.

Because the faculty was willing to accept the challenge of higher expectations of themselves and the students, self-esteem in general was enhanced. The effort that was made to adjust and improve was an important part of the general sense of accomplishment that permeated our school. Something difficult had been tried and achieved. The focus had been on believing in possibilities and increasing self-confidence; in doing both, students and teachers found the good.

Who am I?

We will be in this location for a while. There are some fine young people here, and you will watch them participate in a wonderful exercise designed to help them focus on the good. You will see their excitement as they begin to recognize how to discover their own worth. You will see their self reliance increase along with their personal pride. This will take a little time, but time is one of the most necessary elements in this journey.

One of the reasons Robert's mother and Elizabeth's parents were having trouble being effective parents is that all three of them had lost faith, for one reason or another, in themselves. They didn't believe in their hearts, where true transformation must always take place, that they could be capable parents. They were willing to take the journey, but they were confused about the stages. They didn't realize that each stage takes time.

Time. You have by now noticed that, in this journey, certain words reappear consistently: *honesty, effort, struggle, purpose, time, balance,* and *hope.* As we go through these stages, the persistent use of those words should help you focus on their importance in this whole parent process. Nothing can be improved and negative habits cannot be replaced by positive ones without understanding the value of those important words.

To find the good in anyone or anything takes time. Time to pay attention to the person long enough to discover his or her value. Children, especially those in their teens, tend to focus on what's wrong with them: why they don't fit in; why they don't look the way they would like to look; why they aren't taller or shorter, stronger or prettier, white or black. They and their parents are so busy finding fault that they lose sight of what is right about them. They lose sight not only of their own value, but of what constitutes value. If you want to help your children find self-esteem, then take the time to help them focus on what is truly worthwhile in them.

I discovered a wonderful way to get children started in that positive direction. As with all things you want your children to learn, this one is taught best by example. You have to show them by your example how to value who they are and how to find the good. In speech class one year, in an effort to diffuse some ugly racial and ethnic intolerances that were creeping onto our campus, I developed a simple, highly effective approach to finding the good. I called it "Who am I?" It can and should be done once a week by everyone in the family.

Begin with a sheet of paper for each participant, and allow only five minutes for each member of the family to think of one thing they have accomplished during that past week. At the end of five minutes, ask them to write it down. Parents or older siblings can write for the youngsters who have not yet learned to write. Yes, begin at even that early an age to help your children focus on the good. The rules for this exercise are simple and few:

1. You must be completely honest.
2. You may write down anything that *you* consider to be an accomplishment.
3. You must write the reason *why* you consider it to be an accomplishment.

Before you do this exercise, let me give you some background on the widely diverse racial, ethnic, and economic population served by our small high school. Its children come from an interesting collection of blue-collar workers, farm laborers, hospital personnel, owners of large and small rice and dairy farms, orchardists, college-educated professionals, livestock handlers, and ranchers whose holdings range from 20 to 2,000 acres. We are an unusual mix of Latino, white, black, and various combinations of all three. Politically, we run the gamut from liberal to libertarian, with many moderates and conservatives included in the mix.

On the particular day that I initiated "Who am I?" in my speech class, the particular mix seated before me covered the whole spectrum of our school population. It was a perfect opportunity to prove what I knew to be an important truth about self-worth: The bulk of our self-worth must come from what we do with our lives, not from the things beyond our control such as race, color, or cultural heritage.

Before I began the exercise, I wanted to set the stage for its success. I chose a dramatic way to get their attention, one that would reach all three learning styles. I pointed to one of our fine football athletes. "Now, there's Michael," I began, "sitting there thinking he's pretty terrific. He's black, in a time when black is finally recognized as beautiful, and Michael is good looking!"

Michael squirmed a little and laughed self-consciously, while the class wondered where I was going with this. The year was half over, so they knew me well enough to know that something important was coming and something exciting was going to be expected of them. I was deliberately using superficial, stereotypical ways of describing the students. I definitely had their attention.

While they were still wondering about the point of this exercise, I aimed my finger at another young man a few seats away from Michael. Looking directly at the very tall, blonde boy with a rugged Scandinavian look, I said "Here we have Luke, feeling pretty sure he's got the world by the tail. After all, he's tall, white, and male! And he has a great smile!"

Now it was Luke's turn to feel a little self-conscious. My students knew I would never humiliate or embarrass them in any way, so they sensed this was not an effort to ridicule but was aimed at a much larger lesson. Still, there was some natural uneasiness on the part of those singled out, one by one, as I went around the room, pointing to three others and making similar comments.

My last target was a beautiful dark-eyed Latina named Maria. "There sits our lovely Maria," I swept my arm dramatically in her direction. "She knows how powerful those thick, lush eye lashes are! She sees how they stir the breeze and stir a few hearts as they flutter up and down. Ah, Maria is very proud of herself and her deep dark eyes!"

By now, the room was full of excitement as they wondered who would be next. I turned and walked purposefully to the blackboard at the front of the room and wrote in big, bold letters, "Who am I?"

Then, I asked a question that took them all by surprise. Pointing to each of the previously singled out students as I spoke, I said, "Why are you so puffed up and proud of things over which you had no control? Your color, your height, your eyes? You had absolutely nothing to do with any of those things. Accept them as conditions of your being, but keep them in their true perspective."

I barreled on, moving around the room as I spoke. "You can't take credit, Michael, for being born black. Luke, your height was not something you had anything to do with. Maria, your beautiful eyes are not something you earned. These things I call attention to are simply a condition of your birth. They are certainly part of your identities, but they are accidental things over which none of you had control. Then why let them take such unreasonable importance in your life? They are such a tiny, insignificant part of you! Let's find out, beginning right now, who you *really* are!"

Students were smiling now, sitting up straight, not yet fully understanding where I was heading but knowing I would take them along with me and trusting they would somehow arrive at a place they all wanted to be.

Then I sat on the edge of my desk and spoke very quietly. "How can you all be so preoccupied with such superficial things in yourselves and in others? Your ancestry, your color, your physical size and stature are all beyond your control. They are not things to love yourself for, nor are they things to hate yourself for. They are merely *conditions* of your being that you accept. They are as uncontrollable as the climate or the geography of a place. They are things to recognize for their difficulty or their beauty, but they are too far beyond your control to take up any significant time. They are only one incredibly small part of who you really are, and more importantly, of who you really can be!"

With that, I stood up, and said, "Who are you? I'll tell you," and I pointed again to Michael.

"Stand up please, Michael," I commanded, and as he did I said, "That's Michael, who threw two touchdown passes in last week's game. A game he was sent into cold, not expecting to play that night. That's Michael, who's been working out early every morning to increase his strength and stamina." A puzzled look on his face, Michael stood up straighter, as though at attention.

He had no idea that I had known about his early morning sessions, but his coach confided it to me a few weeks back. I continued, "Michael, through his own effort and mental toughness, made himself ready for the game even with no guarantee he would play. And *that*, Michael, is what should fill you with pride."

My voice was soft now. "That," I went on, as Michael's eyes grew bright with what I knew was the salt of tears, "that is who you are." The class burst into spontaneous applause, then quickly silenced themselves as Michael sat down. They were with me now, following my eyes to Luke, understanding now where we were going. This was about discovery, and they felt the power of its purpose.

Luke rose, knowing I would ask him to, eager to find out who he really was. "That's Luke," I began. "You know him. He plays basketball. No surprise, though, with that tall reach!" Some laughter rippled through the class. Luke smiled, at ease now with his height, already accepting it as a simple fact of his life, nothing more, nothing less.

"That's Luke," I was still pointing toward the lanky blond boy. "He spent half the night last weekend cleaning up a neighbor's yard that he and some friends had toilet-papered earlier that night. His buddies didn't realize that the student they hoped to impress with their stunt had left for the weekend, and only an ailing older relative was in the house that night. Luke found out and knew that seeing toilet paper strewn all over the yard in the morning would have caused her great distress. He took it all down before morning. That," I said firmly, "is who Luke is." There was silence, then Luke sat down to even louder applause.

I proceeded to make known the same sort of discovery for each of the students I had previously singled out. By the time I returned to Maria, no one was in any doubt about my destination. But they were still not sure how to get there. I knew it was time to take them into the game. I gave them the three rules for "Who am I?" and added two conditions. I also insist upon these conditions for families who use this exercise in personal discovery and for my forum attendees who participate in the same exercise.

"After the five minutes are up," I told the class, "You will write your statement and keep it brief. Then you will read it aloud." There was some grumbled reluctance about sharing their personal "Who am I's" with the rest of the class.

I explained, "By reading them aloud, you will not only begin to learn who *you* really are, you will also begin to know who your classmates are. You will be better able to go beyond such unimportant things as skin color, gender, and looks. You'll begin to focus on the good in each individual.

"The second condition," I continued, "is that every week's comment must be saved. At the end of this year, you'll take all of your discoveries about yourself, and you'll write a short essay that summarizes what you have learned about you...who you really are. Its title? What should that final essay have for a title?" I waited for them to tell me.

"This is me," piped up Luke, soon joined by a chorus of other voices. "The real me," called out one extremely shy girl, surprising everyone. Another student volunteered, "The best of me," and suggestions kept coming, until lovely dark-eyed Maria announced her solution.

"We should call the last paper 'Who am I?' like Mrs. Turnbull wrote on the board," she said, "because it's a question we should always be asking ourselves, because we will keep changing and growing into better and better people."

Maria's reason for keeping my original suggestion so completely captured the whole purpose of the exercise, that it quickly won the other students' hearty approval. She had also proved the merits of the exercise. Her intelligent explanation of her choice for the essay title let the other students see a side of her that went beyond the stereotype of her good looks. Maria was already beginning to understand that who she really was had more to do with what she did than how she looked.

As each week came and went, those "Who am I?" sessions proved to be a catalyst for change. With each accomplishment recognized, the students were encouraged to set new and harder goals. Realizing they were really competing with their own personal selves, they began to accept challenge and enjoy it. Once a week, for the first third of our class time, personal discoveries were made. Slowly, attitudes broadened and energies focused on positives rather than self defeating negatives.

Students stopped blaming society and other individuals for their shortcomings. They began to recognize that there is much prejudice and false information that each of us must stumble over and then kick aside in an effort to improve our own situation. They also began to see that discarding the negative and going on with our lives and goals is the only real way to diffuse and defeat those attitudes.

The first time we conducted our "Who am I?" a full third of the class struggled to find something they considered to be an achievement. Sadly, they had been so programmed to disregard themselves as having any real value beyond things like their outward appearance or their parent's financial success or lack of same that they missed the point of what real personal achievement is.

When I saw that someone was unable to focus on any good, I began giving suggestions, such as "Sam, didn't I see you picking up trash in the parking lot when Megan accidentally backed her car into the big trash barrel?"

"Well, yeah," came Sam's answer, "but..."

I interrupted with, "Well, that's a responsible thing to do. It's always a worthwhile achievement to be responsible. Start with that one."

Soon, others were offering suggestions to classmates who seemed to be stalled in their personal assessment. "What about the math test yesterday?" one helpful senior offered to his buddy. "That B was the best grade you got in there so far this year!" His friend laughed and gratefully wrote it down.

"Why was that an accomplishment?" I asked. "What reason will you give?" I had to keep reminding them that it was extremely important to not only write down an accomplishment, but to write down why they considered it to be one. I wanted them to be able to see that the reason they valued something they did always came down to its difficulty. It was a valuable accomplishment because it was hard to do. It was valuable because it required determination, time, courage, kindness, or some similar worthwhile human attribute.

I wanted them to see that effort was something each of them was capable of, and the effort to improve, set goals, and change habits would take them away from external things beyond their control. It would help them focus on the things within themselves that they could control, change, and fix. I saw students who didn't like themselves very much when this project began gradually begin to stand up with increasing pride and confidence as their achievements slowly added up, week after week. These achievements, however small, began building, layer by layer, into a tough core strong enough to deal successfully with external things like skin color, ethnic stereotypes, and social position.

In the forum sessions that I present, I read aloud some of the actual "Who am I?" papers from that first group of students. I select at random six or seven different students. I begin by reading their first tentative declarations; then I read ones they wrote a little later in the progress of the project. I finish with their last summary paragraph. The parents in attendance at the session are as gratified as I am to see the growth in each student's confidence. Always, the parents become very aware of the fact that what the students find to value in themselves is always tied to effort.

Here's a sample, beginning with this student's first week's comment: "I babysat my little sister and stopped complaining about it to my mom, even though my sister is a brat! The reason I think this is an accomplishment is because mom has enough to do with working two jobs since Dad's gone. She doesn't need me to be griping all the time about my sister. It's hard for me to not gripe, but I'm doing it anyway."

When I read her comment written three weeks later, it was apparent to all of those listening that the student was making a real effort toward self-control, and it was allowing her to change her focus from negative to positive.

"I figured if I have to babysit my sister anyway, I might as well teach her some stuff. I'm getting her so she knows almost the whole alphabet. The reason it's an accomplishment is that it's hard to get her to pay attention, but I keep working on it and I come up with ideas to help her. She thinks I'm pretty smart!"

Effort. Purpose. Reward. I pointedly have neglected to mention this girl's color or race. It's not nearly as important to who she is as the positive steps she's taking, by herself, toward growing up, accepting responsibility, and actually enjoying it. If she keeps going in this direction, this child will be able to take control of her own life, to build purpose into it, to set goals, to struggle through problems, and to overcome setbacks.

Once children believe that they are capable because they have proved it to themselves, they will fear failure less. The more good they find in themselves, the more they will be willing to struggle toward even greater good. They will not need to look for the easy, empty answers. Even when those answers are offered, they will have the self-discipline, self-motivation, and self-esteem to stand up to those who offer them and they will be able to turn away from them. Armed with confidence, they will see the struggle as the prize, and they will celebrate the struggle for the value it gives to their lives.

Stage 9

Look in Your Mirror

In this stage, you are far enough along in your journey to reflect on what you have learned. You know the difference now between positive and negative behavior in yourself and your child. In these locations, you will learn how to reinforce the positives and reverse the negatives. There is some history here to help you. Robert and Elizabeth are still with us and their parents' progress will prove that it is possible to improve your relationship with your child by first improving yourself. Like them, you chose not to give up, and you're prepared to move forward.

Why must reward respect the individual?

If we truly want to encourage positive behavior, then we need to reward it when we see evidence of it in our children. Reward is a positive reinforcement of that behavior. We need to reinforce it in a way that also tells our children that their positive behavior is what we expect of them as individuals.

Before we can do that, we need to actually believe that when properly informed of their responsibilities, they will be responsible. Children sense it when we don't give them enough credit, in our minds, for being able to do the right thing at the right time; that is, to do what they know we have a right to expect. When children know they are expected to behave in a certain way and that their parents trust them to behave in that way, the chances that they will fulfill their parents' expectations are extremely good.

That doesn't mean that you take positive behavior for granted. Acknowledgment should always be given. We all appreciate being appreciated. We all want and need occasional recognition that our effort is noticed and although it is expected, it is not taken for granted.

Let me emphasize that even if giving positive acknowledgment is new to you, as a parent you must overcome your reluctance to show proper appreciation. Don't fall back on old habits of only noticing poor performance. If the only time you comment is to criticize, change that habit now. Be willing to praise. If you don't, the behavior you want to encourage will soon wither and die, as any growing thing will do for lack of tending. When your child does the right thing, acknowledge the action with a comment appropriate for that individual and particular situation. Don't go overboard with your praise. As your children might say, "Don't make a big deal out of it."

One evening, years ago, our family had just finished dinner when we heard a commotion outside. One of our cats, confronted by a strange dog that had wandered onto the property, had scaled a tree in record time. We all rushed outside, except for my daughter, who was then 13 years old. The rest of us tried to convince the cat that the intruder was gone, and it took a ladder and considerable coaxing before we were able to bring the cat safely to the ground. After the adventure was resolved, I headed for the kitchen. I expected to find everything just as I'd left it, with dinner dishes still on the table, the kitchen in disarray, and pots and pans from the meal's preparation still stacked in the sink. I certainly didn't expect my daughter to do them.

I had developed the harmful habit of doing most indoor chores myself, expecting very little in the way of help from my children. I gave myself all the classic excuses. They were too busy. It was too much of a hassle to get their cooperation. The truth is I found it easier and quicker to do things myself and then complain about it later, playing the martyr role. Consequently, knowing nothing was expected of them, my children were often somewhere else when I could have used their help.

But when I walked into the house that evening, my daughter was in the process of finishing up the last of the pots, and the kitchen was spotless. I was surprised and pleased. So pleased, in fact, that I launched into a stream of appreciative words. "What a great surprise!" I gushed, "The kitchen looks terrific! I was expecting a real mess when I came back in. Those pans crust over really fast when I make that casserole if I don't get to them right away."

I went on and on, but instead of being pleased with my effusive praise, she scowled. "Mom, don't make such a big deal out of it! It just makes everyone think that it's a miracle when I do the right thing."

Slowly, it dawned on me that cleaning up the kitchen was her way of redeeming herself for her lack of cooperation during the previous weeks. She knew she had been doing less than her share and getting away with it. She wanted her effort to be noticed but not fussed over. She had only done what I had a right to expect of a member of the family. When I made a big fuss, it told her that I didn't really expect her to do the right thing, and that hurt her.

I have had ample opportunity to redeem myself. As she grew into womanhood, it became very much in character for my daughter to do the right thing, often behind the scenes and without any reward or even any notice. Every time she does, and I discover it or observe it on my own, I remember my lesson from years past, and I keep my comment short. "That's what I would expect you to do," I say.

Also remembering that incident of years ago, her acknowledgment of my appreciation is equally brief: "Thanks, Mom."

That bit of history illustrates the importance of reinforcing positive behavior by verbal acknowledgment. However, when your child does the right thing and does it well, you occasionally want to reward that effort with more than a verbal comment. You don't want to rush out and buy something, as though you feel you have to pay or bribe your child to get the positive behavior to continue. Reward should come in a form considered valuable by the person making the effort. Honor your child's effort by taking some action that shows by its very nature that you respect his or her individuality.

Think of your child as a colleague, a co-worker, a partner in the family unit. You don't rush out and buy a trinket for a co-worker every time that individual does his or her job well. Nor do you "make a big deal" out of it with gushing praise, as though it surprises you that they are responsible. Let your acknowledgment of effort demonstrate some effort itself. How? Let your child's learning pattern lead you. Let your reinforcement of positive behavior come in a way that is compatible with your child's way of looking at the world.

For example: For three straight weeks, your son has kept his promise to mow the lawn in a timely manner, without complaint or procrastination. Don't say "You've mowed the lawn so well, without any nagging, I'll buy you ...(whatever affordable thing you think your child would like.)" If you do that, you undermine the whole idea of work as a worthwhile goal in and of itself. You demean your child by assuming that the chore is done only for obvious reward, not because it is the responsible thing to do. Instead, acknowledge his efforts in the same way you would acknowledge a colleague or co-worker. Show him that you respect his time, and respect him as a person.

Perhaps you've noticed there's a particularly difficult place to mow because of an irregular garden area that juts into the grass in a jagged pattern. The mower can't be easily maneuvered in and out of that area, and your son has to take quite a bit more time to do that one patch of lawn. Offer to simplify that edge of the flower garden with some redwood strips that will give the mower an easier, straighter line to follow. When you do, say something like, "I'm changing this awkward place so you can save some time when you mow."

By approaching it in this manner, you're reinforcing the fact that you consider your son's time to be valuable, and that his work and time are appreciated. The sense of self-esteem that he gains from this approach will last far longer than any trinket or gadget that you buy as a superficial reward.

The time-saving offer in this example would be greatly appreciated by your active, kinesthetic learner. On the other hand, your son may be the visual learner in the family. He may really enjoy and respond to the beauty of the flowers and doesn't really mind cutting in and out of that border. With this particular child, you might want to offer to enlarge the flower area, leaving less lawn to mow. You could even ask him to help you select the flowers with a direct statement like, "Before you mow the lawn next week, help me pick out some flowers to add to the garden. We'll make it bigger, and you'll have less lawn to bother with every week."

Once again, you're showing appreciation of effort and time, and doing so in a way particularly compatible with your child's way of looking at the world. You're expecting something of your child as an individual, and you're respecting that individuality.

Why is giving up not an option?

In my first meeting with them, when I told Robert's mother and Elizabeth's parents that giving up was not an option, I was letting them know that I expected them to continue to be parents. That was an important thing for them to know. By telling them that they couldn't quit, I was telling them what they already knew but hadn't yet admitted to themselves. They did not want to quit. They wanted to do the right thing. That's why they approached me in the first place.

By this ninth stage of our journey, they're ready to see that the right thing to do is to have positive expectations, not only of their children but of themselves. People don't quit when they believe they can change their situation. In this location, you will see how they began to believe in the possibility of positive change. Expectations of our children and ourselves are always the key to our relationships with them.

After the ninth forum session ended, Elizabeth's father came to me and said he was beginning to see some evidence of a turnaround in Elizabeth. "She's taking some after-school aerobics classes put on by the city recreation district," he said, "and she's helping the teacher, sort of like an assistant. She's pretty excited about it, and I told her she could keep doing it if she brings her grades up. It's mainly for kids her age, and she gets to wear some of those fancy outfits and she likes that." He was much happier about his daughter's direction than he was at our first meeting.

I asked him if Elizabeth's stepmother had helped the girl find out about the classes, because I remembered that she and I had discussed finding some way to channel Elizabeth's natural inclination toward gymnastics and aerobic activities. His wife was not feeling well that night, so she wasn't there. Before he answered my question, he hesitated, as though there was something I needed to know. Earlier, his wife had already confided to me that she was not Elizabeth's birth mother, but I had not been told when the child had acquired her new parent.

"Kay's not Elizabeth's mother," he said. "Elizabeth's mother and I divorced three years ago, but we were separated a while before that. She married right after the divorce and she lives in another state. I've been with Kay for two years, and we got married last year."

That would mean Elizabeth was about 9 years old when her world first changed dramatically, I calculated to myself. From what I could gather, it had not been a particularly amicable marriage. But a divorce is a final thing. It means the child can no longer pretend that everything will be all right between her parents. Now, Elizabeth was in the beginning of another significant change in her life, puberty. At the same time, she was adjusting to a new woman as part of the team who was responsible for raising her.

Elizabeth's father continued, "Kay worries about Elizabeth all the time and tries to help her. Elizabeth's coming around a little to treating her decent, but she still talks to Kay like she's trash."

I knew some of that must come from Kay's own habit of belittling herself. Elizabeth was picking up on that and taking advantage of her stepmother's low opinion of herself. If we don't respect ourselves, it's hard for someone else, especially a child, to respect us.

However, I had heard and seen how Elizabeth's father seemed to treat his wife as though she wasn't there. His tone of voice when he spoke to her was usually hard and abrupt, showing a certain impatience. Elizabeth was picking up on that, too. It was time to be certain that he understood what he was teaching Elizabeth about how to treat her stepmother.

I had to be direct again. "It's a habit with Elizabeth. Habits can be changed," I said. Then I said what had to be said. "She'll stop when you stop."

Elizabeth's father looked down. I continued, "It's Kay's fault as much as yours that you talk to her the way you do. She lets it go on. I'm sure you don't realize it, but I notice that you interrupt her and never treat her comments like they matter. It's just a habit with you, and one that I know you can change. It's easy when things are bad at work and you're being treated with disrespect to treat others the way you're being treated. Most of the time, we don't even realize we're doing it. People love us, so they put up with it. But Elizabeth needs to see you treating Kay with more respect before she'll change her attitude."

I held my breath, hoping I'd said what needed to be said in a way Elizabeth's father could understand and accept. I was being honest, not with the intent to hurt, but because honesty is the only way I know to begin to change a negative habit into a positive one. It is ultimately also the only truly respectful way to treat another human being. I knew he understood when he said sheepishly, "Oh yeah, that example thing." We both laughed, and I think his relief was as great as mine.

I sensed that he had realized this all along but found it hard to admit to himself. It took someone on the outside to help him face it, someone he trusted, who believed in his ability to improve and wanted him to become the parent his daughter needed. I knew he was ready to accept it when he confided, "Elizabeth told me that once, when I got after her for her tone of voice to Kay. 'You talk that way to her all the time, Dad!' I guess she was right." Elizabeth's father is moving forward.

Robert's mother is also beginning to glimpse some positives in her situation, and she is learning what she has to do to reinforce them. But first she had to recognize the negatives in her own behavior. By automatically assuming that her son was smoking pot at the party, it was clear that she expected her son to behave in that way. Because she had allowed him to close himself off from her, she really didn't know him. She had no idea of what to expect of her son, because she didn't know her son.

Had Robert known his mother expected him to smoke pot when he was around people who were doing it, he might have fulfilled her expectations. Fortunately for both of them, he had no idea that his mother's opinion of him was such that she saw him as a follower rather than a leader. She did not recognize his individuality, but instead she saw him as a "teenager," and in her fear-fueled mind, "Most teenagers smoke pot, or worse, when they get together."

In fact, Robert was using the party as an excuse to come out of his shell and make people laugh, something he had been unable to do ever since his father left. That he was able to be around others who were drinking and smoking pot and not do it himself told me that he had higher expectations of himself than his mother had of him. She nods her head when I point this out to her.

"Get to know your son better," I advise her, at the end of this session.

"I won't quit," she promises.

"Good," I answer. "Robert is worth knowing. He's a hero." Robert's mother is moving forward.

What is a hero, anyway?

A hero is someone who does the right thing, even when it's difficult to do. A hero is someone who doesn't give up, or give in, even when it would be easier to do both.

Sometimes, the actions of a hero are very obvious, such as saving the life of someone who is drowning or carrying a child from a burning building. Isn't that the behavior of someone who is simply doing the right thing even when it's difficult to do? The important thing to remember is that most people who do the right thing do it without fanfare or praise. It's usually done in a quiet, behind-the-scenes way. It's not done for attention or gain, but because the person doing it knows that it is expected of them, and the knowledge that they have behaved responsibly is their reward.

A few seasons ago, major league baseball honored long-time Baltimore Oriole Cal Ripken Jr. for playing in the most consecutive games of any ballplayer in its history. For years, game after game, regardless of his health or his personal life situation, he showed up and played to the best of his ability. He did both because that's what he believed he was expected to do. He had been raised to be responsible, even when it was inconvenient or downright uncomfortable to do so.

The fact that so much commotion was made over someone who was, in his words, "just doing his job," makes it clear to me that we all recognize what the right thing is, and we are willing to acknowledge it when we find it. Why do we only seem to recognize it in people who are sports figures or celebrities? Why aren't we willing to look around us and within ourselves to find it and acknowledge its presence? Perhaps we've lost sight of what heroism really is, and it takes someone like Cal Ripken Jr. to remind us.

A hero is also someone who is willing to change when change is needed. By that definition, we are all capable of being heroes because heroes believe in possibilities. Teach your children about possibilities and hope. Teach them by your example that change is always possible. Then, if they do start down a destructive path at any point in their life, they will be able to turn back because they will believe that it is possible to make that turn. Let them see by your example that you are willing to change direction when change is needed, no matter how difficult that change might be. Don't give up. Show them how to move forward by doing it yourself.

What is the last 20 percent?

We can't reinforce positives without also reversing negatives. If we don't reverse the negatives, we are losing the vital last 20 percent of our effort. It can be extremely difficult to reverse negatives unless you remind yourself of the lesson learned in the first session. Not only are you your child's first teacher, you are your child's most influential teacher, and your most successful teaching is done by example. Before you can reverse negative behavior in your child, you need to eliminate it from your own conduct. It is not necessarily easy, but it is this last 20 percent of your effort that will ensure a full 100 percent success.

Let me clarify exactly what I mean when I say effort. Perhaps I should qualify the word *effort* by saying *sustained effort*. Most solutions will be successful if we make the effort and sustain that effort long enough to make a real change in our behavior. It's the last 20 percent that makes the difference. When most of us begin new projects, or attempt to change behaviors, we begin with a certain amount of enthusiasm and purpose. That initial thrust of good intention carries us along for a while, especially if we see some small progress.

As we proceed, having invested about 80 percent of the total effort that is going to be required for complete success, we begin to bog down. Our freshness fades and our resolve weakens. This is unfortunate, because it's that last 20 percent, not the first 80, that often means the difference between successful completion and a well-intentioned but unsuccessful attempt.

Make your effort to change count. Give it the full 100 percent. See it as an opportunity to improve your own personal habits. Let the presence of the children in your life be the motivating factor for you to change and reverse the negatives in your own behavior.

How important is the last 20 percent? When my children were preschoolers and the youngest not yet 2 years old, I found the high frequency noise level of their voices increasingly irritating. It seemed they were always screaming at each other, causing me to shout or scream just to get their attention. Even their happy times were shrill and noisy. My husband was working two jobs then, and many days I was the sole parent from dawn to dusk. I was frankly frustrated with the general lack of calm in my house.

One of my neighbors had four children, three of them close in age to my own. Yet when I stepped into her house, it was not overly noisy and there was very little yelling and screaming of the sort that I was being subjected to in my own household. Outside, I noticed that her children were just as boisterous and rambunctious as mine, so I asked her how she was working this miracle.

She looked at me in surprise. "Well, I shoo them out into the yard as often as I can," she laughed, "maybe that's it!" We were living then in a part of Ohio where the winters were hard. "I find it's worth the time it takes to bundle them up," she went on, "to send them outside and burn up some of that energy." I had tried that and knew there was something else that I was missing.

As we talked, her 3-year-old burst into the house from outside, yelling loudly. Her two youngest children were twins, and they were pleasantly occupied in their playpen at that moment. She turned to her 3-year-old, and without raising her voice said, "Inside voice, please." He stopped yelling almost immediately, then repeated his request in a reasonably quiet voice. He wanted some cookies to take outside to his friends in the yard. As she handed him the cookies, I thought of the sound of my own voice of late and compared it to hers.

The solution was struggling to make itself known to me. But I was fighting it, not wanting to admit that it was my own negative behavior that my children were imitating. This was one that I couldn't blame on their father. They were often asleep when he was home, since he left early and arrived late five days out of seven.

If I was going to reverse this yelling habit in my children, I was first going to have to stop doing it myself. I found my voice rising in frustration each time I encountered resistance. This whole concept of inside and outside voices was new to them. But I kept reminding myself of my neighbor's words to her child. Inside voice, please. I said it to myself. Stop one behavior. Start another. It took effort, but it finally worked.

We need to first be certain that the change we're attempting to make is a good solution to the problem. For example: Inside voice. Why? What's the reason for this rule? A house or an apartment is a much smaller space than an outside area. Inside that contained space, sound reverberates, creating din and noise because of the close quarters. Outside, loud voices have a lot more room, more space to be absorbed by, and they are therefore much less disturbing to the ears and the mind. Sometimes, because of sheer distance outside, one has to shout, just to be heard.

These are good reasons for the rule. Any other reasons? Yes. Children must learn how to modify voice levels so that people will pay attention to them when they need to be heard. Inside, it's not necessary to shout to be heard unless everyone else is shouting or the television is too loud. There are other equally defendable reasons for this rule, but you get the idea.

What does this have to do with the concept of 20 percent? Everything. Once you begin to make a positive change and reverse a negative, you must allow enough time for the change to become a fixed form of behavior. My children had to hear my own voice taking on a quiet tone, and they had to hear it enough that it became a constant, before they could see it as a behavior to adopt themselves. I had to stay with the new approach long enough for them to see it as normal, not new, and subject to change.

Eighty percent wouldn't do it. Most change takes a full 100 percent effort to be effective. That last 20 percent may be the most difficult part, but why enter the race if you don't intend to keep a steady momentum until you cross that finish line? If you don't, then not only will that first 80 percent have been wasted effort, but you will still have the original problem.

Before we leave this location, remind yourself that when change is necessary, you must work through the temporary discomfort it takes to affect that change. To help you through that discomfort, keep in mind that your children are always observing and learning from your behavior, even when you're not aware that they are.

Sometimes, the hardest part of change is admitting to our children that there's something about us that needs to change. That's because we're afraid that they'll see us as not perfect. We're being foolish. They already see that. They've observed our flaws, and even when they're very small, our children make their observations known to us with comments like, "Don't holler, Daddy!" or "Mama, you're saying bad words!" They can see our imperfections and still love us. We are the ones who have a hard time believing it. When we deny the truth of what they see, we're only making ourselves more imperfect in their eyes. We're lying about ourselves to ourselves, and they also see that. It's time we take an honest look in our own mirror.

What do you see in your mirror?

Is what you see in your mirror what you want to see in your child? Try this experiment. Immerse an ordinary dry sponge in a glass bowl filled with clear water. Let the sponge stay in the bowl of water in plain view for an hour or so. Then lift the sponge from the bowl, and holding it above the water, begin to squeeze the sponge.

As the water falls back into the bowl, think of yourself as the water and your children as the sponge. The water has not consciously done anything to the sponge, yet the sponge is directly affected by it. Just by being in the water, the sponge has absorbed enough of it to be thoroughly wet. In that same way, a child absorbs a parent's attitudes and behaviors, merely by being in the presence of that parent.

Envision a high mountain lake with the sky reflecting in the lake's surface. However the sky appears, the lake will reflect that appearance. Whether the sky is crystal clear or dark and stormy, the lake will repeat that particular visual effect. If the sky is stormy, the reflection in the lake may be harder to see because the water's surface will be choppy from wind and the storm's disturbance, but the reflection will be there, nevertheless.

As parents, remember that you are the sky and your child is the reflecting pool. You are the water, and your child is the sponge. Be certain the sky is clear, and the water clean.

Is what you are what you want your child to absorb? If not, change. If we are to be good parents, we first have to parent ourselves. All of us come into the role of a parent as a beginner; it's difficult to know exactly how to do it. Children do not arrive in our lives with packaged instructions. Even if they did, each child is so different from one another that the instructions would be confusing at best. Again, when we don't know exactly what to do, we often do what's been done to us.

Without even realizing it, we often repeat both the negative and positive parenting we absorbed from our own parents. Often the behaviors of our parents that they were least aware of are the ones we soaked up most surely and swiftly.

Doing what's been done to us, however, is no excuse for perpetuating the negative aspects of our parents' behavior. Learn from their example. If you had poor parents, then reinvent yourself. Become the parent you wish your parents had been. If you were blessed with good parents, remember how they did it and do the same. Remember, most of us had parents who were neither always bad nor always good examples to follow.

Before the birth of his first child, my son and I sat outside one evening, talking about the joys and the responsibilities of being a parent. I was telling him about the things I was glad I had done and others I would change if I had the opportunity to raise him and his sister again. He was also recalling some of the things that he was determined not to repeat as a parent himself, as well as the positive things about his upbringing that he hoped to pass along to his own children.

As I acknowledged some of my mistakes, he watched me closely. My son is an honest and forthright individual. He usually thinks something through very carefully before he makes any prediction about future behavior, even if it's his own behavior. After a while, he said, "Mom, I won't make the same mistakes you and Dad made."

He paused and looked away before he continued. I knew that he was wrestling with the sobering realization that mistakes would most likely be made, no matter how hard he tried. But he, like most parents, was secretly hoping those mistakes would not be serious ones. As though I had been reading his mind, he continued, "But I know I'll make mistakes of my own."

That statement assured me that he would do just fine. His willingness to acknowledge that the job of being a parent is a difficult one told me he would take it seriously. Knowing that, I knew he would be capable of making thoughtful, deliberate decisions, and he would be willing to change things about himself that needed changing while keeping the good for his child to absorb.

His two sons are 5 years old and 2 years old. He and his wife are very conscious of the role their own example plays in their sons' eyes. As difficult as it sometimes is to make changes, they are both willing to take an honest look at their own habits. As a result, they are both being the effective parents I expected them to be. Most importantly, they both enjoy being parents, even with all its inherent frustrations. They regard parenthood as a joyful duty.

As a parent, it's important to remember that your parents probably struggled as you do to make the right decisions. Your parents also searched for the balance needed to raise children who will become productive, self-reliant, well-adjusted adults. Look in your mirror and keep changing until an honest, confident person returns your searching gaze. Let the person in your mirror become the person you want your child to see.

Stage 10

Be a Beginner

This is the tenth stage of your journey, but it is not your journey's end. You will see that it is, in fact, the place where you ready yourself to begin the next. This is where you step out on your own to put into practice all you have learned from our travels together. This is where you use what you now know, but you also continue to learn and improve. You keep changing what you still need to change in yourself while keeping your purpose steady and true, your values intact, and your goal clear. In these locations, you finally accept the challenge of becoming the teacher your child deserves, not with fear, but with confidence. The answers to the five guiding questions in this stage will take you to that acceptance.

What is lifelong learning?

The lifelong learner is the individual who is always willing to be a beginner. That individual is the one who continues to learn and improve. The surest way to affect positive change in yourself and your child is to let your child see your own willingness to change and begin anew.

The world is full of far too many experts and far too few beginners. Something in our ego makes it difficult to admit to being new at anything and to acknowledge that we still have more to learn. This is unfortunate. Learning is how we grow, how we keep balance in our lives. Learning is also how we keep ourselves vital in mind and body, as well as interesting to ourselves and to others.

I'm certain that a glimpse of my family history has a similar parallel somewhere in your family history. Remember when you were a child and your parents announced that it was time for another one of those obligatory visits to a particular old family friend or relative? I remember vividly. Whenever my parents suggested that it was time for a visit to one aunt in particular, I would moan dramatically, "Do we have to go?"

It was my father's relative, and I always suspected that he felt the same as I did about those visits. However, he would only look at me disapprovingly when I'd urge my parents to postpone the visit for awhile, ideally until I was fully grown and not obligated to go along any more. Why did I feel that way? It wasn't because she was old and I was young. I wasn't the only one in the family who shared that reluctance to spend any significant time with her. The mention of a visit to her house was never greeted with enthusiasm from any of us.

What made that aunt someone to avoid was not her age but her attitude. Her attitude contrasted sharply with a lady who lived in our neighborhood and was well into her seventies. I never really thought of her as old. I loved to sit on her back porch and listen to her stories, and tell her stories of my own. She was always so interesting to listen to because she was always experimenting with some new recipe, just finishing a new book, or learning a different way of doing something. She was badly crippled with arthritis, yet she had about her a vitality that made being with her an energizing experience.

Because of her willingness to grow and learn, this woman was also always interested in what others were doing and learning, and that was one of the things that made a visit to her house something I so thoroughly enjoyed. She seemed so vital and alive.

On the other hand, the aunt I tried to avoid was a lady not given to expanding her knowledge in any way. She was rigidly rooted to only one way of looking at life. She had no stories to tell of new challenges met or places seen. They need not have been worldly places or monumental challenges to have kindled my interest. They could simply have been small indications of a spirit that was willing to learn and look at each day as a beginning.

Had she just once been able to speak about something she was willing to try, like walking with me to the park, just to see if the old swing set was still there, I would have welcomed that as though it was a breath of fresh air in a closed-up room.

Her conversation was never about ideas or experiences. Instead, she gossiped, criticized, and generally concentrated on narrowing her horizons and in so doing, narrowing herself. In short, she shied away from beginning anything that might enlarge the restricted view she had of the world. Because of this, she made herself smaller and smaller, auguring in on the past not in a pleasantly nostalgic way, but with a limiting, stifling grip that kept her from enjoying anything or anyone.

Unless one is willing to run the risk of being a beginner, one runs the risk of being boring. Whenever I'm tempted to turn down an invitation to try a new restaurant or drive home a different way, I remember that aunt. Financially secure, she still struck me as being hopelessly poor. Impoverished by her own unwillingness to grow in any way, she was doomed to become the one in the family whose only visitors came because of obligation rather than interest.

As we become more accomplished and experienced, it's very easy to become rigid in our thinking and our way of doing things. We look at the world through an increasingly narrow window. We become weighted down with our knowledge, losing our sense of balance because there is no new, fresh information to keep us flexible. Our minds close instead of remaining open to absorb and learn from new experiences.

To learn new things does not mean we have to abandon old values or discard favored ways of doing things. Why would one tear out an old but still thriving and obviously well-tended, beautiful garden? It would be a foolish waste. Think how much more attractive that garden might be if a new variety of flowering plant was introduced into a drab northwest corner. We want to keep what is good about what we have learned, but knowledge should be something that has a life. Like anything that lives, we must continually freshen and invigorate it if we want to keep it healthy.

Knowing all this, why then do we sometimes shy away from being a beginner? We fear failure. We fear failure so much that we forgo the risk that goes with learning. What we forget is that wherever there is the risk of failure, there is also the opportunity for success.

Years ago, one of the adult courses I taught at California State University, Chico consisted of two classes: Beginning and Advanced Calligraphy. The course was also available for college credits as part of the graphic design major, so I was stringent in the requirements for completion of those credits. Because of my background as a professional designer and calligrapher, I preferred to have my particular beginning class be a prerequisite for my advanced class. That way, I could be certain that sufficient skills had been acquired before students attempted to do the advanced work. If students had not taken my beginning class, I had to see their portfolio of work so I could see for myself that they were capable of the advanced rigors.

One woman in her early forties wanted to sign up for the advanced class that coming spring. She had taken calligraphy classes elsewhere but had never taken my beginning class. I asked to see her portfolio, and she showed me her work with some hesitation. She had been walking around the room and observing some of the work going on, and she could see the high level of skills the students already had.

When I looked at her samples, I informed her that, while her work showed good promise, it was not yet at the level which would allow her to succeed in my advanced class. I strongly believe in setting my students up for success.

"Sign up for the beginning class," I told her, "and your progress will be good because you've already had some training."

She replied quickly, "Oh no, I can't do that." Something in the sad way she spoke told me that she was someone who did not like to be a beginner.

"Why do you say that?" I was persistent, sensing that she wanted to be a better calligrapher than she was, but her fear was holding her hostage. My mind raced to find the real reason for her resistance, and I suddenly saw that it had to be the name of the class.

"Is it that you don't like the word *beginning*?" I asked. I had hit my mark. She looked at me as though I had opened her soul, letting her suddenly see herself for the first time.

"Why, yes," she was clearly surprised at her own admission. "It's just that my friends think I'm pretty good and I hate to have to go back and tell them that I'm taking a beginning class."

Her relief at her own honesty was encouraging. I reminded her that beginning is never going back. It is always a forward step. "Your friends are right," I quickly assured her. "You are pretty good, but wouldn't you like to be even better?" As she nodded her head, I realized that there must be many others for whom the word *beginning* was a stumbling block, one they did not yet have the courage to overcome.

I believe that there are many people who would like to be beginners, but in this world where only so-called experts seem to have value, they are afraid of being thought of as beginners. I made a very quick, newly informed decision.

"It happens," I told her truthfully, " that I have the option of changing the name of my classes whenever I choose. In this coming semester's course description, my classes will be called Calligraphy I and Calligraphy II." Her face brightened and she did sign up for Calligraphy I that coming spring. She proved to be a worthy student. Her calligraphy improved considerably with her effort, and best of all, she was eager now to be a beginner.

During the course of that semester, we talked about that first encounter. She appreciated the fact that I had changed the name of the class, but she assured me that the whole incident had caused her to realize that it wasn't important if others saw her as a beginner. What was important was her willingness to continue her improvement of her craft, and, in the process, her improvement of herself.

What she didn't realize was that I had also grown by our encounter. Refusing to be held to some rigid notion that a beginning class had to have that word in its title, I was able to expand the numbers of those who were willing to take the class. I had opened my mind and remembered what my purpose was when I began to teach calligraphy. It was to educate more people to the beautiful craft of calligraphy, to introduce its wonderful potential for disciplined skill and artistic beauty into more lives. If changing the name of the class allowed students to focus on their effort and progress rather than be bound by the limitations of their current knowledge, then I would happily change the name of the class.

How can you overcome the fear of failure?

Let me again remind you that the risk of failure is always present whenever we try anything new, but so is the opportunity for success. Overcoming the first leads to the second. Small children are just as fearful of failure as we are, but we do everything in our power to minimize that risk for them. We want them to build faith in their ability to learn new things so we focus less on the act itself and more on the effort.

Walking and talking are very difficult skills that a child must learn at a very early age. As parents, we applaud these early efforts and offer encouragement, even when a child stumbles and falls or pronounces words incorrectly. Rightly, we don't focus on the mistakes, we focus on the effort, the progress toward the larger goal. Yet we seem to forget this truth as the child grows older.

Remember how Sam's father reacted when Sam struck out at the game? He ignored the fact that after a full season of patient effort, Sam finally made the regular lineup. He was making progress in his struggle, but his father focused on the stumble.

The process of becoming a responsible adult requires continual adjustment to new challenges. Older children, particularly those in the extremely self-conscious teenage years, need that encouragement even more. Yet as your children grow, do you notice that you tend to focus exclusively on the result alone, rather than the effort they are making to meet the challenge? You see a stumble as a failure rather than a step toward a greater goal. Then you wonder why your children are afraid to learn new skills.

You are distressed when they don't want to invest the time it takes to get from those faltering first steps to the mastery of a skill. You don't understand it when they begin to look for easy tasks. You deplore the fact that your children are becoming fearful of anything that appears to be hard to do. You see this avoidance expand to include things like self-discipline, a respect for the law, and personal integrity.

Somewhere in the following example, do you see yourself? Are you the parent? Or were you the child? A 13-year-old wants to learn to play the guitar. The parent invests in lessons and sees that the child gets to the music teacher's home. The child, however, is not a naturally gifted musician and the progress is slow.

Nevertheless, the teenager is staying with the lessons and seems to be enjoying the process of learning to play the instrument. One evening, during one of many practice sessions, the parent hears the same struggling version repeatedly of a very simple tune. "That last section doesn't sound right," says the parent. "That's the tenth time you've played that thing, and you still stumble over the last part."

No comment is made on the noticeable improvement in the first section of the song. The parent has focused on the small part of the picture without seeing the importance of the whole view. The child is intelligent enough to realize that more work is needed, but doubt is entering this 13-year-old's mind. The child begins to believe that this is too hard and that even with effort and time, there is no chance for success.

There's no need to resort to insincere praise. A truthful comment like, "That's a nice song. What's the name of it?" would have gone a long way

212 / Be the Parent Your Child Deserves

toward making the child feel confident that it was only a matter of time and practice before the tune would be learned. When parents focus on the mistake instead of encouraging the effort, children gradually learn to do the same thing. They lose sight of how much progress is being made and become increasingly frustrated with the mistakes. They stop believing in their own possibilities.

It wasn't long before the child abandoned the whole idea of learning to play the guitar. "Whose stupid idea was this, anyway?" the child said, pretending that it didn't really matter. The parent who told me this story wasn't talking about his child. He was remembering his own childhood. He remembered that, frustrated because he wasn't learning as fast as his mother thought he should, he stopped trying and quit the lessons. If he had decided to abandon the music lessons because of another interest, that would have been quite a different thing. But when he quit because he felt he wasn't capable of learning something new and difficult, he set a poor precedent for himself. His fear of failure grew, and he still battles it today.

"My folks weren't upset when I quit," he said. "They said they didn't think I could make a career out of it anyway." His parents had missed the point entirely. This wasn't about learning to play the guitar. This was about helping a child learn to believe in himself.

Without faith in our ability to solve problems, we avoid them. When we avoid problems, they only multiply.

When our focus is in the wrong place, it weakens our resolve and doubt begins to gnaw at us. Learning of any kind is essentially a problem-solving experience. Doubt in our ability to solve problems leads to doubt in our ability to do anything that requires effort.

This is especially true when a child is attempting to learn something new, even when it's something the child really wants to learn. When this doubt happens with any kind of frequency, children lose faith in their ability to solve problems. It's such a painful loss that it stifles their desire to acquire new skills and take on new challenges. They narrow their learning experiences to only those they are certain will be easy, with no risk of failure. Unfortunately, avoiding that risk will only lead children to the greater risk of an aimless existence that leads the young to be defeated before they even begin.

In fact, it is not that they will not finish anything that is so disturbing about so many of our frightened young people. The greater tragedy is that they do not have the courage to begin anything. Their inability to be beginners leads them on a search for easy distractions to avoid the pain of their disappointment in themselves. The destination those easy distractions take them to is filled with much more destructive risk than any of the beginnings they abandoned along the way.

At this point in this location, there is a side trip that you must take. It leads to a dangerous neighborhood, but it's one you must visit if you wish to keep your own children from being permanent residents there. Please understand that this neighborhood is not limited to ethnic stereotypes. This is a neighborhood any child can wander into once the child has learned to put limits on his or her learning.

Any child who is afraid of being a beginner, who has no faith in his or her own problem-solving ability will find this place a magnet.

This is where gangs, cults, and cliques, with their unhealthy emphasis on elite estrangement from society, originate and flourish. They come in all colors, sizes, and degrees of affluence. Why is their call so alluring? That's something you need to understand if you want to have any hope of curbing their power. Let's understand it by examining the gang, the more notorious of these groups that pull children into such ultimately destructive lifestyles. As you read, be aware that in most cases you could easily substitute the word *gang* with *cult* or *clique* and the information would still apply.

The typical gang member wants to create the impression that he or she is someone who knows everything. They call themselves "street smart" as though that rudimentary knowledge is all the knowledge they will need. Their aggressive, antisocial behavior is actually full of fear, the fear of their own individual failure. Gang members want the world to believe that they can get what they want and need without going beyond their present knowledge. In truth, they are full of the fear of learning anything new.

The fact that they so jealously guard their turf, a relatively small area that they have restricted themselves to, shows again their fear of anything outside their narrow, limited vision of themselves. Their fear of failure results in skills that are severely limited. It does not require great skill to learn to pull a trigger, nor does it require any sort of complex thought process to hurt or steal from those who are unable to defend themselves.

These are the sort of activities pursued by those who have no confidence in their ability to be anything more than what they are at this particular point in their lives. The gang tattoo is a very strong visual statement attesting to that lack of confidence.

I believe that it is highly symbolic, in a way gang members would not wish it to be, that they use tattoos to signify their gang membership. To me, the tattoo is a tangible symbol of their unwillingness to change. It is a stamp that symbolizes a stop in their growth as individuals, an indelible mark that announces to all who see it that they have effectively sealed off their potential as productive human beings. Why else would they brand themselves like cattle? Their particular tattoos are not an individual expression of their uniqueness, as some tattoos are. A gang tattoo is a sign to the world that its wearer has lost his or her individuality, traded it away for membership in a herd. A mindless herd that can be easily stampeded into violently destructive behavior, often to itself, as well as those who are caught in its path.

This willingness to stay where they are in terms of personal growth is especially sad to observe in children. Sadder still is that often it is an attitude they have learned from observing their parents. Parents who are unwilling to take on new challenges are seen by their children as leading an uneventful, boring existence. For the young who crave excitement, this makes adulthood seem like a stage of life they want to avoid. So they take drastic measures to keep themselves from entering it, and they join the gang or the clique instead. It offers them an opportunity to stay safe from effort, in the limited, but familiar role they know, the role of the defiant teenager.

They have no fear of failure there, because they already know that being defiant and destructive is something they can do well. One of the strongest deterrents for keeping children away from these destructive groups is for them to see their parents and other role models in their community as individuals who are continually willing to learn, change, and improve.

Perhaps the truly criminal part of losing a child to gang membership is the loss to the world of the incredible contribution that might have been made by that individual. At this young age, many who seem to have nothing to offer to society could become, with proper direction, worthwhile human beings, responsible parents, contributors to the best of the human spirit.

Children who join gangs are giving up. They are leaving a society that does not seem to want them. We need to make them see their choice to leave as the negative behavior that it is. We need to let them know they have a positive place in the larger society of humanity.

We do need them. Somewhere within their ranks, there may be another Albert Einstein, who was told as a child that he would never make it in math. Somewhere within their ranks, there may be another Michelangelo, creator of the Sistine Chapel masterpieces, whose passionate, rebellious nature could easily have led him to a destructive life. Some where within their ranks are responsible fathers, nurturing mothers, capable teachers, skilled farmhands, lawyers, carpenters, doctors, plumbers, accountants, mechanics, and any number of equally useful, self-reliant individuals so desperately needed in our society.

We have no way of knowing what positive contributions these young people could make as individuals if only they believed in their own unique potential. If your child has followed the dark lure of the gang or is caught in the insidious clutches of a campus cult or clique, don't give up. Call that child back before his individuality is completely obliterated by his need to belong. Give him a reason to believe in himself. Give him a family worthy of belonging to. Convince him that he can begin again. Show him, by your own willingness to begin again to be the parent he needs, that it is not too late. Show him by your own courage what true courage really is. Let your visit to this neighborhood give you that courage.

What is the common ground in all learning?

In order for learning to take place, one must make an effort to learn because there will be no progress without effort. Effort is the common ground, the foundation for all learning. Whether our teaching is done in the role of a parent, classroom teacher, athletics coach, minister, scout leader, or any other role that offers us the opportunity to teach, we are most effective when we focus on the student's progress.

Successful teachers quickly realize that recognizing effort produces more and greater effort on the part of the student, which results in the student ultimately reaching the goal to which they are directing that effort. Without exception, effective teachers are always the ones who motivate their students toward effort. Without exception, that effort will always result in improvement, which results ultimately in achievement. Achievement that boosts self-confidence and helps the child take on new challenges because of that confidence.

Take a quick look inside my freehand drawing class for an excellent example of this truth. At the beginning of each semester, I ask every student to select an object in the classroom and draw it. The object they select is entirely their choice. Beginning and advanced students alike are asked to do this. I tell them I want honest effort to do the very best they can. When their drawings are completed, I collect them and put each one in a file that will belong to that student for the rest of that semester.

I explain to them that this first drawing of the session tells me exactly where they are now in terms of their skill. It is neither good nor bad; it is simply where they are now. We always want to go forward from where we are if we intend to add to our skills. Their grade will be determined by how much progress they make beyond their present skill level.

"You are competing with yourself," I advise them. As the semester progresses, their first drawing will be compared to the next, and that one, in turn, to the one following it. "You are in complete control of your own progress." I make this point very clear. Excuses for lack of effort are not accepted. They know this and it discourages them from counting on anyone but themselves. It's a wonderful way to level the playing field, because students who believe they have a chance to be successful usually are.

It's my personal crusade to expose as many students as possible not only to the beauty of art but to its discipline as well. I want them to appreciate the thought and craft that make art such a necessary part of our existence. I want them to understand that there is art in all things that are done well. Everything, from a perfectly executed double play in baseball to an exquisitely timed dance sequence in a musical, to the masterful marble forms of a Renaissance sculpture, is the result of skill that is the result of effort.

Much is made in our society of talent, yet talent is nothing without what I call the three P's. They are practice, patience, and perseverance. Practice is nothing more than effort directed toward a certain goal. Patience is what the beginner must have with himself, giving himself enough time to learn. Perseverance simply means not quitting just because something is difficult.

Those three things are necessary in all endeavors, but in art, they also produce tangible, beautiful results that a child can see and keep, and use as constant reminders of what he or she has personally accomplished. Those results show effort and help others learn to trust effort as a way to achieve goals.

These are visual results that can translate into all other areas of their lives. A basketball coach hopes his team's endless practice sessions will help his players learn that those sessions can translate into achievement. If the coach's practice sessions with his team help to produce an NBA player in the process, that's fine. If my practice sessions in the classroom help to produce a great designer in the process, that's also fine. However, our main purpose, and the one that drives us most passionately, is to train children to take the risk and be beginners!

The parent, the sports coach, the classroom teacher, and the dance instructor are all teaching life lessons. In effect, we should all be saying, "I don't care how much or how little talent you have. Come to every practice. Be mentally and physically ready to play at every game. Attend every lesson and perform at every concert. Learn every step and dance at every dance. I want you to do your best with what you have. If you do these things and follow my instructions, you will improve. You will realize your dreams, step by step, goal by goal!"

All of the arts have the same potential as sports to serve as excellent, highly visual or dramatic ways to teach children to be beginners. They can see the actual result of their efforts, in plain view, and better understand the principle of applied effort. It's not uncommon for me to say to a student who is failing math, for example, "Do you realize how much better you will do in math class if you take the same amount of time with your math homework as you have taken with this drawing?"

The student can see, right before his eyes, what happens when time is spent productively. Things get done. It's not a hard thing for them to see that they could probably learn a science theory or a math rule in much the same way. Very often, success in my class translates into increased effort in some of their other classes, because they have seen the proof of their ability to improve if they put in the necessary time.

Time and again, I've seen this same transfer of effort occur because of a child's success with music. One student was encouraged by her music teacher to develop an idea she had for a tune. Working with her instructor after school, she honed the melody into a lovely, haunting theme, and added a beat that made it particularly appealing to her peers. The music teacher frequently pointed out to her the connection between the time she was putting into this song and the time she needed to put into some of her other subjects in order to be able to graduate with her class.

Her success with what she was willing to invest her time in made it very clear to her that time and effort could also be the difference between passing and failing in her problem classes. It was a logical conclusion drawn from tangible proof. She had done the work. She could hear her song. She could transfer its lesson. She was able to graduate with her class.

Sports programs also offer this same opportunity for tangible proof of the connection between practice and positive results. Using a child's favorite sport as a place to begin, you can bring this same point home to your children in a similar way.

Meet Brad, who loves to play basketball but needed improvement on his set shots. He tended to tighten up when his toes were touching that line and all eyes were focused on him. His father advised his son to take one hour every day and practice nothing but making shots from that line.

He gave Brad two weeks to stick to that time frame. He asked his son to write down his starting and ending times for each practice session. At the end of the two weeks, both father and son were delighted with the improvement.

Interestingly, when the father checked the son's time sheets, he found the hour sessions were often stretching into 80 or 90 minutes as the end of the two weeks approached. His father was absolutely right with the following interpretation of his son's willingness to increase the practice times. "Brad was seeing that the practice was making a difference, and it made him want to do more of it."

Then the father said to his son, "If your English grade doesn't come up by the end of this quarter, you know you'll be off the team."

"But, Dad," Brad argued, "we're writing essays right now, and I hate writing essays!"

The father stood his ground. "You used to hate set shots, too. For the next two weeks, whether you have homework or not in English, I want you to give one hour to writing essays every day."

The son moaned, "Ah, Dad! What a drag!"

The father said simply, "Write about what you know and love, basketball. Follow the format your teacher gave you, but write about basketball." His father was asking Brad to take something he knew a lot about—basketball—and use it to help him learn how to do something he knew little about—writing essays. This is a process we'll discuss just a little farther along in this stage of our journey.

The point is that once Brad felt more comfortable with the essay-writing process, he gained confidence in his ability to do it, no matter what subject matter he was given to discuss. It wouldn't have happened without the extra time and effort. The father was using basketball to teach his son that time and effort is an important part of the common ground in all learning. Brad saw that learning anything new is simply a matter of accepting a challenge, whether it's set shots or essays. Once he accepted that fact he lost much of his fear.

As adults, we are often as fearful of new challenges as any teenager, sometimes for different reasons. Before we move to the next location, let's examine some of those reasons, because your children need to see that you are willing to take on new challenges if you are going to teach them effectively by your example.

One reason we avoid new challenges is we're afraid that if our children see us struggling with something new, they will no longer think of us as more knowledgeable than they are. They will lose respect for us. Nothing can be more false. The truth is that seeing your willingness to be a beginner will only increase your child's good opinion of you.

More importantly, the child will see that taking one difficult step at a time and straightening back up after every stumble is the only way to get from one place to the other. A person, adult or child, who is busy learning new things, accepting new challenges, and learning to find a balance is a person who has no time to be tempted by the easy path of instant gratification. As a parent, if you continually strive to improve yourself by learning new skills, you accomplish two things with one effort. You grow as an individual and your example encourages your child to do the same.

Another reason we sidestep new challenges is that we become complacent. After all, we've been alive quite a while and we have learned quite a bit. We're comfortable with what we know. We seem to be functioning fairly well, so why do we need to add to our information? We don't particularly want to find out that maybe we need to change some things about how we conduct our lives. That would mean that we have to admit that we were wrong, or at least misguided, about some of the decisions we made.

We need to chalk those decisions up to being human, and not let them cripple our efforts to grow in whatever way we need to grow. Mentally, physically, and emotionally, we need to keep pushing our limits and developing our potential to keep our health in all three areas.

If, as adults, we're afraid of failure when we take on a new challenge, it's because we forget that we already have formed some learning pattern that we can tap into and use. The very fact that we are older and have developed some significant skills can be used to our advantage. As adults, we have had to learn many new things just to have arrived at where we are now. We can use that past experience to move us forward, instead of restricting ourselves by our own complacency. We can let it help us discover how we learned what we already know.

Remember, there are many different ways you can be a beginner besides the traditional route of taking a class or joining a club. Ask yourself, what new and difficult challenges have you accepted in the last six months? In the last year? In the last two years? How far back did you have to go to find one? If you had to go back further than a year, what kind of example are you setting for your child?

Is this a familiar scenario? Your 14-year-old is refusing to do his math because he is convinced he will fail. Why is he so convinced? Because he's never been " any good at math," he says, so why bother. He has asked you to join him in his computer games, but you refuse, telling him you aren't "any good at computers."

Your complacency is setting a poor example. You're missing a golden opportunity to teach him something about possibilities. Turn off the TV set and ask him to show you how to play the game. Children of all ages love to be the ones to teach their parents some new skill. Show him you are willing to go into new uncharted territory. Who knows, in the process you may find some intriguing way of using computer games to help with math learning skills. Let your child be the teacher, the expert, while you show him, by your example, how to be the beginner. Both of you will get past the crippling inertia that forces us to be content with self-imposed limitations.

I developed a simple series of questions that can help you move forward toward some unrealized dreams of your own. They need not be grand dreams of fame or fortune; they can be small goals you dream of realizing, brief adventures you always wanted to have. Keep this in your mind as you answer these questions. Be completely honest.

1. What new skill would you like to learn?
2. Why do you want to learn it?
3. Why haven't you done it yet? (Identifying your fears can help them disappear.)
4. What can you use from your own past experience to help you learn this skill? (The answer to this question is in the next location.)

How can your past experience lead you forward?

Understanding how we have learned things in the past can help us be less fearful of future learning. In other words, remind yourself that you have already been successful. How did you learn the skills you already know? By observation? By practice? By reading instructions? By apprenticeship? By repetition? By some method not yet mentioned? By a combination of methods? You know you can learn, but by answering these questions and others like them, you can figure out exactly how, as an individual, you learn best. This exercise will strengthen your confidence as we look at your past success, step by step.

First, select three skills that you feel you know how to do fairly well. Remember, these should be skills that are of particular value to *you,* not necessarily to others. They should be skills that give you cause for pride.

Are you drawing a blank when you try to list three valuable skills that you have mastered? Then, start off by naming some things that you probably take for granted. Like most of us, you probably tend to regard what you already know how to do as having less value, so I'm certain there are many things you may have mastered yet fail to acknowledge as important skills. It's important to acknowledge them before you can learn from them.

Are you the one in the family who balances the checkbook? Are you the one who organizes all the family get-togethers? When there's a birthday, are you the one who bakes the cake from scratch? These are useful skills. Don't take them for granted. Ask yourself how you learned to do these things.

Let's pretend two different people, Louise and Steven, have listed the same three skills:

1. Balance the family checkbook.
2. Refinish furniture.
3. Bake cakes from scratch.

The skills are the same, but each one learned to do them by following a slightly different learning pattern.

Louise's learning pattern

Louise balances the family checkbook every month, and she learned how by reading the instructions on the back of the bank statement and then following them, step by step. She also recently refinished two bureau dressers for her guest bedroom. To learn how, she bought a how-to book on furniture restoring and faithfully followed it as her guide.

Those birthday cakes she baked last year for three different parties? She relied on her trusty *Good Housekeeping* cookbook and followed the steps for three different cakes she always wanted to try. At this point, it's obvious that Louise used a definite learning pattern common to all three skills.

She is a learner who reads manuals and is comfortable following written instructions, then practicing in a hands-on way. Knowing this about herself, Louise can master that new skill she wants to learn by using the same learning pattern. She wants to learn how to use a computer well enough to do her household budget. For her most direct route to success, she should begin by thoroughly reading the manual. She should follow it from cover to cover, as she actually uses the computer, step by step, until it becomes a mastered skill. This is the way Louise has learned before. Chances are very good that it will work again.

Steven's learning pattern

Steven learned how to balance his checkbook by watching his sister do it. He followed her lead, doing it with her several times until he was comfortable enough to try it on his own. That coffee table he refinished? He read the labels on the lacquer and stain containers, but other than that, he basically learned how to refinish that piece of furniture by helping his uncle refinish an old dining table. From working with his uncle, he picked up some of his little tricks such as using old dishtowels for the stain wipe off part. They still had texture to them, but no lint left to stick to the stain as the surface was wiped down.

The cakes? Simple. As a boy, Steven often helped his mom on baking day. When he did, he got the first crack at licking the bowl. In the process of helping his mom with the hand mixing, he also learned to "feel" when the batter was just the right consistency for the cake to emerge light as well as tasty.

Once again, the learning pattern is clear. Steven acquires skills by actually doing the thing, by plunging in, making some mistakes but getting the feel for it as he goes along. He will learn his basic computer skills by buying a user-friendly one and starting right in to use it! He'll probably lose some material on it from time to time, but with a few sessions of hands on help from his computer whiz son, he'll gradually understand what it can and can't do. Louise would not be comfortable with this way of learning, but Steven is quite happy with it.

Once Louise and Steven are aware of their most natural learning style, there's no need for either one of them to fear failure when they want to learn something new. They can simply study *how* they've learned what they already know and apply those same principles to acquiring the new skill. This is a great way for each individual to build the confidence it takes to try something new. You remind yourself that you can learn and furthermore, you now have a better understanding of how. So be a beginner and begin!

This same confidence-building approach to learning something new will also work for your child. Even as a very young person of 6 or 7 years old, your child will have mastered at least three new skills. List them, as your child tells you what they are. Help her remember them.

"You dress yourself every morning, don't you? You help clear the table after dinner, don't you? You know how to add and subtract some numbers, don't you?"

Be certain to select skills your child knows she can do. As your child answers yes to each one you mention, you can then help her remember how she learned those skills. What did she do with each one that can be used to help her learn how to ride her bike, the new thing she wants so very much to learn but is afraid to try.

Remember that your goal is to bolster your child's confidence so she will lose her fear of failure. You want her to remember that effort was made and mistakes were made, but because she kept at it, she did learn how to do those things you and she just recalled. She needs to be reminded of past successes and made to see how unimportant the mistakes were because she didn't let them stop her from learning. As you help her remember, be specific.

"Remember when you put your play shorts on backward and how you laughed when you couldn't find your pocket? Now, you get your pockets in the right place every time. Remember the first time you helped with the table clearing, you could hardly reach and I had to help with the big dishes? Now, you can do it all by yourself.

"Remember how you used your wooden blocks to learn to count to 10? The blocks kept falling down but you just piled them back up again and started counting all over until you got all 10. So what if your bike tips over a time or two? Here, I'll show you how to catch yourself when you feel it begin to tip."

Remember, your child wants to learn. She just needs to have her confidence boosted beyond that fear of falling. Reminding her that she got past her fears before will help her get beyond the more crippling fear of failing. Help her understand that the stumbles and backward pockets and tumbled blocks are all part of the process and nothing to avoid. Rather, they are something to celebrate, because they mean we are breaking new ground, making an effort, making progress, and being a beginner.

How exciting it is to watch the hope come alive in your children's eyes when they begin to believe in their own possibilities. How exciting it is to look in the mirror and see the hope rekindled in your own eyes when you begin to realize that you've only begun to tap your own potential.

If you tell your child, as many of us do, that he or she can be whatever they want to be, then you must show them by your own example how to do it. If you honestly believe it, then you must prove it to your child. If they are to trust what you tell them, if they are to have faith in your word, then you must keep your word.

When Robert's mother finally realized that her son wanted to be a performer and make people laugh with his funny stories, she kept urging him to sign up for drama class. "That way you'll learn something about what it's like to perform in front of people, and you'll find out if you really like it." He seemed to think about it, but he let that semester go by without signing up for the class. She knew he was afraid that he couldn't do it, but she didn't know how to help him get over that hurdle. Then, after this last session, she suddenly knew how to help Robert help himself.

She called me three weeks later and asked if I remembered what she said she had always wanted to do. I did. She always wanted to learn how to read music, so she could play the old upright piano that she inherited when her father died.

"He never had the patience to teach me, and I was such a slow learner," she said. "I never wanted to take lessons because most people who take piano lessons are kids. I was afraid they would think I was too old to start at the beginning."

We both smiled. "I'm ready now to be a beginner," she said. She signed up for an adult education class in piano at the community college.

"What did Robert say?" I asked her.

She beamed, "He said, 'Cool, Mom.' Maybe he'll get up the courage to go after his dream too." Then she was very quiet for a minute or two. "At least we're talking now," she said softly. "It's a good start." Yes, I thought, a beginning.

Conclusion

Parting Thoughts

What will become of Robert and Elizabeth? I can't say. I do know they will not go through the rest of their lives believing that they have nothing of singular value to offer to the world. They will be less likely to point to others as their reason for not realizing their potential. They will no longer need to wonder what their lives might have been like if they had been blessed with parents who loved them enough to raise them, because they have discovered that they do have parents who are willing to be worthy of the name.

It's been a difficult journey for Robert's mother, this journey toward self-reliance for her and her son. She is stronger for the effort and comes closer every day to the journey's goal. Elizabeth's father and stepmother are closer too, not only to the goal, but to each other. That unity gives Elizabeth hope that there will be some security in her life while she struggles with adolescence. This book is, after all, about hope.

For as often misguided and always challenging as parenting has become today, most of us are desperately driven to do it right. There is no lack of love for our children. Somehow we forgot that our children also need parents. Somehow we forgot that to be a parent is to be a teacher. To be a teacher is to be a builder of character, and the best way to build character in our children is by building character in ourselves. It is my fervent hope that this book will help us remember these things. Remembering them, we will be free to be the teachers our children need us to be.

It is my personal hope to make up for my own mistakes by bringing them into the light, where others can see them and learn from them. This book is part of my own sometimes painful process of self-discovery and the struggle it took to find the courage to keep what I needed to keep and change what I needed to change. I've taken this journey for the sake of the children in my classroom, for the sake of my own children who still look to me for guidance, and for the sake of my beloved grandchildren. It's an ongoing journey, one I no longer fear.

Where once I believed courage to be the absence of fear, I have come to believe that my daughter's definition is more accurate: Courage is the abandonment of fear in the name of love.

For the only thing more powerful than fear is love, and the most powerful love is the love we have for our children. For the sake of those children, we must be patient with ourselves as we try to become the parents our children deserve. We must practice every day being the person we want to see in our mirror. We must persevere, never giving up on ourselves or our children. As I told Robert's mother and Elizabeth's parents long ago, giving up is not an option.

You know now there is no need to give up. You realize that you have the skills to do this job. You have traveled through 10 stages of a remarkable journey. One that led you to understand why you are your child's most influential teacher. You learned what you need to do to have that influence be a positive one. You believe in your own abilities. You want to use those abilities to become the parent your child needs. You can continue with confidence, armed with what you learned from each stage. You know that you can return to any stage at any time to refresh your memory and strengthen your resolve.

Stage one gave you the foundation for reclaiming your primary parental role as teacher of your child. You learned to see the power of example as a teacher. You understood why there were many stages you must go through to become a worthy teacher, but you were willing to **Take the journey**.

Stage two explained why it's important to discover the individuality of your child, and how to pay attention to the clues that are always there. You learned that you will only find them if you're willing to be patient and **Take the time**.

Stage three taught you how to inspire your child and encourage your child's journey to self-reliance. You know that it's sometimes a difficult road to travel, but you realized the best way to help your child is to **Be the guide**.

Stage four explained the challenge of choices and helped you understand the importance of rules to help your children make positive choices. You believe now in the necessity of individual responsibility, and you see how rules encourage responsibility. When they apply evenhandedly to everyone, they help parents **Build trust.**

Stage five emphasized the value of work as a way to gain personal satisfaction and learn to set goals and achieve them. You learned about the miraculous power of effort and the significance of gaining what we need in life through our own effort. You know your children can find joy in their work if you are willing to **Show the way**.

Stage six showed you why your children must be responsible for their own work, and how to get the help they need to fulfill that responsibility. You understand that they will believe they are capable if you show them by your actions that you **Have faith.**

Stage seven helped you understand how to curb the negative influence of the media and how to make the media become a servant rather than a master. You accept the fact that parents must monitor who and what is influencing their children, and others will follow if you **Take the lead**.

Stage eight gave you the true definition of self-esteem and self-confidence and explained how self-discipline leads to both. You began to see that achievement is the key for your child to find his own worth. You know now how to help your child **Find the good.**

Stage nine moved you forward by showing you how to reinforce positives and reverse negatives in yourself and your child. It strengthened your resolve to teach your child by your own positive example. You realize that you must keep changing until you are proud of what you see when you **Look in your mirror.**

Stage ten introduced you to true lifelong learning. It showed you how to lead your child by your own example away from the fear of failure. You have a better understanding of how you learn, and how your willingness to continue to learn teaches your child to do the same. You know now why you must always be willing to **Be a beginner**.

In this process of understanding your parental responsibilities, you discovered the teacher in yourself and accepted that role for the extremely important one that it is. Because the best way to teach is by example, it is clear that everything you want your children to be, you must be yourself. That you are *always* the teacher of your children, is something you learned to see as one of the true gifts of parenthood.

Thankfully, parenthood is a job from which you will never be forced to retire. It is a role you can continually re-invent, revitalizing your own life in the process. Because you must be an example, don't look on that as a burden. Rather, regard it as a form of freedom. Accepting the responsibility of being your child's teacher means that you are free to continually strive toward your own self-improvement.

You need not be an expert in child psychology to motivate your children in positive directions. You need not be a professional teacher to guide your children to the wonders of learning. You need not be a perfect human being in order to inspire your children. What you *do* need to be is a willing parent, willing to keep your focus honest and keep the pledge you made at the beginning of this journey:

I will be the teacher my children deserve. I will prepare them for their eventual independence by teaching them how to become self reliant, self confident adults, able to love themselves and others, willing to lead decent, useful lives, and capable of pursuing their own happiness.

There are many career paths you can follow. There are many life choices you can make. There are many magnificent successes you can achieve. But none will ever present as great an opportunity for a significant contribution to society as the singular accomplishment that it is to raise a child. Be grateful for this opportunity. No task is more challenging. No task is more far reaching in its potential to influence future generations, and amazingly, through it all, you will find that being the teacher your child deserves will be its own reward.

Index

E

example,
    learning by, 28
    negative, 33
    setting for your children, 28
    teaching by, 33-38, 49-50, 93,
    103-104, 106, 132

F

failure, fear of, 210-215
fear of failure, 210-215

G

gangs, 213-215
goals, 73
government agencies, 19

H

happiness, 79
health, 131-133
help, teaching your children to ask
    for, 150-152
heroes, 196-197
homework, 23-24, 138-141
honesty, 38-40

I

individuality, 22
    understanding your
        child's, 57-63
inspiration, 23
inspiring your child, 68-72
interest, discouraging your
        children's, 83
interests,
    learning about your
        children's, 83-84
    why parents discourage their
        children's, 83

K

keeping your word, 28-33
kinesthetic learning, 46, 128

L

leaning, 65
    auditory, 127
    foundation of, 216
    kinesthetic, 128
    lifelong, 206-210
    visual, 128
learning styles, 46-50
    categories of, 46
limits, known, 142

M

manipulation, 70
media, 19-20, 24, 153-167
   as a tool of commerce, 156
   balancing the message
     of, 154-157
   controlling quality and
     content of, 160-163
   persuasive power of, 154
mentors, 83-89

P

parent,
   as provider, 78-83
   as teacher, 18, 22, 23, 78-79
   primary role of, 18, 23
parental ability, having faith in
   your, 137-153
parental pledge, 24-25
parenthood, 18
parents, fears of, 75
parents' expectations of
   children, 34-35
physical health, 131-133
preparing your child for
   success, 133-136

R

rewarding positive behavior,
   190-193
risks, 68-77, 141
   emotional, 68, 89
   importance of children taking,
     72-77
   physical, 68, 89
rules, 92-94, 101-116
   compromised, 101-103
   consistent, 101-103
   making respected, 103-111
   secrets of effective, 94-101

S

self-confidence, 143-144, 216
self-discipline, 24, 173
   value of, 174-177
self-esteem, 24, 39, 169
   link with self-discipline, 169
   promoting, 177-179
   struggle for, 170-174
self-reliance, 24, 31-33, 77-83, 148
self-respect, 79
standards, 146-150
student study team, 54-55
success, preparing your child
   for, 133-136

T

V

W